MW01714376

This book is dedicated to my husband Paolo, who patiently, and tirelessly, listens to me read aloud the first draft of everything I write. He's my best friend and cheerleader. I'd also like to thank A.L., my mentor, for believing in me and helping me find my literary confidence, and for sharing his knowledge with me.

Finally, I dedicate this to the reader that chose this book, out of the *thousands* of options available, and gave this first time, self-publisher a chance. Thank you, from the bottom of my heart. I hope you will stick with me on my adventures.

Follow my journey...

jennifervettor.com

CHAPTER 1

Meg

It had taken a lot of purging, planning and preparation but she was finally there, standing on the porch of her brand new, old house, waiting for a shipment from the airline to arrive. She didn't have a lot to move in, she'd purchased the house furnished, but still had a few personal items shipped from home. As hard as she'd tried to downsize, there was one heirloom she couldn't part with, an antique, walnut dressing table passed down from her Scottish grandmother, to her father, and then to her. She wasn't sure of its history, but her grandmother said it came from Scotland.

People thought she was crazy for moving half way around the world, but for twenty-eight year old Meg Miller, it was exactly what she needed. She'd always been curiously pulled to Scotland, as far back as she could remember. Her grandmother would share stories about the homeland, and she'd always made it sound so beautiful, and mysterious. She'd painted a picture of a country dotted with deep glens surrounded by mountains, shimmering lochs, thick woodlands, and miles and miles of lush farmland.

Not many people knew this, but Meg was born in Scotland (to American parents), a fact Meg had only come to realize herself a few years before her father's death. Her father was a musician when he was younger, moderately successful, and had been touring in the United Kingdom with his pregnant wife in tow. Most people would have discouraged a young woman from following her husband on tour, especially if she was with child, but her mother was a stubborn, strong-willed woman, and didn't imagine her baby would birth six weeks early. Her parents waited nearly a month after Meg's birth, sorting through all the red tape, before bringing their baby home to America; but it must have been long enough for Meg to bond with the country.

The house was a wreck, but it had good bones and plenty of heart, much like Meg. Anyone with a healthy imagination, unshakeable determination, and plenty of tenacity could see that beneath all those layers of dust and cobwebs was a little diamond in the rough, waiting to be transformed into a palace. Meg had seen its potential the moment she'd walked into the run down bookstore/cottage seven weeks earlier. She'd selected a dozen different homes online to look at and connected with a little fire cracker of an estate agent named Bonnie. After a seven hour flight, she and Bonnie were combing the countryside, searching for Meg's forever home.

The truth was, Meg wasn't picky on location as long as it was quaint, sparsely populated (in comparison to where she was coming from) and had a spectacular view, but Fort William was secretly on the top of her list. It was where her grandmother grew up, and for some reason, Meg thought it might be romantic to return to where her ancestors had lived long ago.

As soon as Meg stepped onto the porch of the wee, hilltop cottage, she instantly fell in love with the sweeping views of Loch Linnhe. She could imagine sitting on the porch watching the sun setting over the water, a steaming cup of earl grey in one hand, and a richly delicious novel in the other, glancing up every now and then to take in the vista. She knew beyond a shadow of a doubt that she could grow old and die on that porch, without a single regret, even if she had to do it alone. So after a quick home inspection she signed an offer. Two days later she and Bonnie were toasting her new purchase, and her new life, over a dram of Dalwhinnie scotch. She wasn't much of a drinker, but what the hell, when in Rome...or Scotland, in her case!

The best part about living in Scotland was that it was 3500 miles away from Nathan. She would have preferred separate planets, but separate continents was the best she could do. Nathan could no longer influence her. Period. He'd been a difficult boyfriend. She never knew where things stood with him, he was all over the map. From week to week she never knew whether he would be hot or cold.

Nathan was a cop, a detective, and as handsome as they come, but inconsistent as hell. One day he would ask her to dress more provocative for him, accusing her of letting herself go, and the next day get angry because she was showing too much cleavage. He'd pout if she wanted to go out without him, even if she was just grabbing a drink with coworkers, but then accuse her of being too clingy if she suggested they spend more time together.

It had taken her three years to realize that she wasn't crazy, that maybe he was a control-freak. She never knew where she stood with him, and spent the better part of their relationship second guessing herself. When she'd first met him he wasn't controlling. He was charming, funny, and attentive, and for the longest time she'd held on to that. Maybe, in a small way, she still wished he could have stayed that way. When they first met, he made her feel desirable and beautiful, a tall order given her insecurities.

A shy, self-described book-worm, Meg felt like a plain-jane her whole life. It wasn't that she was unattractive, not at all. She was cute, in an XL-Emma Stone sort of way; quirky, auburn hair, hazel eyes, and faded freckles. She was the quintessential girl next door, not a knock-out, but all in all, not a bad package. When she dolled up, she actually thought she looked rather nice; but sexy she wasn't. She'd always thought herself as two sizes too big, and three inches too tall. Not a head-turner, more of an acquired taste. She'd had a few boyfriends, but nothing substantial. At least until she'd met Nathan.

They met at a fund raising event, *Hope for Heroes*. A friend's husband had suffered a debilitating injury while serving in Afghanistan, and the foundation had been an absolute god-send for him. Meg was volunteering at the door, selling tickets and taking donations. She wasn't expecting to meet anyone that day, let alone a handsome police officer, but Nathan had other ideas. He was there as a guest, along with fellow officers, firefighters, soldiers and paramedics. It was one of the largest fundraisers in the district and fully supported by the community. Meg was proud to be a part of it.

Once everyone was inside, enjoying the festivities and listening to speeches, Nathan slipped out to see her. At first she didn't realize he was flirting with her, it wasn't a common occurrence. As usual, her head was in a book, and he dropped into the empty chair beside her, feigning interest in what she was reading. Initially she was irritated to be interrupted, until she looked into his warm, brown eyes. He was sweet and charming, and something about his devilish grin screamed danger, in the best way possible. The way he looked at her, hell, she didn't stand a chance. While he was imagining peeling off her clothes, layer by layer, she'd been focusing on the fact that she was wearing practical underwear. That's just how she rolled.

They didn't sleep together that night, in spite of Nathan's efforts, but he did take her out for a drink after the fundraiser; a drink that rolled into pancakes and coffee at an all-night diner on the highway. They talked into the morning and really got to know one another, and before the sun came up, Meg had fallen for him. It was only years later that she realized that she might not have known him at all, only the parts he wanted her to see. While she was being completely transparent and honest, Nathan was studying her, and in turn offering her the man he thought she wanted. The man *she thought* she wanted.

In retrospect, he was actually quite gifted. He could make her feel beautiful and vulnerable; both wildly confident, yet completely insecure at the same time. Little did she know he was grooming her into exactly the kind of woman he needed to feed his ego. Worst of all, there was a small part of her that still loved him, in spite of herself.

The delivery arrived a few minutes later, but not without incident. The crate, containing the dressing table, slipped out of the mover's hands while being hoisted up the porch steps. Meg had wrapped the mirror up snugly, but still cringed when the box hit the ground with a thud.

"Oh, please be careful," she blurted, unconsciously raising a hand to her lips.

"Aye, no worries lassie. It's not broken," the burly one assured, tossing her a cheeky wink. Skeptically, Meg nodded while they readjusted their grip, taking a step back to make room.

"Canadian?" the thinner man asked, his voice strained from his efforts.

"American." She opened the front door for them, certain the cumbersome crate wouldn't pass through.

"Ah, that's ok," he grinned, in what she assumed was meant to be charming. "I won't hold it against ya...unless ya want me to." She wondered briefly if he might have lost his front tooth in a bar fight, maybe flirting with another man's woman. In spite of the gap, he wasn't a bad looking guy.

"Thank-you?" she shrugged, not sure what to make of the remark.

“Never mind him,” the bigger man teased. “He’s got a thing for Canadian girls, don’t you Archie?”

“Do you meet many Canadian girls?” Meg smirked, flattered by the harmless teasing. The accent helped.

“A few,” Archie admitted, gently setting the crate down, “but you could persuade me to try something new.”

“Easy there, Archie,” Meg chuckled. “You don’t want me to think all Scots are randy horn-dogs, do you?”

The larger man dropped his end, assessing the door frame. “Dinna bother about him, he's a wee bit daft,” he remarked casually, as though reprimanding Archie was a common occurrence, and he was his handler.

“Eejit, can’t you see I’m charmin’ the pants off her,” Archie retorted playfully, knowing full well Meg wasn’t buying it.

“I think I’ll keep my pants on, Archie,” Meg laughed, turning towards his buddy. “So what are you thinking...um...sir?” His name tag read Euan, but Meg had no clue how to pronounce it. "Will it fit?"

“Nay, we’ll have to unpack it on the porch. Do ya mind?” Euan asked, pulling a long, sturdy screw driver out of his back pocket.

“No, no, please do,” Meg agreed, closing the door to keep out the flies.

A few minutes later they had the crate open and the dressing table out of its safe confines. It looked no worse for wear, but Meg was more concerned about the mirror. She unwrapped it carefully, praying it hadn’t shattered in export. Carefully peeling the packing material away, she was pleased to see her reflection intact.

“What’s this then,” Archie asked, raising a silver locket from a tiny drawer that had popped open in transit. Meg had never seen it before, nor had she been aware of that particular compartment.

"May I?" she asked, holding her palm out for him. Archie grinned at her as though she was asking him to place something else in her hand. She didn't mind a little flirting, she was no prude, but he was starting to make her uncomfortable.

Euan impatiently snatched the locket from his partner's hand. "Stop acting like a knob and give the lady her necklace before I kick yer arse," he insisted. His tone was light, his expression was not. "Sorry, miss. Apparently Archie left his manners at home today." Euan handed her the piece very carefully, ensuring not to drop it.

Meg cradled the locket in her hand, and quickly looked over it, giddy with the discovery. It was tarnished and very old, but it was still beautiful. She attempted to open it, but the latch was seized. She clasped it around her neck for safe keeping, patting it with her palm as it fell against her chest. She wondered who it belonged to, or how far back it came. Maybe it belonged to her grandmother? One thing was certain, there was a story behind it. There always was.

The boys brought the antique inside, skirting around the shelves and piles of old books in the front shop. It was currently a disaster, but she had visions of a quaint, charming, little bookery filled with treasures, trinkets, and novels, old and new. Something that appealed to both locals and tourists alike. Her grandmother had always encouraged her to follow her heart, and her heart was all about books. She adored reading, all the better if the ending was a happily ever after! Even if true love evaded her in her real life, she could always find it in her books.

As soon as they placed the dresser in her bedroom, Euan and Archie left, but not before Archie made one more attempt to seduce her with his blue collar charm.

"If ya need a tour guide, lass, or ya be wantin' a bit of a shag, here's my number," he chirped, pressing his card into her hand. He lingered a moment too long.

"Git out of here, ya wee tadger," Euan shouted, giving Archie a shove. Meg couldn't help but laugh, certain their schtick was performed time and time again. She wasn't the first lady Archie had tried to pick up, and she was certain she wouldn't be the last. She didn't know what a tadger was, but she guessed it to be unflattering.

Meg made her way to the kitchen. She picked up the bottle of wine that Bonnie had gifted her, reading the card.

'Welcome to Scotland. I don't know what ya left behind, but I do know what's in front of ya. Good times. Whit's fur ya'll no go past ya! (Google it!)
Love, Bonnie.'

Smiling, Meg dropped the card on the aged countertop, promising herself to look up the saying later. She was sure she would have to 'Google' plenty, until she got used to the customs and quirks of her new town. She grabbed a glass out of the cupboard, rinsing it well under the tap. There wasn't a tea towel in sight, but that wouldn't stop her from enjoying a glass of wine. Finding a corkscrew, however, proved a little more challenging. She opened every drawer, but to her dismay, there was nothing she could use to uncork the lovely chardonnay.

"Well," Meg whispered under her breath, "there's no time like the present to meet the locals." She snatched her purse off the old formica kitchen table, mentally noting that she'd need to replace it. She would add it to the million and one things she needed to tackle on her *honey-do-it-yourself* list.

CHAPTER 2

Meg

The pub was exactly how Meg imagined an old Scottish pub would be. With it's dark wood furnishings, tacky wallpaper, and brass fittings, she felt like she'd stepped through a time machine, probably to the very day the pub opened. She sat on an old stool at the bar, smoothly worn down by the asses of many drinkers. The bar was tacky, not from uncleanliness, just years of residue from many spilled pints. It didn't bother her in the least, in fact, she found it kind of nostalgic, romantic in a way. She wondered how many stories the old bar could tell her. The angles, the edges, the intricate carvings, it was spectacular and offered the pub it's warmth, as well as a touch of class.

"What can I get you," the bartender asked kindly, setting a coaster in front of her. She was a petite little blond with a disproportionate rack, androgynous in her features, but not unattractive. Her long bangs, which hung loosely over one eye, were a sharp contrast to the rest of her shortly coiffed hairstyle.

"Um, I'm not sure?" Meg hedged. Like a kid at an ice-cream counter, she eyed the shelf behind the bar. There was every type of alcohol she could imagine, but it was the whiskey that was proudly displayed up front, Meg assumed for easy access.

"American?" the bartender grinned, reaching for the Jack Daniels.

"Yes," Meg grinned, waving off the Jack, "how did you know?"

"The accent. It's pretty exotic," she flirted, raising her brows. Meg giggled nervously, resting her purse in front of her. She'd never considered that it would be she with with the accent, not the other way around.

"I guess I never thought of it that way."

"So, no to the Jack?" the bartender asked, shaking the bottle provocatively in front of her.

"Just a glass of chardonnay, if you have it."

"We've got everything here, whatever your heart desires," the flirtatious barkeep winked, as though sizing Meg up. She was cute, and Meg was flattered, but she firmly played for the other team.

"I'm good with wine," Meg nodded kindly, hoping to let her down gently. She wasn't looking for a girlfriend, but could definitely use a friend.

"That's too bad," she smirked, retrieving the wine from the fridge behind her.

When she turned back, Meg was relieved to see she was still smiling. "What's your name?" Meg asked, catching her eye.

"Isla. Proud owner of The Hairy Coo," she boasted, setting a wineglass in front of her. She filled it right to the rim. Meg immediately approved of the way Scots eyeballed their ounces.

"Great name for a pub! I'll bet that raises a few eyebrows!" Meg laughed, raising her glass in a toast. Isla poured herself a dram of whiskey, clinked Meg's glass, and tossed it back like a champ.

"Aye," she sighed heavily, allowing the whiskey burn down her pipe. “It’s meant to!”

“There’s a decent sized crowd in here,” Meg observed, glancing around the room.

“It won’t stay this way. This is just the calm before the storm. It’s bound to get busier once the locals roll in for supper. It’s roast beef and Yorkshire pudding night. So Red, you never gave me your name?”

“Meg...Miller. I’m from Virginia. It’s on the east coast of the U.S.?” Meg offered, holding out her hand. Isla looked down at her long fingers and smiled, gently taking her hand.

“Very nice to meet you. The truth is, if you hadn’t spoken, I would have pegged you as a local. You look like a Scot,” Isla confessed, softly shaking her hand, leaving no doubt of her attraction.

“Actually, my family is originally from here. I’ve been told I resemble my paternal grandmother, she grew up in Fort William.”

“Wow, what brings you back? A holiday?” Isla asked, pouring a beer for another patron.

“I bought the old Sealladh Cottage, at the end of Hill Road? The one with the little shop on the side, do you know it?” Meg asked, wiping the condensation off her wine glass. It was mid June, and quite warm inside the pub.

“Aye, that old dump has been for sale three years. An old bookstore if I’m not mistaken. The old guy who owned it passed it on to his only son, an ungrateful little prick who lives in Glasgow. He wouldn’t even come back to clean the place out. Let it fall into disrepair. And you say you bought it?” Isla asked, completely unaware that her words might be considered insensitive. Meg was starting to see that Scots had notoriously honest opinions, and held very little back. Although they sounded abrasive, they typically didn’t mean any harm. To be honest, she kind of liked it. It was a welcome change.

“Yes, I bought it. It’s a bit of a fixer-upper, but I'm hoping to restore it to it’s former glory. It really is a lovely house. Quite solid. It came with everything—right down to the dishes,” Meg boasted. She didn’t care if it was a dump. It was her dump. “No cork-screw though. That’s why I’m here.”

“Win for me,” Isla winked, topping up her wine. “Welcome to the neighbourhood.”

She left Meg to enjoy her wine while she took care of some new customers seated at the table behind her. Meg looked around the room, casually as possible. She didn’t want to seem rude, but her curiosity got the best of her. She loved to people watch, a side effect of her shyness. She found it difficult to strike up conversations, but was determined to push through. She was ready to reinvent herself. That’s what the move had been all about, wasn’t it? A fresh start?

There were several tables occupied with locals, who clearly knew one another well. Their unapologetic laughter animated the room. Every now and then they would erupt in cheers, or curses, depending on which team on the big screen scored a goal. By the look of things they were cheering for blue, jeering and trash-talking random insults to their opponents. Meg knew nothing about soccer but promised to learn, especially if she wanted to fit in.

“Are you ordering food, Red?” Isla asked, dropping a menu in front of her. Meg quite liked the nickname, it made her feel welcomed. She was ravenous. She’d flown in the night before, on the red eye, and had woken only moments before the delivery arrived. She hadn’t eaten a thing since her tasteless, mushy, airline meal.

“I’ll take the special,” Meg agreed, waving away the menu.

“Good choice. You’ll love it,” Isla praised, ringing in her order.

"Isla, you must know a lot of the locals, right? I'm wondering if you might recommend a tradesperson that could help me with some renovations?"

"Ya mean a carpenter?" Isla asked, nodding her head. She filled four pints into frosty mugs, and walked around the bar, delivering them to her customers.

"Sure," Meg nodded, adding, "maybe more of a jack-of-all-trades. I'm sure the place will need some plumbing, and electrical improvements too. I just have no idea where to start."

"Yes, I think I can help ya find someone. Give me a minute, I'll be right back."

She wandered off again, this time to clear a table of empty glasses. She wiped it down thoroughly, hoisting the tray over her shoulder, and disappeared into the kitchen.

"Yer looking for a carpenter are you, Birdie?"

Meg turned. The man beside her smiled, and held out a hand, his fingers stained amber from years of smoking. His teeth were crooked and badly tarnished as well, and he was obviously drunk. Meg offered him a quick nod, avoiding his handshake.

"Are ya looking to get nailed," he chortled tastelessly, banging his palm on the bar. Amused, he unleashed a dirty laugh that rang throughout the room, rotating every head in their direction. Meg could feel her blush rising, staining her cheeks the colour of her hair. Speechless, she picked up her glass and took a long sip, hoping to thwart his advances. Too polite to tell him, or anyone, to piss off, she hoped gracious indifference would send the message for her.

"Ya look like you could use a good fecking," he slurred, swallowing back another mouthful of beer. "American's are so tight."

Meg shrugged her shoulders uncomfortably and turned away,

unsure how to handle him. No one had ever spoken to her quite that way.

“Come on, Birdie, I’ll take you to my truck and show you my hammer—”

“That’s enough, Robert.”

Meg glanced up to find a man standing over the drunk, an arm loosely framing his shoulder. He was smiling at her warmly, his kind, blue eyes twinkling with humour.

“That’s no way to treat a lady. This fine young woman is trying to enjoy her drink in peace. What do you say you leave her be.”

“Feck off. I’m just having a little fun. She doesn’t mind, do ya?” Robert insisted, glaring at them both.

“Oh, I think she does. Come on now, let me buy you a coffee.”

Robert brushed at the good samaritan, roughly knocking away his arm. “I don’t want a fecking coffee. Go to hell. I’m on a date with this pretty thing. Isn’t that right, Birdie?”

Meg shook her head, easing her purse into her lap, ready to spring off her barstool. She despised being the centre of attention, but hated confrontation even more. Just then, the drunk reached over, roughly caressing her arm.

“Where you going. Let me take you home—”

The good samaritan had clearly seen enough. He grabbed Robert by the collar and hoisted him off his stool, escorting him not so gently across the room. It probably would have seemed less aggressive had the drunk not kicked and screamed the entire way. As soon as he was out the door the room erupted in a fit of laughter, applauding their hero. Meg just stared, her mouth hanging open in a state of shock.

“What the hell is going on here” Isla shouted, pushing her way through the kitchen door, her tray filled with food. She set it on the bar, and stared at Meg, as though she trusted no one else to speak the truth.

"Um, I..." Meg mumbled, searching for words.

"It's alright, Isla. I handled it. Robert was being a pain in the arse again," the man soothed, walking towards the barkeep, his composed smile settling her. Isla grinned back at him, reluctantly allowing him to hug her. She barely reached his chest.

"Yer always causing trouble. Why the hell can't you go one night without raising hell," she teased.

"It wasn't me," he answered innocently, turning to meet Meg's stare. "I was defending this young woman's honour!"

"Were you now?" Isla turned to Meg and smiled. "Will you be needing yer glass filled again? Settle yer nerves?"

Meg continued hugging her purse, unsure whether to stay or go.

"Of course she does," the man laughed. "And give it to her on the house."

"Bite your tongue. I'm not running a soup kitchen," Isla laughed, placing the chardonnay in front of him. "Why don't you buy her a drink, if yer feeling so generous?"

"Don't mind if I do," he winked, filling Meg's glass.

"Let me introduce you," Isla offered, picking her tray back up. "Meg, this is Kade Campbell. He's a good friend of mine. He'll help fix you up."

"Fix me up?" Meg choked, still finding her voice.

For the first time, she really looked him over, pleased by what she saw. Kade was unpolished, but very attractive, with the sexiest dimples hiding beneath a five o'clock shadow. She appreciated his height. A long-limbed woman herself, it wasn't uncommon for her to stand an inch or two above most men. Most of the time she found herself slouching to appear more petite, feminine.

His dark chestnut hair, wavy and disheveled, kissed his collar, offering him a youthful appearance. Meg pegged him for early thirties, certainly younger than forty. It was hard to tell under dim lights. He was muscular too, not in an obscene way, but just right. Aside from needing a haircut, the man was damn near perfect.

“Aye,” Isla said, walking away, “ya said you needed a good carpenter? Kade’s yer man.”

CHAPTER 3

Kade

Kade noticed her as soon as he'd walked into The Hairy Coo. It wasn't every day that a woman was sitting alone in his favourite hang out, especially one so beautiful. He knew almost everyone in town, and he'd definitely never seen her before. He would have remembered those curves! She was voluptuous, tall, thick, and solid, just the way he liked them, with hips a man could really hold on to. Her long auburn hair, swinging loosely down her back, was like a beacon from across the room. God, she was a fine woman!

He actually had no idea that Robert, the town sot, was harassing her until he approached the bar. He recognized the tone. The man had a reputation for being a lecherous, old bastard. Most women avoided him like the plague, another clue that Meg was a newcomer. She was sitting right beside him. No lady he knew would give ole Robbie the time of day.

"Mind if I sit down?" he asked, gesturing to the stool previously occupied by her assailant. A wordless invitation, she dropped her purse back on the bar, smiling sweetly at him. Sitting, he signalled for a drink. "Scotch, Isla, neat."

"You got it," she winked, dropping a glass in front of him. She filled it with the finesse of a someone who'd poured a million drams, smiling before taking her leave.

"So Meggie, what brings you into this fine establishment," he asked, holding his glass up in greeting. She raised her own glass, allowing him to clink it.

"I live a few blocks away, saw the sign and thought it looked like a fun place. I've never been to a pub like this before."

Kade raised his brows, surprised by the cute American accent. It made her even more alluring, but he kept himself in check. The last thing she needed was another stranger coming on too strong.

"Where are you from?" he asked, playing it cool.

"Virginia?" she replied, as though uncertain he'd know where that was. Geography was one of his best subjects in school. Although he couldn't point out every state on a map, he had a general idea where Virginia was.

"Yes, I've heard of it. What brings you to Fort William? You're living here, you say?"

"I am, just bought a house on Hill Road. The Sealladh?"

Her smile was beautiful, curiously changing her entire appearance. She had one of those rare smiles that could instantly set a person at ease. It denoted intelligence, kindness, and hopefully, a quick wit. Kade couldn't resist a beautiful woman with a smart-ass sense of humour. He needed it to match his own.

"I'm familiar with the place. It hasn't been open for many years, even before the old owner passed. Some say he became a recluse after his wife died. Closed the book store and stopped running the bed and breakfast. Is it in rough shape?" he asked thoughtfully, recalling why Isla had introduced them in the first place. He was a whiz at restoring old properties. Probably the best in town. He wasn't the fastest, or the cheapest, but he took great pride in his work and it showed. He considered himself a craftsman. A dying breed.

"It could definitely use some work. I've the vision but not the skill, I'm afraid. There's a lot of woodwork in the home I'd like to save. Are you any good?" Meg asked innocently. Blushing, she dropped her eyes, as though suddenly realizing her question could be taken many ways.

Kade chuckled under his breath, amused by her embarrassment. The devil in him wanted to flirt with the remark, redden her cheeks further. He was no fool, he knew the effect he had on women, but he was a humble guy. Besides, he wasn't sure teasing her was appropriate, especially given the circumstances of their meeting.

"I've been told I'm pretty good," he grinned, hoping she'd raise her eyes to see he was harmless. Lifting her chin cautiously, she didn't disappoint him. In spite of her glasses, he could see she had beautiful eyes. They were hazel, with little flecks of green and gold weaving through them, and lashes for days. Her eyes held a lot of depth, making him even more curious. There was definitely a story behind them and he was game to learn more.

"Do you have references?" she asked, searching deep into her purse. She pulled out a pad and pen, opening it to a blank page, then turned to look up at him. He cleared his throat, once again clipped by her smile.

"I...um...sure," he said, having never been asked for a reference before. "What do you think of this bar," he asked, running his hand seductively across it's surface.

"It's incredible! I was just admiring the craftsmanship," she admitted, noting his eyes lighting up. "You?"

"Yes," he beamed, pleased by her reaction.

"I thought it was original. It has such so much personality, I'd swear it has a heartbeat! It blends in flawlessly with the rest of the pub."

"That's probably the best compliment I've ever received," he gushed, touched by her sincerity. He'd often thought, as he was creating a piece, that he was breathing life into it, but he never shared that with another living soul, afraid they would mock him, or think him crazy. His mates weren't the mushy type.

"How did you get the wood to match so well?" she asked.

"The wood is from the old bar. It was still there under all the old scratches, scabs, and stains. I knew, as soon as I started removing the chipped paint, that with enough coaxing it's true beauty would reveal itself. Sometimes it just takes patience, and imagination to see the magic in something, you know?"

Meg inhaled slowly, locking her eyes with his, as though moved by his words. He wasn't sure why he felt so comfortable opening up to her, being vulnerable, but something told him she would appreciate it.

"I do know," she finally choked, pulling her eyes away. "I saw it the minute I walked into the house. It was like the walls were whispering to me, begging me to love it, to see it's potential. Most people would have been too disgusted by the boxes of old books, the clutter, old peeling wallpaper, and deep cracks to see past it. But I did! The intricate woodwork, the incredible claw foot tub, the beautiful old ceiling fixtures, perfectly preserved under all that filth—maybe it can all be brought back to life, and maybe not, but it's beauty can't be denied."

"You must hire me, Meggie," Kade insisted, sitting higher on his stool, as though better posture would emphasize his intention. He needed to get his hands on that old house, a project worthy of sinking his teeth into. Plus, working with a woman with that kind of integrity fired him up! Most of his customers just wanted to gut and replace. It broke his heart to swap out oak with M.D.F, glass with plastic, wrought iron with stainless steel. It sucked the very soul out of the home, as far as he was concerned.

"Oh," she gasped, raising a hand to her chest, her fingers winding around an old locket. "I haven't begun interviewing trades. You haven't even seen the house..."

"I know, and I'm sorry to come on so strong, but something tells me you and I will make a good team. I won't let you down, I promise ya," he urged, surprised by his passion. He was usually so much cooler.

"Ok," she giggled, her eyes regarding him curiously. "Do you want to come by the house Monday, offer me a quote?"

"I do," he grinned. Money hadn't even crossed his mind. If he didn't need to eat, he'd probably have done it for free.

"Here's yer roast beef, Red," Isla interrupted, setting a plate in front of her. Surprised, Meg looked up and chuckled. The Yorkshire Pudding was the size of the dinner plate it was sitting on. Kade laughed along with her, amused by her shock.

"You won't go hungry at The Coo," he quipped.

"No, I suppose not," she chuckled, taking the cutlery from Isla's hands. "Not sure I can eat all of this!"

"Come on, lass, give it a go!" he encouraged, topping up her wine.

"Will you split it with me," she offered. Normally he would have politely refused, but there was something about her that intrigued him, and the food smelled bloody delicious.

"Don't mind it I do," he grinned, gesturing Isla for another plate. She nodded at him knowingly, returning to the kitchen. "But I'm only going to share it with you if you allow me to treat you to dinner."

"No way! You've already done enough. I'm happy to share!" Meg pressed, sliding her purse out of the way to make room for his place setting.

Kade held up a callused palm, the hand of a strong, hard working man. "I insist. Consider it the start of a promising friendship, a welcome to Fort William."

CHAPTER 4

Meg

Meg had to admit, Kade was a great guy. If she hadn't sworn off men, she might have been attracted to him, but the last thing she needed was to get caught up in a romance. She was definitely not ready for that again. She wasn't sure she ever would be.

No, she'd spent too many years navigating every shadowy corner of her relationship with Nathan, trying to circumvent all the pitfalls and sink holes. It was too much work, and emotionally draining. If only she were thinner, prettier, smarter, more loyal, less clingy, a better cook, more health conscious, more communicative, less argumentative, more out-going, less flirtatious, and a better lover; his list of demands was ever changing and never ending, and she bit the hook every single time, too afraid of losing him to stand her ground. She'd spent so much time trying to be the right woman for him, to be good enough for him, that she never saw how wrong he was for her.

But she'd promised herself that no man would ever hold her hostage like that again, dangling that happily ever after in front of her like a proverbial carrot. She wouldn't dumb herself down, or dim her shine, for anyone ever again. If any man wanted her, he'd have to love her exactly the way she was; quirky, independent, and intelligent, with a healthy appetite for life, tasty food, and good wine. *Oh darling, you have cellulite? Well get over here and let me read you like braille.*

Since she had a better chance of winning the lottery or getting hit by lighting than finding a man confident enough to accept her, Meg was content building a life for herself. In fact, she welcomed it. She was ready to step back into the light, push herself farther than she ever had, reach higher than she ever thought possible, trust her own capabilities. Nathan tried to convince her that she would be nothing without him, but the truth was, she often felt like she was nothing with him. Several days before she'd walked out, he even told her so, and for a split second she'd believed him; until a little voice whispered in her head: *prove him wrong, Meg.*

After their dinner, Kade took her number and promised to arrive early the following Monday morning, his tool belt in hand. There were probably people who would caution her to interview several prospects and get multiple quotes, but she had a good feeling about him, and she had to start trusting her gut again. He seemed like a salt-of-the-earth guy, with an obvious passion for his work—and he wasn't hard on the eyes either. Although she had no interest in a meal, there was no harm reading the menu.

Meg spent the weekend sorting, organizing, and cleaning. Clearing as much space as she could for Kade to move around. As she went through her little cottage, she was overwhelmed by the amount of work ahead of her and several times had to calm herself on the porch with a cup of tea, just to stave off a panic attack. Although she might have bitten off more than she could chew, she'd much rather choke on ambition than swallowed by apathy. She'd just take things a day at a time.

It was late Sunday evening. She was sitting cross legged on the floor, searching through boxes of old books, piled two and three rows high. She was hoping to salvage much of their contents for the shelves of the bookery, maybe even find a treasure or two, but much of what she found was questionable in it's usefulness. Dusty, old fashioned books, perfumed with a musty aroma of decay and neglect. She assumed most of the books were donated castaways the previous owner never had the time, or the desire, to sort through. He seemed more a hoarder than a collector, Meg thought ruefully. Most of the boxes were untouched, still sealed with yellowed, crumbling packing tape that had long ago lost its sticky residue.

She was about to push aside a box, certain she wouldn't find anything interesting, when something caught her eye. It was a vintage diary, the kind that would have been filled with the longings, secrets, and fantasies of a young girl; red leather with a gold scroll design, long ago faded. It was locked, but the leather was compromised, cracked along the flap that held the metal edge in place. She took a moment to search the bottom of the box for the key, piling the remaining books around her, but found nothing, even after turning it upside down. She placed the box down and retrieved the diary, inquisitively rolling it over in her hands. It seemed a shame to break it, almost impolite, but Meg was curious about it's contents. She carried the book with her into the kitchen, hoping to find a tool to unlatch it.

"This should work," she spoke out loud, to no one in particular. She slipped a small butter knife behind the seal and it easily popped open on the first try, as though its secrets begged to be revealed. She slowly opened the book, pleasantly surprised by the soft texture of the paper. It was quite extraordinary, made even more striking by the elegant script decorating the pages. Meg felt the familiar flutter of excitement that always happened whenever she first opened the pages of a new book; the promise of a new adventure waiting to be devoured, fresh mysteries to unfold, and delicious characters to fall in love with.

It had been years since Meg had read cursive, raised in a computer generation, but there was something mysteriously beautiful about those swirling consonants and vowels. It struck a deep chord with her, luring her into an era where things were simpler, slower, with more attention paid to detail. An idyllic world where folks really took the time to engage with each other; computers, cell phones, and Instagram just a cold, distant, impossible reality. She often felt like she'd been born in the wrong era, dropped onto the planet generations later than she should have been. She longed for those deeper connections.

Excited, she opened the first page, allowing the words to transport her like a literary time machine.

CHAPTER 5

Katherine

February 1, 1961

Dear Diary,

It's me, Katherine. Mum gave me a diary for my birthday, and I couldn't wait to write my first entry. She asked me what I wanted and this was all I asked for. I wanted one so badly, but I think mum had reservations, preferring I didn't keep secrets from her. A girl needs to have a place to call her own, hidden away from prying eyes of disapproving of adults, doesn't she? Especially now that I'm seventeen? I'm nearly a woman!

My friend Esme has the exact same one and reads me her entries all the time, although I'm sure she makes up most stuff. She can be quite naughty and I'm sure the nuns would wrap her knuckles if they knew how sinful she was. I don't mind though. Even though she makes me blush, I admire how plucky she is. She doesn't worry about silly things, like going to hell. Then again, her mum isn't as strict as mine. My mum isn't fond of Esme. She considers her a bad influence, and you know what, I'm thankful she is, but I would never admit it or mum would never let us socialize. It's bad enough that her parents are divorced. Mum has strong opinions about that, she's so old fashioned. It's not Esme's fault that her father deserted them, is it?

I'm looking forward to sharing all of my adventures with you, diary. I just hope something wonderful happens soon, so I can fill the pages. You can be sure I won't share you with anyone. What I write stays between us. As for today, I have nothing exciting to confess. I'm just a girl who's never been kissed, but wants so badly to be! Esme has already been kissed so many times, by different boys! I think I'm just as pretty as she is, although she does have that lovely blonde hair. I'm so jealous! She tells me it's because I'm too shy. She might be right.

Anyway, Mum said I could go out tonight to celebrate, and I don't have to be home until 10:00! We're going to see a film and then after to Argyle's for milkshakes. Now that I have a diary, something exciting HAS to happen, right? Wish me luck!

* * *

Katherine stood in front of the mirror assessing her third outfit change. She hated her clothes, all of them! They were so childish. Esme's mum let her wear whatever she wanted, even skirts above the knee! No wonder the boys were more interested in Esme. If it were up to Katherine's mum, she'd make Katherine wear skirts to the floor!

She cursed the plaid skirt she was wearing, slowly pleating the fabric at the waist to raise it over her knees. It looked better that way. She continued to tuck the excess material until the hemline was exactly where she wanted it, securing it with a skinny belt before pulling her cardigan over top. She quickly ran a brush through her long hair, wishing it was a glowing blonde instead of the colour of rusty water. Normally she would have pulled it into a pony-tail, brushing her bangs down straight, but that night she wanted to look more mature, like a woman. Satisfied with her appearance, she grabbed her purse off the bed, hesitating just long enough to hide her diary under the mattress. She'd already hidden the key inside her jewelry box, underneath the velvet liner. Although she didn't think her mother would snoop, she wouldn't put it past her either.

"Katherine Margaret! Where do you think yer going?" Mary shouted, a stern, disapproving expression on her pinched face. "Douglas, did you see what your daughter's wearing?" Katherine stood at the bottom of the stairs, her arms crossed defiantly across her chest, her mum blocking the front door.

Douglas raised up from his paper, feigning interest. "Aye," he answered, before dropping his eyes.

"Well, aren't you going to say something?" Mary pressed, her frustration growing. He glanced up impatiently, and shrugged.

Her father, a much respected economics professor at the University of Edinburgh, worked in the city every Monday through Thursday. When he came home on weekends, the last thing he wanted was to play referee for his wife and daughter. Katherine briefly caught his eye and smiled, hoping to charm him to her side. She should have just changed at the theatre, but hoped, with the passing of her birthday, that her mother would cut her a tiny amount of slack.

"Katherine, do as yer mum says," he scolded, thrusting his paper back up in front of him, a gesture implying his work was done. Irritated, Mary sighed, shaking her head. Katherine rolled her eyes in defiance, certain she would catch flack for that too.

"Don't sass, young lady. Now march up those stairs and put on something decent before I change my mind about letting you out!" Mary disapproved, pointing a stern finger towards the staircase.

"Mum, all the girls dress this way!"

"Well, if all the girls were jumping in the loch, would you do the same?"

Katherine glanced towards her father once more, hoping he'd step in. He had, on occasion, taken her side, but it was clear he was content hiding behind his paper, wise enough to pick his battles. "Of course not, Mum! I just want to fit in. Why can't you just let me be?"

Exasperated, Mary shook her head, as though she couldn't believe how daft her daughter was behaving. "Well if you want to fit in with trollops, yer doin' a fine job. Wipe off that lipstick too, while yer at it. Now go!"

Certain she wouldn't make headway, Katherine turned and stormed up the stairs, allowing her heavy footfalls to speak for her.

"Oh, the kids these days!" Mary complained, turning towards her husband for support. "In our day we'd never dream of giving our parents lip, fearing a beatin'!"

Katherine listened to her mother prattle on, all the way to her bedroom, anger burning in her chest. She wanted to slam the door but wisely thought better of it, certain her defiance wouldn't go unpunished. The last thing she wanted was to push her mother into a grounding, especially that night. Rumour had it that her crush, Mack, might be at the movies.

It didn't take long to make herself presentable. She simply tied her hair back and dropped the hem of her skirt, slipping the belt into her purse for a quick change once she was out of Mary's sight. She grabbed a hanky and wiped away the lipstick, shaking her head at her reflection in the mirror.

She was a good girl and rarely gave her parents reason to mistrust her, and yet they refused to give her even the tiniest inch. Her grades were exceptional, she never swore or snuck cigarettes, like so many of her friends did, and she followed her curfew to the letter. She was sick of never having any fun; it hurt that her mum treated her like a child. What the hell was the point of trying so hard if her mum didn't trust her anyway?

Finally able to pass inspection, Katherine grabbed her coat and ran down the porch steps to freedom, walking the four blocks to the theatre as quickly as she could. As soon as she was out of sight she pulled the ribbon out of her hair and pinched her cheeks, trying to add some colour.

"Kat, over here!" Esme shouted, waving frantically. Smiling, Katherine skipped over to her friend, pulling back once she realized she wasn't alone. Alec Thomson slipped an arm around Esme, casually nodding a welcome. Awkward around boys, Katherine tried not to blush, staring at her friend for support. Esme grinned, taking a long drag off her cigarette.

"I didn't think you were going to get here on time," she chirped, blowing the smoke glamorously into the air. She waved the cloud away, making eye contact. Katherine shrugged, as if to say, 'you know how it is'.

"Aye, did yer mum not want you to come then?" Esme asked, rolling her eyes playfully. Alec's laughter forced Katherine to look away, her shame revealed in another blush.

"No, it's fine. I just had to tidy up. I lost track of time. I didn't know you were coming, Alec?" Katherine offered quietly, wishing he hadn't. She hated being a third wheel, but something told her Esme liked it that way. She enjoyed making Katherine a wee bit envious.

"Aye, I hope it's okay. I know it's yer birthday and all, but I've been wanting to see this movie," Alec replied, not even looking at her.

"You want to see *Pollyanna*?" Katherine asked, trying to hide her surprise. Alec and Esme laughed in unison, as though she'd said something stupid.

"No, of course not," Esme chirped, speaking for the boy. "We're seeing *Spartacus*. Kirk Douglas is so handsome!"

"Really? You like those gladiator types, do ya?" Alec teased, feigning jealousy. He tickled Esme under the ribs, surprising Katherine with his forwardness.

"I'm just saying he's fine, that's all," she giggled, squirming out of his clutches.

"I thought we were seeing Pollyanna?" Katherine shrugged, appearing indifferent. It wasn't the first time Esme changed plans without discussing it with her first, and Katherine conceded to her whims far too often, afraid of confrontation.

"Do you want to see that?" Esme smirked, raising a disapproving brow. "It's for children, really."

"I suppose it is," Katherine agreed, embarrassed that she'd been looking forward to it. Alec chuckled under his breath, catching an elbow to the ribs from Esme. It was all too much. Katherine didn't like the way things were unfolding, and worse, that Esme didn't seem to care that it was *her* birthday. Sometimes she was a really bad friend, and yet she was the coolest one she had. Esme raised Katherine's status, and she knew it.

"I think I might just skip it," Katherine shrugged, wishing she could start her birthday all over. Nothing was working out the way she'd hoped.

"Why? Don't be daft. It will be fun," Esme coaxed, not very persuasively.

"No, no, it's fine. You two enjoy the film," she urged, forcing a smile. "I think I'll just go to Argyle's and get a soda."

"No, it's yer birthday. Stay and hang out with us. We'll go to Argyle's after and Alec will treat us to a milkshake, right?" Esme asked flirtatiously, batting her eyelashes at him.

"Huh? Oh, sure," he agreed, half-heartedly.

Katherine shook her head, even more determined to bow out. It was clear from his body language that Alec would much rather be alone in a dark theatre with Esme, than to placate her spinster friend. Katherine wasn't jealous of Esme, she just wished she had someone too.

"Really, it's fine. I don't mind," she insisted one last time. Esme drew her into a hug, offering an indifferent peck on the cheek.

"Well, if that's how you'd prefer it, I'll call on ya tomorrow."

Katherine smiled awkwardly and spun around, wistfully hoping Esme would call her back. Of course she didn't, and Katherine was too proud to change her own mind.

As she rounded the corner, she leaned against the building and sobbed, sorry she'd even left the house that night. How silly was she, believing that seventeen would be any better? After a few minutes, she wiped her eyes, hunting in her purse for a tissue.

"Are ya crying?" a deep voice summoned from the dark. Katherine quickly shut the clasps on her purse and straightened up, not sure whether to reply, or run as fast as she could.

'Who's asking?" she choked, wiping the remaining tears off her cheeks, bracing to flee. A tall figure stepped forward, out of the shadows, a cloud of smoke haloing his head. He took another drag off his cigarette, tossing it into the curb before facing her.

Katherine sucked in her breath, certain her legs would puddle beneath her. It was Mack, looking finer than she'd ever seen. Usually he was surrounded by mates, a gang of rebel rousers typically up to no good. A man of few words, Mack was their leader, holding their respect just by sheer size, and an air of indifference. He was the epitome of cool, sexy, in a James Dean sort of way, a rebel without a cause in his own right. And Katherine was completely smitten with him.

"I'm asking. What's yer name?" he asked, slowly ambling towards her.

Part of her did want to run, afraid to make a fool of herself, but she was certain her legs would never hold her up. She'd been crushing on Mack since she was thirteen, when she'd first noticed him standing outside Argyle's with his gang. He was a year older than she, and attended the public high school. At least she assumed he did, Katherine didn't know many kids outside the Catholic school. All she knew was that he was nothing like other boys. Most of them were short, irritating little twits; and when not playing football, spent their free time tormenting the girls. Katherine was often an easy target because she was quiet, and rarely made a fuss or tattled.

Mack was different, intriguing. Discreetly, she'd often watch him through the windows at Argyle's, careful not to reveal her feelings. Of course Esme was quick to notice, and would tease her mercilessly, sometimes to the point of humiliation. She often carried things too far, especially when it came to talking about sex. Katherine was more naive than her friend, often blushing when Esme talked about what boys liked to do to girls in the dark.

"Yer name?" Mack asked again, offering reassurance with his smile. Although she couldn't explain, it set her instantly at ease.

"Katherine," she squeaked, her voice betraying her. Mack nodded, offering her a cigarette. She shook her head, waving him off. "No thank you. I don't smoke."

"Probably smart," he chuckled, closing the pack. "Do you want to know my name?"

"I know yer name," Katherine gushed, leaning against the wall, her eyes riveted to him. He was even better in person, his blue eyes framed with the longest lashes she'd ever seen on a boy.

"Do ya now," he laughed, running a hand through his dark, curly hair. Her mother would have disproved of the length, among other things. She thought anyone without a crew cut was a thug.

"Yer Mack, right?"

He raised his brows in surprise. "That's right, have we met?"

"No, I've seen you around though."

"Have ya?" He leaned up against the wall, right beside her, so close she could feel his body heat.

"Aye, with your mates. Where are they? Yer alone?" Katherine asked, afraid to move an inch, for fear he'd move away.

"I dunno. I guess they'll be here soon. Why are you crying?" His concern was moving, even a little surprising.

"It's stupid," Katherine shrugged, waving off the question.

"Of course it's not stupid. You're obviously upset. Who's ass do I need to kick?" he quipped, nudging her flirtatiously. Amused, Katherine giggled, his touch releasing the butterflies in her belly.

"It's my birthday today and my friend ditched me for a boy. I guess it's silly to be crying over it, but it hurt my feelings," she admitted, struggling to look at him. He was too beautiful, and she was too nervous.

"Your friend? Ditched you on yer birthday? Wow—"

"Ya, I guess it is bad."

"I'd be raging," he pressed, smiling down at her. "What do you say I take you for a soda? It's the least I can do for ya."

Katherine glanced up and smiled, still shocked he was there. "What about yer mates? Won't they be looking for you?"

"They'll catch up later. No big deal. Making a girl smile on her birthday is more important, don't you think?"

"I suppose," Katherine agreed, wondering how the hell she'd

gotten so lucky. Not only was Mack handsome as hell, he was a gentleman too. It was a pleasant surprise. She wondered, for a split second, how her mum would feel if she wandered off with a strange boy instead of being at the pictures with Esme. Mortified, no doubt. She quickly brushed the thought away, before Catholic guilt could change it. She'd never been on a date before, and wasn't about to blow it.

"Come on, Kat," Mack encouraged, placing a confident arm around her. "Let's get out of here."

She nodded, allowing a sigh to slip past her lips. Her mother would have a bird if she heard anyone call her Kat, but then again, she'd be none too happy that Mack was taking her out anyway. In for a penny in for a pound, she thought, following him out of the alley. Her birthday was shaping up great after all.

CHAPTER 6

Meg

"Well I'd say this was a productive day," Kade boomed, running a dusty hand through his messy hair.

Meg looked up from her task to offer a smile. He was a damn hard worker, and in spite of the huge amount of work in front of them, his enthusiasm had not waned at all. It was actually fun working with him; he had a great sense of humour and kept her laughing.

They'd been tackling her bedroom; him removing the avocado shag carpet and chipping away old paint from the woodwork, while she peeled the yellowed wallpaper. She nearly cried when she realized that there were at least three layers on the wall. Kade teased that it was quite possibly the only thing holding the plaster together.

They'd decided to start in her room, Kade insisting a woman needed a beautiful space to sleep in. If she had a pleasant place to lay her head at night, everything else would seem less daunting. She couldn't disagree. At the moment she was sleeping on a cot in the living room, and had been for the past week. She was looking forward to having her bedroom back. The bathroom would be next. While she loved the old clawfoot tub, the bathroom desperately needed a facelift. She needed a sensual space to bathe and unwind, and had full confidence that Kade could make it happen.

“I don’t know about you, but I’m ready for supper, and a pint. Care to join me?” he asked, unbuckling his tool belt. She discreetly watched his strong hands pull the leather strap, dangerously flirting with her imagination. He eyed her curiously, a smile tugging at the corner of his mouth. Turning away, she recovered quickly.

Kade had asked her to join him for dinner the past three nights, and each time she’d politely declined, unsure it was wise to mix business with pleasure. She didn’t want to give the wrong idea. She’d hired him for a job, not to date him.

Yet, he genuinely seemed interested in a friendship with her and admittedly, she needed some friends. They’d developed a great rapport and she was curious about him, about his life. She stood up and stretched, wiping her sticky hands with a towel. Although sore all over, her hunger pains yelled the loudest.

“I was going to make a sandwich and get right back at it,” she shrugged, tossing the towel at him, a small part of her wishing she wasn’t so conventional. But she’d let her guard down once before, and it had turned into a shit show. She’d learned her lesson.

Amused, Kade wiped his hand before dropping the towel. “You can’t work all night, lass. We’ve been at it more than nine hours.”

“I know. I guess I’m just anxious to get it done,” she admitted, looking around at the work left to do.

“Meggie, even Rome wasn’t built in a day. Come out and get a drink with me,” he coaxed, walking towards her, “just a friendly dinner. I’ll be on my best behaviour. I promise.”

Meg chuckled, running a hand through her tangled hair. "I'm a mess. I can't go out like this!"

"Nonsense! You look like a woman who's not afraid to get dirty," he grinned, raising a coquettish brow.

"Is this you behaving?" she smirked, in mock disbelief, the flirtatious innuendo not lost on her. She had to admit, she didn't mind so much.

"Aye, I am being good. I just call it like I see it. Seriously, you look grand."

Meg sighed, her resolve slipping. Would it hurt to get a drink and fill her belly? Besides, she was being presumptuous. It was more likely he was offering a gesture of friendship than flirting, and she appreciated that.

"Fine, but I need to freshen up. Can I meet you at The Coo?" she conceded, noting his eyes light up.

"Of course. I'll head over and get a table," he offered triumphantly, not bothering to hide his joy. Unaccustomed to such transparency, it caught Meg a little off guard. Nathan had always played it cool, regardless of how he was feeling. He liked her to guess, and lord help her if she got it wrong.

"Okay," she nodded, leading him out of the room.

"You won't change yer mind?" he asked, offering her a playfully stern look.

His infectious smile was disarming, and she couldn't help but return it.

"I promise. I'll be there in twenty minutes," she insisted, holding the front door open. He walked though, turning sideways to slip his full figure through the tiny opening. She'd asked him once about the small doorways in Scottish dwellings and Kade explained that years ago they were designed that way to keep the heat inside; the smaller the gap, the less chance for a draft to blow in. A minor inconvenience to save comfort, he'd teased, after whacking his skull on the door jam.

Meg shut the door behind him, looking down at her dusty, stained clothes. What a mess, she thought. How the hell do I make this presentable in twenty minutes? Leaving a trail of discarded clothes, she made her way to the bathroom, taking the fastest bath of her life.

CHAPTER 7

Kade

Oh, boy, Meggie was a feisty woman. Kade leaned against the bar, his first pint already half swallowed. He was talking with a few mates, but his heart was only half way in, his mind preoccupied with thoughts of the spunky American.

She came off as a strong, hard working, independent woman, and yet there was a soft vulnerable side to her that occasionally revealed itself, in the tiniest glimpses. It intrigued him. He wasn't sure, but his gut told him she was protecting herself; from what he didn't know. They got on well enough, but as soon as he found a tiny crack to charm his way in, she sealed up tight again. He was determined to find another opening, dig a little deeper. Hearing that laugh? Watching her bonnie eyes light with humour? It was well worth the excavation.

She challenged him in ways he hadn't expected. She didn't consider herself a beauty. It was obvious, in the way she carried herself. She walked with her shoulders rolled forward, as though shrinking herself. She was almost as tall as he, but it was clear she hadn't yet embraced her sex appeal. Or maybe she'd never met a man that appreciated it.

Until now. He was enchanted. In truth, he had to constantly

check himself to make sure his admiration wasn't obvious. He sensed she spooked easily and would shy away from any sort of advances. Fair enough. She was in a strange country starting over; that would be daunting for any one. He would keep things light, playful, friendly, and get to know what made her tick, learn her story.

"Fancy meeting you here, stranger."

Kade recognized the voice, but didn't smile. He took another gulp off his beer, turning around slowly. Lorna was standing before him, dressed to the nines, her cleavage greeting him provocatively.

"Lorna," he nodded, averting his eyes.

"Not even a hug?" she taunted, arms open wide. He would have preferred a hand shake, or even better, a wave from across the room, but he offered a half-hearted embrace, avoiding the scene she would surely cause if he denied her.

"It's been awhile," she observed coyly, plopping herself on the barstool beside him.

"Has it?" He glanced casually towards the door. The last thing he wanted was Meggie to walk in and see him talking with Lorna. He didn't want to give her the wrong idea, or worse, have to make an introduction.

"Aye, its been awhile. You haven't called—"

"Right," he interrupted, his cheeks reddening. He hadn't called her after their last encounter because he hoped to avoid seeing her. He'd made a mistake in a moment of weakness. Lorna could manipulate him in a way no one else ever could, and he wasn't proud of it. Actually it was downright embarrassing.

"No matter, you're here now. Buy me a drink?" she asked, wrapping a hand flirtatiously around his waist. Kade shifted, wordlessly expressing discomfort, a gesture meant to avoid her touch. It didn't.

"Sure," he shrugged, gesturing Isla to take Lorna's order. Isla offered a look that said, '*What the hell are you doing?*' He grimaced in response, Lorna missing the entire exchange.

Isla dropped the draft in front of her, splashing the cold amber over the frosted rim. Lorna ignored her, refusing to meet her disapproving gaze, no love lost between them. Kade caught Isla's eyes and offered a look of regret, along with a five pound note that he slid across the bar.

"So how've you been?" Lorna asked coyly, taking a sip.

"I've been great," his cold reply.

"Really?"

"Right as rain," he assured, setting his empty mug in front of him.

"I've been fine too. Are you going to order another?" she asked, gesturing to his glass. "You don't want me to drink alone, do ya?"

"Actually, I'm expecting someone," he answered curtly, glancing towards the door. He hoped she'd take the hint and make herself scarce, but Lorna rarely gave him a break, and he was pretty sure that day would be no different.

"Oh, a mate?" she asked, knowing full well it wasn't. Refusing to answer, Kade turned back, smiling flatly. "Really, a woman is it? A date?"

"Just a client," he dropped quickly, his tone leaving no doubt he wanted their exchange to end. No surprise, Lorna ignored the signal.

"Why didn't you call me? I really missed you," she pouted, gently touching him again. He clasped her hand, removing it off his chest, and dropped it into her lap.

"You know why."

She sighed deeply, frustrated. "Don't be cross, Kade. I've honestly missed you. I thought after we hooked up you'd finally end this charade. The sooner you stop pouting the sooner we can move on. We're good together."

She wasn't completely wrong. At one time they were good together, and he couldn't deny their chemistry. There was even a time he thought they might marry—until she cheated on him. He tried to forgive her, to forget her indiscretion, because he had loved her, but the truth was, Lorna was toxic. The last time they were together he realized it was truly over. He felt nothing, and he knew he'd finally gotten over her. He tried to tell her that night, but she kept dismissing him, changing the subject. He ended up walking out, certain his words fell on deaf ears. Lorna was like that. If it wasn't what she wanted to hear, or things weren't going her way, it would go one of two ways; she'd either avoid him or make an emotional scene until he conceded.

"If you recall, we didn't hook up. I left before things got carried away. I'm done Lorna. What happened was a mistake, and I regret it. I'm sorry you got the wrong idea, but we're really over."

"Oh, Kade. We'll never be over. You know that," she taunted, her eyes penetrating his resolve.

He tore away, half convinced she'd never pull her claws out of him. He tried to be a decent man, and prided his integrity, but he wasn't perfect. Although they hadn't slept together that night, they came damn close. He'd been drunk and feeling extra lonely, and Lorna exposed his weakness to her advantage. He wasn't making excuses, he was definitely responsible for his own actions. He just didn't want to be cruel, and maybe that was his downfall.

"Kade?"

Lorna whipped around first, the moment she heard the strange American accent. At first she appeared angry, almost threatened, but as she assessed her competition, her features suddenly relaxed, as though deciding she had nothing to worry about. It pissed Kade off, and he almost called her out, but thought wiser to ignore it.

"Hey," he greeted, a little too loudly. Lorna raised her brows and chuckled, sensing his nervousness.

"Hi," Meg replied. Staring between the two of them, she smiled cautiously. He could see her wheels turning, perhaps gauging the connection between him and the mysterious, dark haired beauty at the bar. He was quiet for a moment, madly flipping through his own brain for the best way to handle the situation. To his relief Meg rectified the situation.

"I'm Meg Miller," she offered sweetly, holding her hand towards Lorna. Lorna glanced down, grimacing as though the hand was covered in boils. She shook it without enthusiasm. It didn't seem to deter Meg at all, who continued to smile. She waited a moment for Lorna to introduce herself before asking, "and you are?"

"Lorna Stewart. I'm Kade's—"

"Friend." Kade interjected, throwing Lorna a stern, warning look. She smirked scornfully, turning her attention to Meg.

"I hope I'm not interrupting?" Meg hesitated, pushing her glasses up the bridge of her nose. Kade found the gesture endearing.

"Actually we were just catching up," Lorna challenged tightly. Kade knew that look, and took his cue to end the interaction, worried Lorna would say something inappropriate. It wouldn't be the first time.

"We were just finishing up. Join me Meggie, Isla saved us a table," he chimed in, gesturing her to lead the way. He placed his hand in the small of her back, directing her away from trouble.

“Nice to meet you,” Meg chirped politely, craning her neck around. Lorna offered an indifferent wave, eyes pooled with mischief. Thankfully Meg didn’t seem to notice.

“I’m glad you didn’t change yer mind,” Kade said, pulling out Meg’s chair, his voice returning to normal. He glanced across the room once more, to make sure that Lorna was behaving herself. She was engaged in an animated conversation with his mates, her hands gesturing wildly. He only hoped her madness would remain in check.

“A girl’s got to eat.” She offered a cheeky wink.

“Aye, that she does. What do you fancy to drink?” he asked, gesturing for one of the servers to swing by. “Chardonnay?”

“That would be perfect.” She seemed pleased he remembered.

He ordered the drinks along with two dinner specials, before sitting down to join her. She’d taken a shower, her damp hair curling loosely over her shoulders. He swallowed down his arousal, images of her wet, naked body flirting with his libido.

“So tell me how old ya are?” Kade asked, unaware that the blunt question might be considered rude. Scots were not known for their diplomacy.

“I’m twenty-eight. Soon to be twenty-nine. My birthday is in December. Why how old are you?” she asked, returning his directness.

“I turned thirty a few weeks ago, he admitted, recalling the embarrassing night once more.

“Ah, I pegged you much older,” she teased.

“Did ya now?” Asked Kade, his smile challenging her, “I guess all those years of hard living aged me.”

"Oh, has life been hard on you?" she asked, her eyes twinkling with mischief. He liked that she didn't take herself, or him, too seriously.

"Not really," he confessed, "I've had it pretty easy, I guess. Three square meals a day and ne'er without a roof over my head. My parents are still married and only beat me on occasion."

"I'm guessing only when was much deserved?" she teased. He didn't mind.

"Oh, I'm sure it was. I was a wee bugger. The oldest of four boys. All of us gave mum a run for her money. The only reason we're still alive was her strict discipline. We were a rowdy bunch."

"I'm sure you were," Meg winked, her voice trailing off as the server approached with their drinks. Kade received them, handing Meg a very full wine glass.

"I'll say one thing, you Scots know how to pour a drink!" she observed, mindful not to spill a drop.

"That we do, Lass." He raised his beer and carefully toasted her glass, their eyes meeting. Unglued, he cleared his throat and set his beer in front of him. "So Meggie, you haven't told me, what ever possessed you to move halfway around the world. And why Scotland?"

"Hmm," she hesitated. She took another sip of wine, convincing him she was stalling. It must have been a good story.

"You don't have to tell me, if ya prefer not to. I'm just curious."

"No, no. It's fine. It's just not very compelling."

"I disagree," Kade pressed. "It must be a tiny bit exciting. It's not everyday a person takes on such a big adventure by themselves, let alone a woman."

Meg raised her eyes and smirked, hesitating as though carefully choosing her words. "Well, I'm not your average woman."

"I've gathered that, Meggie," Kade agreed, with a bit too much enthusiasm. She quickly averted her eyes, confirming his earlier suspicion that she had no idea how fascinating she was. He cleared his throat, urging her to continue.

"I guess I just needed a fresh start. I've had a few losses recently, and there was really nothing holding me back anymore. Scotland has been calling to me for a long time," she offered quietly, her eyes searching for the waitress, as though a hot meal placed in front of them might change the subject.

"Do ya mind if I ask about your losses?" asked Kade, unwilling to let her off the hook. He was anxious to know more, but promised himself to tread softly.

"My father passed away," she dropped flatly, her mouth twisting at the corners, as though holding back tears.

"I'm sorry. We're you close then?"

"Yes, he was a good man. One of the few," she added, inhaling sharply as though regretting her words.

Kade was not the most intuitive man, but he knew the sound of a broken heart. Someone had wronged her, no doubt. He wondered if he dare ask, but quickly decided against it. Her truth would reveal itself in time, if he was meant to know.

"He was young when he passed. Only fifty," she continued, her eyes pooling with grief. "Dad was an electrician and was killed on the job. He was working on the high wires when a miscommunication occurred. He died instantly."

"My God," Kade offered, wanting to take her hand, only too aware that Lorna was probably watching. That, and certain it was too soon for such affection.

"It was life-altering, to say the least. It made me take a good long look at where I was in my life. Grief will do that to you."

"Aye," he nodded. Although he'd never experienced the same level of grief, he could only imagine. Both his parents were alive and well, and although they didn't always see eye to eye, he was grateful to still have them.

"I was in the throws of a complicated relationship at the time, and just not happy. I'd been going through the motions a long time, hoping things would get better..."

That he could relate to.

"...and my father's death just added to the tension."

The server arrived with two heaping bowls of stew, with thick, with chunky bread for dipping. She set a dish in front of Meg, who immediately stopped talking. She smiled appreciatively, as though grateful for the interruption.

"Thank you, sweetheart," Kade acknowledged, nodding pleasantly at the young woman. Blushing, she grinned back, thoroughly charmed. He was used to that kind of response. Women adored him, which frustrated his parents even more that he'd yet to choose a wife. They were old-fashioned and wanted nothing more than for all their sons to be married and crank out babies.They loved their grandchildren, and the more the merrier. Being the oldest, and last of their boys to wed, they were constantly pressuring him. Not that he minded, but it could be frustrating at times. Things were much easier when he and Lorna were a couple. That small modicum of hope had kept his parents off his back. Since the break up, they'd turned up the pressure considerably. God love 'em.

"This looks delicious," Meg observed, rolling her cutlery out of the napkin. "The food is so homey in Scotland, don't you think?"

"I suppose it is. I've never really been anywhere else, so I can't compare."

"Trust me, it is," she chirped, popping a gravy soaked knob of bread into her mouth. He loved her enthusiasm for food. It was rare to see a woman expressing her joy for a good meal, and he didn't have the heart to interrupt her feasting with more questions.

They ate slowly, making small talk and just enjoying one another's company. She asked about his family, his parents and his brothers, laughing when he told her that along with four sons, his parents were blessed with four grandsons, nary a girl in sight. They were desperate for a bonnie lass to spoil.

"My goodness that Y chromosome is strong in your family!" Meg giggled, sitting back in her chair, a satisfied glow on her face.

"Aye, it is. So much testosterone. She was the only daughter in her family, and even my dad came from a family of sons! My poor mum. I think that's why she wanted her boys to marry, so she'd have some daughter-in-laws to help share the women's work," he grinned sheepishly.

"Did you just say that?" Meg tittered, tossing a spoon at him. Kade chuckled impishly, ducking just in time, pleased to raise her ire. He quite enjoyed teasing her.

"I'm kidding! I'm kidding. My mum would never have raised lazy sons. You'll know what I mean once you meet her," he slipped, the corners of his mouth dropping as soon as he realized what he'd said. Meg raised her brows curiously.

"Oh, I'm meeting your mum, am I?" she grinned, enjoying a long sip of wine.

"Well you never know, it's a small town," he bounced back. He pushed his plate away, pleased with his recovery.

"That would be nice. It would be lovely to meet your family. I could use some friends. It's strange starting over with no one, but oddly hopeful too. Do you know what I mean?" she asked sincerely.

"I don't suppose I do Meggie. I doubt I'd ever have the courage to start over from scratch. It's admirable."

"It was more self-preservation," she shrugged, not accepting the compliment well.

"What about your mum?" Kade asked, confident the timing was right to pick up where they'd left off.

"My mom left us when I was five. I was told she just couldn't settle into marriage and motherhood. They were both so young! She married a rock star and ended up with an electrician. She disappeared and I haven't heard from her since, not even when my father died. My grandmother was really the only mother I knew. She raised me," Meg looked away again, and sighed.

Kade could sense her raising the veil again, but at least they'd made progress. He was pleased enough with that, and didn't want to press much further, but he had to know— "So, this relationship you were in, was it a marriage?"

Shaking her head, Meg grinned at him, demonstrating he wasn't as slick as he thought. "No, definitely not marriage. He wasn't the marrying kind. I suppose it was a blessing."

"Aye," he offered, trying to play it cool. The man was clearly an eejit to let a woman like Meggie slip away, but it wasn't his place to say.

"I should probably head home," Meg offered suddenly, reaching behind her chair for her purse. "What's my share for dinner?"

"What? No dessert? Come on Meggie, sticky toffee pudding. How can you say no to that?" he tempted, not ready to say goodbye. She smirked at him playfully, her eyes urging him to 'keep talking'. He took it as a positive sign. "A little vanilla custard on the side. You haven't lived until you've tried Isla's sticky toffee pudding."

"Okay, okay. Twist my rubber arm," she laughed, easing back into her seat. "So what about you? Ever been married?"

"Oh god no," he blurted, a little too quickly, his mind flirting on the bullet he'd dodged with Lorna. He looked up and saw her smile fade, instantly regretting his tone. "Not that I'm opposed to marriage. I just haven't found the right woman."

CHAPTER 8

Meg

Meg had seen that look before, that anti-marriage, eyes glazed over stare. It actually surprised her, how quickly he'd answered. The way talked about his parents, and how happily married they were, and his brothers too, she'd pegged him the marrying kind. Not that it was any of her business, but it did raise a tiny red flag. She'd wondered if Nathan had felt the same way. If that would be his pat response to any woman he dated after her. She had to admit, it made her a little sad. Maybe she just wasn't the right woman for him. Maybe she wasn't the right woman for anyone.

The server returned to the table and Kade ordered dessert and coffee, before turning his attention to the woman at the bar. Lorna, if she remembered correctly. The pretty woman was looking at her, a curious expression on her face, her hand resting on the thigh of the man sitting beside her. Kade cleared his throat and shifted back to Meg, offering a weak smile.

She wondered if there was more to their relationship than Kade had alluded, if they were an item. If nothing else there was a history there, she was sure of it. She'd seen that territorial look before, when Nathan felt threatened; usually when any man spoke to her, even a coworker. Once they got home he would drill her for hours, making her feel guilty for no reason. She started to question her own instincts when it came to the opposite sex, wonder if she was unknowingly being flirtatious. After awhile she stopped talking to men altogether, keeping her head down when she was out with Nathan. It was easier that way.

"So now that the carpeting is ripped out, I can bring in a sander and clean up those hard wood floors. Those boards are in great shape. Once I re-stain them they'll look amazing," Kade insisted. She noticed that his eyes always lit up when he talked about work. He was definitely passionate about his work. She'd little doubt she'd chosen right.

"I should be finished with the wallpaper in a few days," she chimed in, grateful to shift the conversation away from her personal stuff. It wasn't that she wasn't open, but everything was still so raw. Bringing up the past was a painful reminder, and she wanted to leave it behind her. Besides, she didn't want to saddle Kade with negativity. He was her carpenter, not her therapist.

"No worries. I won't stain the floors until we finish stripping the walls and painting. That will be the last thing we do in the room. Tomorrow I'll strip the old paint off those wide baseboards and get them ready to stain. It will give you more time to finish. Whatever you don't get done, I'll help you with. Sound like a plan?" he asked, just as their dessert was set down in front of them.The sweet smell of toffee wafted towards her, assaulting her senses, momentarily distracting her. She couldn't wait to taste the rich, buttery cake.

"Hmm?" she responded, barely registering his words. Kade laughed whole-heartedly, drawing her eyes upwards. She felt her cheeks redden, embarrassed by her desire for the decadent dessert.

"Never-mind. First things first, pleasure before business. Take a bite," he chuckled, smiling playfully at her. "Go on."

She smiled bashfully, but did as she was told, sinking her fork into the moist cake. Kade seemed happy just to watch her reaction so she took a bite with flourish. A deep, guttural moan escaped her lips as the rich, buttery flavour seduced her tongue. It was quite possibly the best thing she'd ever eaten. Kade nodded, as though her response was exactly what he'd hoped for.

"This dessert is sex on a plate," she blurted, digging for another bite. "Seriously!"

"That it is," Kade agreed, quite pleased with himself for suggesting it. He took a bite of his own, and rolled his eyes for effect, making her laugh. It was fun sharing a meal with someone who appreciated food as much as she did. Nathan, a strict health nut, was no fun to eat with at all, often rolling his eyes for very different reasons. He hated when she ordered dessert, and would chastise her when she did.

She took another bite, just to spite her memories. *Why had she denied herself such simple pleasures to make that man happy?*

Kade offered to walk her home, but Meg insisted she was fine. She actually preferred to walk alone, she told him, thanking him again for dinner. It wasn't that she didn't like him, just the opposite in fact. He was the kind of guy a woman could easily fall in love with, if she wasn't careful. But Meg was careful.

As soon as she got home she grabbed herself a cup of tea and made her way to the front porch to watch the sun set, Katherine's diary in hand. She hadn't made much time for reading over the past week and was anxious to delve deeper into the young woman's story. As she opened the delicate pages, she passively wondered where she was now, what she'd grown up to be; if she was even still alive.

CHAPTER 9

Katherine

April 21, 1961

Dear Diary,

I wish I could talk to mum about Mack, but she'd never understand. Sometimes a girl has questions, or just needs someone to run things by, but mum is definitely not someone I could ever talk to about this stuff. She would have a fit if she knew. It's unlikely she would approve of anyone I chose, but Mack would definitely be a disappointment to her. He isn't the type of boy she'd want me to date. He's not from a well to do family, and he's not even Catholic!

But none of that bothers me. Mack is different. The funny thing is, I've been crushing on him for years, imagining him to be this quiet, allusive, brooding boy that would be hard to talk to, but he is nothing like that. He's warm and thoughtful and funny, and always such a gentleman when we're out together. He insists on taking care of me, opening doors, pulling out my chair, so concerned for my comfort.

We've seen each other almost every day for months. It's been hard hiding it from my parents, but we make it work. He meets me after school and walks me (almost) home, and he always has a bottle of soda for me to sip on. I think Esme is beyond jealous. I know this shouldn't make me happy, but it secretly does. I slept at her house last Saturday and she was actually quite supportive, so I shouldn't be so mean. She told me I could use her as an alibi anytime I wanted to spend time with Mack, that she would happily cover for me. She's being a good friend so I try not to be too boastful when I talk about him, but it's nice being on this side of things for a change. It's always been the other way around, and Esme is not as concerned about my feelings when she brags about her boyfriends. Still, I'm grateful for her help. Without her I'm certain I wouldn't be able to spend time with Mack.

We're going to the movies tonight. Although we've held hands, and we cuddle a lot, we've not kissed on the mouth yet. We came close once. We were sitting on a bench at the park and he leaned in close, his lips only inches from mine, then he just gave me the sweetest, most provocative smile and pulled away. It felt so daring, right out there in public, and left me gasping for air! I'm hoping that tonight will be the night. I'm ready! He's more restrained than I imagined him to be, but that's fine. I actually appreciate that he's not an octopus. If he doesn't try to kiss me tonight I will be disappointed, but I won't ever make the first move. As much as I want to, I'm just not that kind of girl.

I'll be sure to write tomorrow, Diary! Wish me luck!

* * *

"You're going out?" Mary asked, one eyebrow raised. She was assessing Katherine's outfit, disappointed she'd nothing to scold her for.

"Aye Mum. I told you, Esme and I are going to see a movie tonight," Katherine acknowledged carefully, mindful not to give her mother any fuel to pick a fight. Recently, her mother had been giving her a little more space. Katherine wondered if her dad had anything to do with that, quietly reminding Mary that their daughter was not a child anymore. It seemed like something he would do. She felt almost guilty that she was hiding the truth from them, but she preferred to think of it as being creatively discreet, rather than full out fibbing.

"You'll come right home after though." Mary said, as an order more than a question.

"We thought we'd go for a soda, just for a bit. If ya don't object?" Katherine offered, carefully walking over egg shells. "I promise to be home by ten."

"Hmph," Mary mumbled, biting her tongue. She raised her eyes, searching for her husband, but found him wisely hiding behind his novel, listening but not interfering. Katherine could tell her mum was irritated. Every emotion Mary felt was always etched across her face. She called it her blessing and curse. Katherine was grateful she took more after her father in that respect, and was able to mask her feelings from the world when necessary, especially from her mother. "I suppose that's fine," she continued, though her teeth were clenched.

"Thank you mum," Katherine trilled, quickly kissing her cheek before she could add any more, or worse, change her mind. "Bye Dad! Love you both!"

She slipped her purse over her shoulder and closed the door behind her, smiling to herself. She was enjoying her new found freedom, but knew it was driving her mum crazy. Although it probably shouldn't have, it made it all the more rewarding.

Mack was waiting around the corner, smiling as she approached. He looked nice, forgoing his usual black t-shirt for a flattering collared shirt. His hair was combed back, and as she approached she appreciated the pleasant scent of aftershave. She was flattered that he'd put some thought into his appearance for their date.

"You look bonnie," he complimented, taking her hand.

"Thanks, so do you," she smiled, still wondering how she'd gotten so lucky.

"Men aren't bonnie," he teased, flashing his signature smile, a cocky half-grin that always made her knees weak.

"Aye, they can be," she insisted, squeezing his fingers.

"No" he continued, swinging their arms as they walked, "we're handsome, dapper, even sexy, but ne'er bonnie. That's no compliment."

"Well, it should be. Bonnie is such a happy word, and you make me happy," she blushed, surprised by her boldness. She couldn't help it, she was giddy in love.

He looked down at her and shrugged, clearly flattered. "I can't argue with that!" he agreed, pulling her close enough for their arms to brush together. The sensation made her heart flutter.

"Come on," he purred, we can be bonnie together, but let's get moving or we'll miss the news reel, and the coming attractions."

Before long they were inside the theatre, sitting way in the back. Katherine didn't mind. She relished the privacy, nervous someone might see them and report back to her mum. For that, she was grateful for the dim lighting. If someone was to see them, she had a story ready. She would just tell her mum that Mack was Esme's date, and that Esme must have been at the snack bar, or in the powder room when they were spotted. It would be fine.

Mack held her hand through the whole movie, except when they were sharing popcorn. At first he'd placed the carton in his lap, but Katherine had been too embarrassed to reach between his thighs. As soon as he realized his mistake, he tossed her one of his sexy, signature smiles and held the popcorn between them, forcing them to release hands. It was a silly moments they would laugh about later. She was sure of it. Mack never took himself too seriously. She loved that about him.

After the film was over they walked to Argyle's, only to find Esme there with a couple of friends from school. After a quick greeting, Esme eyed them critically, a tight smile on her lips. Katherine almost dropped Mack's hand, suddenly embarrassed by the innocent display of affection, but he just held her tighter, not intimidated by Esme in the least. His confidence was infectious and Katherine couldn't help but stand a little straighter.

Esme invited them to sit down, as though she was doing them a huge favour, but Mack just shook his head and said, "thank you, no. We're going to sit in a booth alone, if ya don't mind." She opened her mouth to insist, but quickly shut it again as though she thought better of it. Katherine shrugged innocently. Although she wasn't that sorry, she smiled apologetically. Kat found Mack's assertiveness irresistible, and by the look on Esme's face, she might have felt the same way.

As the waitress left with their order, he asked nervously, "did you enjoy the movie?"

"Of course! It was grand! Did you?" Katherine asked, searching for a clue to his uneasiness.

"Aye..." his eyes shifted around the room before landing on hers again. He took her hands in his, forcing heat to rise up her chest.

"What's the matter?" she asked, hoping her cheeks had not flushed. He shrugged nonchalantly, but he wasn't fooling her. Something was up. She caught his eye and grinned, hoping to set him at ease. It had the desired effect, she noticed, as she watched his shoulders drop, his mouth turning up at the corners.

"Don't sweat it," he shrugged, shaking it off. She wondered if he was thinking about their first kiss too. She hoped so. He held her hand gently, but kept his thoughts closely guarded. It wasn't like him to be so quiet. She was the shy one.

They sat across from each other, words unspoken, until the server arrived with their soda and chips. She reached for the ketchup bottle, unscrewing the cap, then tipped it over their shared plate. Nothing happened. She hammered the bottom of the bottle with her palm, hoping to get the stick unstuck. One, two, three hard swats—before the ketchup erupted from the bottle, splashing off the plate onto Mack's crisp white shirt.

"Oh!" Katherine gasped, her eyes wide with regret. She tried not to giggle, stifling her embarrassment. On Mack's face, a combination of shock and amusement, with a little mischief thrown in.

"Did you want a little ketchup then?" she asked playfully, carefully setting the bottle in front of her.

"Aye," he chirped, examining his soiled shirt, "but I was thinking I'd eat it off the plate."

"I'm so sorry, here, let me clean that up." She reached for a napkin and dipped it into her water glass, desperate to find a solution.

"No bother. I'll just go clean up. Don't move you wee beast. I'll be back for you," he teased, slipping out of the booth. His sexy command warmed her insides as though she'd just swallowed a mouthful of creamy hot chocolate.

"I'll be here. I might even save you some chips," she quipped, pleased her words weren't drowned out by the arousal she felt. He threw her a wink and slipped out of sight.

"Well, did he kiss you yet?" Esme asked, dropping into the booth across from her, not at all concerned with discretion.

"Shhh, someone will hear you," Katherine blushed, glancing uncomfortably around the room.

Smirking, she helped herself to a chip. "Don't be daft, no one's listening! So spill it, did he finally give up the goods? Did he cop a feel? What was it like?"

"Esme, stop!"

"Tell me," she insisted, lowering her voice.

"No, not yet."

Her friend looked sceptical, trying to read the truth in her eyes.

"Seriously? What's his problem? You've been seeing each other for ages! Do you think he might be—?" Esme dropped her wrist in an unmistakeable gesture, trying to get a rise out of her.

"No! He's just a gentleman, that's all," Katherine insisted, not at all pleased with the suggestion, especially from Esme. Sometimes she could be so mean.

"How disappointing. I thought for sure he'd be more exciting."

"He is exciting. Maybe he just respects me—"

Esme rolled her eyes impatiently. "Please, plenty of boys respect me and still want to fool around."

Katherine disagreed, but wisely kept her opinion to herself. True to form, she kept the peace. "I know. I guess he just wants it to be special. I can't answer for him," she offered, apologetically.

"Well it better be damn special if he's making you wait so long," Esme spat. Katherine wondered why she was so concerned anyway. It wasn't like she was the one waiting for a kiss.

"It's okay. I'm sure it'll be worth the wait. I don't mind, really," Katherine assured, hoping to placate her. In truth, she just wanted the conversation over. With Mack returning any second, she would just die if Esme said anything to embarrass her, or him. "Go, now, before he comes back," she pleaded.

She saw the look of disappointment on her friend's face, and suddenly wished she'd been a more sensitive. She didn't want to hurt Esme's feelings. Not at all.

"I'm going already. *I'm* no a third wheel..."

Katherine wondered if Esme meant the words so harshly, and if the crack was personal. She'd often been the one awkwardly tagging along with Esme and her boy of the week, feeling much like the spare wheel. Was Esme jealous—of her?

"Of course not. I didn't mean it that way," Katherine soothed. As the care-taker of their friendship, she did that a lot. She prayed Esme would cut her some slack, and graciously accept her apology.

"Hmph—I suppose not," she pouted, "just remember that I'm the one watching out for you. I'm only trying to help."

"I know," Katherine nodded, tossing an appreciative smile. "I'll call you tomorrow and tell you all about it, I promise. Please, don't be upset."

"Okay, first thing in the morning—"

"Of course," Katherine agreed, knowing she had little choice in the matter. "Thanks for covering for me tonight."

"Yes, and don't you forget it. You owe me!" Esme winked, sliding towards the edge of the booth. "I'll expect all the details."

"I know, I know," Katherine laughed, pushing down her discomfort. She hated feeling beholden to Esme, so submissive, but at the moment she was just grateful her friend was leaving without a scene. "Thank you."

Satisfied, Esme slipped away, gesturing her approval with a wave.

"What was that about?" Mack asked, sidling up behind her, his mistrustful eyes following Esme out the door.

"Nothing. She just came over to say hello," Katherine assured, taking a sip of soda, trying to calm her nerves. Mack sat down, curiously assessing her.

"You seem agitated," he observed, his words edged with concern. That was one of the things she liked about Mack, he was so intuitive when it came to her feelings.

"It's okay. It was just Esme...being Esme. We've been friends a very long time and this is the first time she's had to share me with someone else. I suppose it'll take some getting used to," Katherine assured, kindly offering the benefit of the doubt. There was no way Esme would ever hurt her. Mack wasn't convinced but shrugged it off anyway. It was just as well, Katherine didn't want to focus on Esme.

"Did the stain come out?" she asked, changing the subject. She pushed the plate of chips towards him. Nodding, he popped one into his mouth.

"It's fine. Don't stress about it. If you wanted to get my shirt off of me, all you needed to do was ask," he grinned puckishly, raising the blood to her cheeks.

"I—uh," she choked, suddenly wondering what that would look like. Those were not thoughts of a proper Catholic girl, but they were impossible to curb.

"I'm only kidding, Kat," he smiled, reaching for her hand. "At least for the most part. Here, share these chips with me."

The hour flew by, Katherine wishing for time to slow down. She kept one eye on her watch hoping she wasn't being too obvious. The last thing she needed was to miss her curfew, and truth be told, she hoped for a slow walk home, and God-willing, a kiss at the end of the night. When Mack finally suggested they leave, she practically jumped out of the booth.

Their walk home was peaceful, Mack gently holding her hand. Although not unwelcome, there was a palpable tension, impossible to ignore. She sensed it burning in the space between them, lulling her into a romantic trance, a quiet space to fantasize...

"Kat?"

Startled, Katherine stopped in her tracks, his deep voice filling the silence. Despite shaking off her fantasy, the evidence of it stained her flushed cheeks. She stared up at him, eyes glazed, wordlessly questioning him.

"Oh god, when you look at me like that—"

Without a word, he hurried her into the alley and pushed her against the wall, anxiously pressing his soft lips against hers. Surprised, she let out a tiny moan, the world she knew changing in a heartbeat. Until that moment it was as though her entire life had been black and white...and then suddenly thrust into an ethereal, technicolour dreamland, like Dorothy in the Wizard of Oz. From one heartbeat to the next, she'd been altered. She sensed Mack breathing new life into her, filling her with a curiosity unlike anything she'd ever felt before, every cell in her body charged with his need. She was no longer a girl anticipating her first kiss. She was a woman.

He pulled himself away, and stared at her with an intensity she didn't understand. It nearly took her breath away, and she wanted another kiss. Forgetting her shyness, she wrapped around him, offering her mouth, this time focusing on the physical sensations, the feather touch of his warm lips, the sweet taste of his tongue, the heat of his hands as they slipped under her blouse. She was surprised how little control she had as her knees buckled beneath her, modesty softly closing the door and slipping silently into the furthest corner of her mind. How easy it would be to lose herself in him, to release herself from the bonds of chastity. It was a seductive thought...

"Kat, we need to stop—I need to stop," Mack whispered, his words greedily swallowed by her kisses. He moaned his regret but continued kissing her, knitting his fingers through her hair. He eased her head back, exposing her delicate neck before gently sinking in his teeth, a sensation she didn't hate at all.

What would her mother say, if she saw her daughter so untethered, allowing a boy to test her principles with such abandon? Surely she would be mortified, perhaps even ground her for life. Images of her mother's disapproving glare quickly forced her back to reality, to the alley, to her good, Catholic girl senses. Abruptly, her body stiffened, involuntarily scrutinizing her. She paused—just long enough for Mack to take notice.

"I'm sorry," he apologized.

And just like that the passion drifted away, like a delicate feather swirling upwards in a gust of wind. Remorsefully, he peeled away, courteously straightening her blouse.

"No," Katherine pleaded, still dizzy from his touch. She didn't understand his apology, or his regret. Did she do something wrong? Did he not enjoy it? Touching her? Kissing her? Mack picked up her handbag, so carelessly dropped in the street, and offered it back, still avoiding her eyes.

"Mack?"

"I shouldn't have done that. I didn't mean to—"

"—to kiss me?" Katherine whispered, her naive thoughts questioning everything. Her cheeks, pink from passion, suddenly reddened with embarrassment.

"I don't know what I was thinking Kat." His words, spilling too quickly, did nothing to ease her shame. She took a step backwards, and stared at him, her teeth pulling anxiously at her bottom lip. What was he saying?

"Did I do something wrong?" she cried, unable to stop her tears.

"Oh god no, woman, no. Why would you think that?" he asked, finally meeting her eyes. "That's not what I meant at all. I thought I came on too strong, that maybe I offended ya?" he insisted sheepishly. Reaching for her trembling hands, he tenderly eased her back into his arms. "Sweet Kat, I waited so long to kiss you, I think I may have lost my mind. I just needed you so bad. It was me that did something wrong."

Katherine sank into his embrace, wishing that along with her first kiss, came all the insight and wisdom of womanhood. Life would be much simpler if it all came at once, she thought, releasing the breath she'd been holding.

"Do ya think it possible that ya can love someone before you've even met them?" he whispered softly, his breath hot in her ear.

"Aye, I think it's possible," she replied, raising her head.

"I know this may sound daft," he cautioned, "but I felt like the moment I met you, we were meant to be. I've been so cynical Kat, all my life. I've never had those romantic notions, but with you, everything makes sense. Like we're promised souls. I feel like I could grow into an old, old man and still love you with every bone in my broken down body. I see it Kat."

She'd seen it too, but thought them only the silly inspirations of a romantic child. But hearing him voice it, affirming everything she'd felt, suddenly made it all seem possible. They'd only been together a short time, but she'd always been drawn to Mack, from the moment she saw him so many years earlier. Something had captivated her, beckoned her towards him; a feeling, a force, an invisible string that bound them together as soul mates. Yes, she had loved him before they'd even met, but didn't understand it until just that moment.

"I can't explain it, but the chemistry I felt when we kissed. It was as though my whole world opened up. God, I sound like I'm off me heid..." he laughed, dropping a playful peck on her forehead.

"No you don't, Mack. You sound brilliant."

"I want to say...I love you—" he balked, as though the words might be ill-fated. She smiled at him warmly and nodded.

"So say it—"

"I love you Katherine Margaret. I can promise ya that."

"I love you, Mack. I promise you, too."

CHAPTER 10

Meg

The loch was still as glass. From her vantage point, the water appeared black as onyx, light glistening off the surface like precious gem stones, in the early afternoon sun. It was Sunday, and after a long week of heavy work, she insisted they take the day off, instructing Kade not to come in despite his protest. He was working hard. In truth, the project seemed almost personal for him. She didn't mind, it was endearing. He took great pride in his work and her home was really starting to take shape.

They'd accomplished a lot in the weeks they'd been plugging away. Her bedroom was finally finished and she'd rewarded herself by purchasing a brand new mattress. In time she'd replace the frame, but it was still liberating, picking something for herself, without anyone's input or approval. She topped it with crisp white linens, making the indigo walls pop. Bold colours made her happy and she planned to paint them throughout the entire house. When she'd lived with Nathan he permitted only neutral colours, insisting that anything else would ruin the home's appeal.

Once, soon after she'd moved in, Nathan went fishing for a week in Georgia. She thought she'd surprise him by freshly painting their bedroom a playful shade of yellow. She honestly considered it a good compromise, not too feminine but better than the uninspiring grey that dulled the room. She wanted to brighten things up and thought he'd be thrilled with the woman's touch she was offering.

She couldn't wait for him to come home, to show him what she'd done. It was her way of saying, *I'm here. I'm a part of your life*. Instead, when he walked in and saw it, he pitched a fit and told her to never do anything to the house without his approval. She was mortified. At first she was angry at him for reacting unreasonably, but it didn't take long for her to turn it around and blame herself. Of course she'd over stepped her bounds. Couples always consulted one another before making big decisions, didn't they? Even decorating ones? She should've been more considerate, and after that she made sure to check in with him before doing anything, even buying something as mundane as a new spatula. Not surprising really, that even after living together for a few years, she always felt like a guest in their home. Correction, Nathan's home.

It was a sunny day, not as humid as a mid-August day back home, but balmy by Scottish standards. Kade had told her it was a rare occurrence for temperatures to rise above seventy degrees, even in the deep summer months. In fact Fort William's weather was fairly moderate all year round, with more rain hitting the ground than snow. He about died when she told him that summers in Virginia could hit a sweltering ninety degrees, sometime even toppling a hundred! He said he couldn't even imagine how hot that was, having never experienced it. Meg laughed and told him he'd probably melt on the spot with all that cool, Scottish blood running through his veins.

Taking advantage of the 'heat', Meg made her way down to the water, bringing a small picnic lunch and a good book to relax the afternoon away. She had to leave the house or she'd find herself working on one project or another, and she was determined to unwind. There was a decent crowd enjoying the park, boating, playing with their kids, or just throwing around frisbees. The fact that she was alone didn't trouble her in the least, she quite liked the solitude, but she couldn't help thinking about Kade. She wondered what he was up to on such a glorious day.

She'd grown accustomed to having him around. His cheerful bantering and teasing made their long days more bearable, even fun. In fact, she was really starting to like it. She'd never felt completely at ease around Nathan and just assumed she was incapable of it. He'd often told her she was too anxious and high strung, a worry-wart. He'd taunt her if she relaxed, calling her lazy and unmotivated. And if she was pre-occupied with a project or task, he'd complain that she wasn't giving him enough attention. Of course, when she called him out on it, he chalked it up to teasing, accusing her of being humourless.

But with Kade it was different. He seemed content in her company, often complimenting her work, or patiently teaching her something new. He never made her feel clumsy or stupid, even when she messed up. Well trained by Nathan, she'd kept her guard up, waiting for Kade to grow impatient or criticize her, but he never did. It was easy with him, and in some ways his praise offered her confidence, but more importantly, *permission* to like herself.

They talked a lot too, about everything, philosophical and silly things alike. Kade was an open book, outgoing and curious, and genuinely interested in her ideas. He was also very direct, but not unkindly so. He was never boastful or rude, just a man who knew who he was, with the confidence to show it. She admired that. The old Meg would have censored her thoughts, second guessed herself. But that was changing. The truth was, she was starting over with nothing, her life in Scotland a fresh chapter, so she had nothing to lose. She could just be herself, honour her own truth, and that felt remarkable. The more she relaxed, the more comfortable she grew into her own skin. She was really starting to like herself. Perhaps even love. Maybe it was Kade's gift for restoring old homes, but she couldn't help but think he was bringing new life to her as well, patiently stripping away her insecurity and chipping away at her walls. She was grateful they'd met.

"Hello there, do you remember me?"

Meg looked up from the book she wasn't reading, shielding her eyes from the sun. "Oh, hello. You're Kade's friend. I'm sorry, I've forgotten your name?"

"Aye, it's Lorna. Mind if I join you?" Lorna grinned, plunking down in the grass beside her, not waiting for an invitation. "Meg, right?"

Meg quickly moved the picnic basket to offer the woman more room, before sharing a curious smile. Although surprised by the interruption, she was pleased Lorna had stopped to say hello. Busy renovations did not leave much time to socialize, or make new friends. Normally she would've been too nervous to strike up a conversation, but any friend of Kade's was probably alright. Besides, if she'd learned nothing else since being in Scotland, it's inhabitants were never short of words and could carry a conversation with anyone, friend or foe. It was actually quite endearing.

"You're out here by yourself, are you?" Lorna asked, her eyes scoping the beach.

"Yes, it was too lovely to stay home," Meg admitted. She picked up a bag of roasted almonds, wordlessly offering them to her new friend. Lorna waved her away, picking up the bottle of wine between them instead.

"Do ya mind?" she asked.

"Sure, let me grab you a glass," Meg smiled, flipping the tea towel off her basket. She handed her a plastic cup, knocking a blade of grass out of it first. “Sorry,” she said, shrugging apologetically.

“No Kade?” Lorna asked, filling the cup to the brim.

“Kade?” Meg asked innocently, wishing the wine was colder.

Lorna grinned. “I just assumed you’d be together?”

“No, of course not. It’s Sunday.” Meg caught the woman’s eye, wondering why she’d made the assumption. She and Kade were only friends. They worked together, nothing more.

“You don’t talk on Sunday?”

Laughing nervously, Meg shook her head, trying to read Lorna’s expression. She’d seen the look before; a smile just an inch short of sincere, flat eyes masking the real questions, not the spoken ones. Did the woman have reason to feel threatened? Even though Kade had introduced Lorna as his friend, Meg recalled wondering if there was something more. If there was, the last thing she wanted was to make waves, especially being the newcomer.

“Kade just works for me. Sunday is typically his day off. I suppose he’s with his family or something,” she assured, as delicately as possible. “Are you and he close?”

“You might say that,” Lorna chuckled, leaning back on her elbow. She carefully set her glass down in the grass before meeting Meg’s eyes again, her face softening. “You’re from America,” she continued, more as a statement than a question.

“Yes, did the accent give me away?” Meg responded timidly, adjusting her glasses. She wasn’t sure why the woman made her so nervous, but she did her best to mask it.

“Aye,” Lorna chuckled, “You might say that. It’s quite exotic.”

Returning the compliment, Meg smiled sweetly. “Oh? Thank you, but it’s not quite as pretty as yours.”

"Hmmm. Which part?"

"Which part? Of America you mean?" Meg asked, seeking clarity.

"Yes. Where are you from?"

Meg hesitated for a moment. She avoided thinking about home, and wasn't sure she wanted to discuss that part of her life with Lorna, but being rude was less appealing. "Just a little suburban town in Virginia, outside Richmond."

"You're quite lovely, I can see why Kade fancies you," Lorna challenged, a flat smirk on her face. Meg shrugged awkwardly, surprised by the out-of-place compliment—and the observation.

"I'm not sure what you mean?"

"Dinna fash yerself, I'm only teasing," Lorna chuckled softly, as though satisfied with the reply.

Still trying to get a handle on the conversation, Meg nervously bit her lip.

"We go way back. He didn't tell you?"

"You and Kade? No."

"Oh, that's so like him. Did he not mention his girlfriend to you, then?"

Meg felt a fleeting pang of disappointment, just enough to make her question her feelings for Kade. We're they more than just friendly? Of course she was flattered by his innocent flirting, and yes, she enjoyed his company, but didn't she chalk it up to friendship? She didn't want more than that, did she?

Recovering quickly, Meg turned up her southern charm. "Well, that's wonderful! He's just a lovely man. You must be so proud of him."

"I am. Of course we've had our ups and downs like every couple. But we've been together a long time. High school sweethearts. We've broken up a time or two, mostly because Kade thinks he's missing out on something, but eventually, when he doesn't find me in another, he comes crawling back on his hands and knees," she offered lightly. "With his tail tucked between his legs, of course. We're on a bit of a break right now."

Meg smiled politely, wondering if they were talking about the same person. Kade didn't seem like the kind of man that would tuck tail for anyone, but she was only just getting to know him. She was definitely uncomfortable with all the information being fed to her, but nodded nevertheless, trying her best not to reveal any emotion. She still wasn't sure about the woman, but her instincts were firing on all cylinders. Her old triggers, like long, bony fingers, poked at her gut, and she knew enough not to offer any ammunition. She chalked it up to self-preservation. Old habits died hard.

"Anyway, I hope ya don't mind me stopping by to say hello. I was with my friends over there," Lorna paused long enough to point out a group of people sitting together at a picnic table. "I thought I recognized you from the pub."

"Of course not, I'm glad you did. I haven't had time to make many friends since moving here—"

"Just Kade," Lorna interrupted, her smile fading.

"Yes."

"Well, no matter. Come, let me introduce you to the gang," Lorna offered, downing the rest of her wine. She quickly stood up and held out her hand before Meg could decline.

And she wanted to. Not because she was shy, that was true, but because something warned her to be careful. She hesitated before taking Lorna's hand, looking down at the book in her lap.

"Come on now, it won't take long. Your stuff will be fine, I promise ya, no one will take it," Lorna offered sincerely, her smile so sweet Meg wondered if she was crazy for feeling so wary. The woman was obviously making a kind gesture and it would be rude to turn her away, she decided.

"Ok, maybe for just a minute."

"You know, I think you and I could be good friends." Lorna said, helping Meg to her feet. "Would ya like that?"

Meg smiled cautiously. She wasn't sure if she would, but knew damn well the right answer was yes.

* * *

Meeting Lorna's friends wasn't as intimidating as Meg thought it would be. They were friendly and inviting, and had her laughing within minutes. It felt good to be welcomed and Meg couldn't help but like them. Even Lorna seemed more genuine around them, and they were certainly enamoured with her.

It wasn't a mystery why Kade was drawn to her too, why he always went back to her. Who wouldn't be attracted to a woman like that? She was sexy, dynamic, and confident. The word that came to mind was seductive, not sexually per se, but captivating. A strong alpha female. Lorna was everything Meg wasn't, and that made her all the more intriguing.

Surprising herself, Meg visited more than an hour before excusing herself. Like a good southern woman, she knew not to wear out her welcome. After she left them she packed up her things and went straight home, opting to make herself a simple dinner rather than going to The Coo. If she was being honest, she didn't want to bump into Kade. Spending time with Lorna that afternoon had made her question her feelings for Kade. Was she drawn to him, in spite of the promise she'd made to swear off men? How could she not be, they'd been spending so much time together.

Yes, she was attracted to him, plain and simple, and he wasn't available. Certainly not emotionally, if what Lorna claimed was true. No, it was better to keep things professional, keep her emotions in check. It was a small community and the last thing she needed was to be thrust into the middle of a love-triangle, especially considering she'd ultimately be the one getting hurt. Lorna said that Kade always found his way back, didn't she? Maybe they were apart for the moment, but surely it was only a matter of time.

She was sitting at the kitchen table looking over her budget when Kade walked in, smelling of fresh air and spicy cologne. He had a huge smile on his face and she couldn't help but grin back, ignoring the sudden surge in her lower half. He walked over to the coffee pot, pouring himself a cup. God he looked good, his hair, still wet from the shower, curling just over his collar; his tool belt swinging low on his hips, framing his perfect ass—

"Did you want some of this?"

"What?" she blushed, embarrassed to be caught staring. *Did he know what she was thinking?*

He raised his mug in salute. "Coffee?"

"Coffee? Uh—no. I just had some." She cleared her throat, quickly dropping her eyes to her spreadsheets.

"Did you have a good day yesterday?" he asked, pulling up a chair, closing the gap between them. His leg brushed against her.

"Um, ya—you know I was thinking that it might make sense to repurpose those shelves in the bookstore instead of building new ones. Just to make the budget go further. And I know I said I wanted to get new door knobs, but you're right, the old glass ones add so much character—"

"Well, you're getting right down to it this morning. Doesn't a guy get any foreplay around here?" he flirted, teasing a smile out of her.

"Sorry, Kade, I have a lot on my mind. Do you mind if we just get to work?"

"All work and no play then, is it? Not even a good morning? How was your day off? A thank you for the gift?"

"Gift?" she asked, looking up from her notes.

"Aye, I bought you a present. It's just something I saw at the antique shop yesterday. It made me think of you," he grinned, unwilling to be deterred.

"You bought me a gift?" she repeated, unable to mask her astonishment. She didn't care what the gift was, she was just touched that he thought of her.

"Come with me, I left it in the shop."

She followed him through the house, doing her best to not stare at his swaying tool belt, until he stopped at the double pocket doors. Sliding them open, he gestured for her to pass, smiling like the Cheshire Cat.

"Kade, it's beautiful!" she shrieked, wide eyed and happy. Sitting on the counter was a beautiful, antique brass cash register, in mint condition, with every key intact. "Does it work?"

"The man who sold it assured me it did. He gave me a demonstration. Look I'll show you."

He walked behind the counter, gesturing her to follow, a huge grin on his face. "You see here, you press the keys for the dollar amount and then turn the handle on the side to register the next item. You'll have to key in the tax manually, and of course count back the change the old fashioned way—when you're ready you push the *cash out* key, and voila, the till will open," he explained, demonstrating each step along the way.

Ting, the register chimed, just as the drawer sprung open with force, unceremoniously hitting him in the groin. Thankfully his tool belt took most of the impact.

"Jesus, don't let it hit ya like that or you may never have babies," he chuckled, tossing her a cheeky wink. Meg let out a hearty laugh and threw her arms around him, wordlessly expressing her gratitude. It was quite possibly the coolest, most thoughtful thing anyone ever did for her.

"I don't know what to say, I love it!" she gushed, properly easing out of the hug, seconds before it became awkward. Instead Kade held her tightly, connecting just a moment longer. It was subtle but there was no mistaking his intention, even for an inexperienced woman like herself. It had been a long time since a man held her like that, and she felt herself swoon like one of her old-fashioned, storybook heroines. If she hadn't felt so pitiful, it might have been comical. *What was wrong with her?* Her body acted like a spoiled child, wanting precisely what it couldn't have.

"I'm glad you like it," he choked, his words catching. Forcing herself away, she quickly turned her attention back to the register. The tender encounter left her vulnerable.

"It must have been expensive, Kade. It's way too much. I really shouldn't accept it."

"Nonsense. As soon as I saw it, I knew it belonged to you. It'll go perfectly with your vision for the shop," he insisted, stepping out of the way. "Here, you try it—"

"I...don't...it's just that...I shouldn't..." she stammered, conflicted. He was so sweet, and the gift was very thoughtful. She didn't want to hurt his feelings, or seem ungrateful, but his generosity confused her. What did it mean?

"It's no a big deal, Meggie. It's just a wee housewarming gift. Do people in America not do that?"

Meg smiled, feeling silly for reading too much into it. "No— I mean yes, of course they do. It's just that, where I come from, we're taught to act humble...and undeserving when someone offers a gift. It's the American way," she offered lightly, hoping to salvage the situation.

In true Scottish fashion, directly, not unkindly, he retorted, "don't be daft."

"Okay, you're right. Thank you...for the present," she conceded, warming a little. It was impossible to keep things strictly professional with Kade, he was just too likeable. So friends they would be, she thought, but nothing more.

The rest of the day went smoothly, the two of them easily falling back into their comfortable routine. Flirting, teasing, and playing harmless practical jokes on each other made the hard work more fun. Meg was working in the bathroom, preparing the walls for paint. Kade had drywalled and taped a few days earlier, and she needed to sand the seams before priming. It was a messy job, but she didn't mind.

"Like I said, I love a woman who doesn't mind getting dirty—" Kade growled, sneaking up behind her.

"Jesus, you scared me," she jumped, spinning around too quickly, her foot slipping off the stool. She tumbled to the floor, falling hard on her ass.

"Christ, I'm sorry," he snickered, trying to suppress a laugh. He picked her up as though she weighed nothing, setting her back on her feet. "You want a kiss to make you feel better?" he winked.

"Oh? Ya want to kiss me arse, do ya?" Meg quipped without missing a beat, using the best Scottish accent she could summon.

“Nay, but I’ll spank it for ya,” Kade laughed, his arms still around her.

Meg giggled, desperate to stop her traitorous, quickening heartbeats. “If you can catch a moving target, old man,” she chirped, gently shoving him aside. He reached for her hand, but she was too quick for him, slipping out of his reach in the nick of time.

“You’re a wee beast, Meggie. You have to stop running sometime…” he shouted after her.

“I’m getting primer,” she trilled back. “Finish sanding that drywall or you’ll be the one getting spanked.”

“Promises, promises!”

She couldn’t stop smiling.

CHAPTER 11

Meg

"So are you ready for that bubble bath?" Kade asked, looking proudly around the finished bathroom. It looked straight out of a magazine.

"You read my mind. I plan to do just that as soon as you get your ass out of here," Meg agreed, poking him in the chest with the butt end of her hammer.

"Well that's not very nice," Kade pouted. "There's room enough in that tub for two, maybe even three people."

"Yes, me, myself and I," she laughed, imagining how sexy it would be to soak in the tub with the handyman. She cleared her throat, and looked around the room, pretending to offer a closer inspection. He did a fantastic job restoring the old tub and cleaning up the vintage tiles that surrounded it. It had a mid-century modern feel to it that was currently all the trend. A nod to the past, the bright yellow walls were a passive-aggressive *'fuck you'* to Nathan. She smiled to herself before turning back towards Kade.

"It looks amazing. You did great work."

"*We* did great work. I've never had a client pitch in as much as you. I'm actually quite impressed," he praised, rubbing her shoulder.

"Well, I had no choice. I can't afford your prices."

"Well I may not be cheap, but I am easy," he winked. "I don't know about you, but I'm ready for the pub."

"Go,go. I'm just going to finish packing up the kitchen so we can start in there on Monday."

"Woman, you need a break. Don't you ever stop?" He was teasing, but she could see his humour was knit with concern.

"I don't mind Kade, it's a labor of love for me. It makes me happy seeing it all come together."

"Why does it mean so much to you, Meggie?"

The question, laced with so much sincerity, touched her. He'd earned a little vulnerability.

"Remember I told you that when I was a little girl my mother left me and my dad? It was a tough time for both of us, so we moved in with my grandmother. I know my dad needed the help. I'm sure he was terrified to raise a daughter on his own. My grandmother was an amazing woman. She was like a mother to me, caring for me, teaching me, loving me unconditionally. One day, when I came home from school, she surprised me with a doll house, a little cottage. I loved that little house, played with it for years. It fuelled my imagination and offered me a safe place to work through all those complicated feelings. My house had a family, with two parents who loved each other—who loved me. I was always safe there, comforted. No one fought, or called each other names, or abandoned their kids..." Meg paused for a moment, and glanced at Kade, solemnly gathering her thoughts.

"Go on," he encouraged, tenderly.

"This house reminds me of that doll house, and of my grandmother. As soon as I walked in it took me back to that safe place again, where I was in control of my destiny. Maybe it sounds crazy, but this house is helping me figure out who I am."

Kade smiled warmly. "It doesn't sound crazy at all," he soothed, reaching for her hand. She allowed him to take it. Much like when he gave her the cash register, she wanted to resist, to question the intent, to deny his generosity, but she was learning to accept his acts of kindness.

"So it doesn't feel like work to me Kade, you see? It's more like therapy." She looked up at him and grinned, "and trust me, as expensive as you are, you're still cheaper than paying any therapist."

"I'm in the wrong line of work, I guess," he chuckled, caressing her fingers. His eyes softened, taking in the honesty. She sensed a shift, an invisible but undeniable chemistry, altering the air between them. *Did he want to kiss her?*

His desire was unspoken but she sensed it in every cell of her body. And she wanted it too, but she was terrified. He seemed to be everything she wanted, and yet, she'd been so wrong before. Her friends tried to warn her about Nathan, but she didn't listen. At one time *he* was everything she wanted, but things changed. She couldn't go through that again. And what about Lorna?

"Well, I'm going to pour myself a glass of wine and tackle that kitchen. You should go..." she announced abruptly, casually pulling her hand away.

"Meggie."

Kade paused, a moment longer than comfortable. She knew what he wanted but had to deny him. It was uncomfortable to leave things that way, but she had to protect her heart. For her sake, and his.

"I'm fine, Kade. Go be with your mates. It's been a long day," she offered instead. She lead him to the front door before turning back. "I'll see you Monday?"

"Meggie, I have something to ask." She met his eyes cautiously, encouraging him to continue. "Will you go to my cousin's wedding with me tomorrow night?"

"Wedding?"

"Aye. I know I should have asked you sooner, but I wasn't sure I wanted to go," he hesitated. His reluctancy made her curious; apprehension was out of character for him.

"Why?"

"Well, my family will be there of course, all my married brothers, and their wives. Showing up without a date might be awkward. Not to mention, it'll make my mother fuss all over me. I thought I might avoid the whole thing, but I know my cousin will ne'er forgive me if I bail on her wedding," he explained, offering a tender smile.

"Oh," Meg hesitated, trying to process his circumstances, and the invitation, studying his intentions.

"It's not a date," he assured, his laughter easing the tension, his eyes twinkling with amusement. "You look mortified."

Her worries drifting away, she grinned back. "So, you need me to be a decoy?" she asked, suddenly understanding.

"Aye! You can pretend to be my girlfriend. I'll promise you a feast! We'll fill our bellies, have a turn around the dance floor, and I'll bring ya home, completely unscathed," he assured, his enthusiasm infectious.

"Won't your mom ask a lot of questions? That might be a lot of heavy lifting!"

"It's almost certain, but you can handle it Meggie. You're a tough bird. I've seen you haul drywall!"

“Hmmm...” she hummed, thinking it over. She hadn’t been dancing in years.

“That’s a yes...” Kade chuckled.

“Wait! How do you know?” she asked, unable to mask her amusement.

“I’ve been working side by side with you for many weeks, Meggie. I think I know ya by now. You don’t have to say a word, I know what yer thinking!”

Meggie narrowed her eyes. “Really, smart ass! What am I think now?”

“Your thinking, ‘get your ass to the pub before I turn you over my knee’...” he goaded playfully, his hand reaching for the door knob.

“Wow, you are clever.”

“I’ll pick you up at four. It’s nothing fancy so don’t fuss. And thank you, Meggie. I owe you,” he beamed, kissing her on the cheek, his confidence back in full swing.

“Okay, okay,” she agreed, certain she had little choice, “but you’d better be a good dancer!”

“Oh, I am,” he purred, closing the door behind him. She couldn’t help but think he was eluding to something else. Leaning against the wall, she shook her head, wondering exactly what she’d just agreed to.

CHAPTER 12

Kade

"The service was perfect. Short, sweet, and romantic. Your cousin is a beauty."

Kade looked away from the road, for just a second, to observe the woman beside him. His cousin wasn't the only beauty. He'd told Meg not to fuss, but she didn't listen. Her silky auburn hair, loose around her shoulders, framed her pretty face just right, with just a trace of makeup. She didn't need cosmetics, she was a natural beauty. He was accustomed to seeing her in dirty, old coveralls, covered in plaster or paint, her hair tied back in a pony-tail, so when she'd opened the door in a dress earlier that evening, it took everything in him not to gawk. Her beauty sucked the air right out of his lungs.

She chose to wear a modest dress, kelly green silk, with only her pretty locket adorning her neck. He was pleased to see some cleavage too, although just a hint. More of a suggestion really.

"You look beautiful too," he offered nonchalantly. He'd learned, over time, that Meggie was squeamish with compliments, especially when it came to her appearance. She was nothing like other women he'd dated, who craved compliments, priding themselves on their looks. They expected appreciation. Meggie was not dazzled with cheap compliments, she consider them low-hanging fruit. No, he had to dig deeper, work harder to impress her, but when he did, it made the apples all the sweeter. "I almost didn't recognize you without dirt on your face."

"Very funny. You clean up pretty nice yourself. I almost expected you to show up with a tool belt under your suit jacket."

"Oh, it's there. You never know when I might need my screw driver," he laughed, pulling into the reception parking lot. She stared at him sideways, as though thinking him daft. Her expression making it that much funnier.

"You just keep your screwdriver tucked away, mister. Don't forget, I'm just arm candy tonight, a decoy," she grinned, playfully pulling her wrap a little tighter.

"Oh, I haven't forgotten. Not to worry, sweet Meggie. You'll go home with your virtue intact," he teased, rolling into a free parking space. "Now it's time to party. You ready?"

"Yes," she grimaced, shaking her head no. Kade laughed cheerfully, popping open the car door.

"Come on, it will be fun. Just follow my lead."

* * *

"Meg, it's nice to meet you finally. Kade has told us so much about you."

Meg smiled sweetly, sitting down in a chair Kade pulled out for her.

"Has he?" she asked, catching his eye, surprised by the admission.

"It was all good, Meggie. No worries. Mum and Dad were interested in the job I've been doing for ya. I might have boasted about how great you are," he offered, sharing a wink for her eyes only.

"Yes, it must have been quite a culture shock for you, coming from America. Are you enjoying Fort William?" Kade's mother asked, eyeing her curiously.

"I love it here, but yes, it's quite different from home Mrs. Campbell," Meg answered timidly. Kade, sensing her apprehension, lightly caressed her knee for support. She stiffened beneath his touch, and while it probably shouldn't have, it enflamed him. He wondered if the response was favourable, or if she was simply warning him to stop. He assumed it was the latter, respectfully slipping his hand away.

"Please, call us Norma and Thom."

"Of course, thank you," Meg smiled, shyly glancing at Kade. He nodded back, encouraging her to just be herself. He'd little doubt she'd make a fine impression.

Norma caught the look and grinned, not concealing her thoughts in the least. There was no question in Kade's mind that his mum was already planning their nuptials.

"Well, we're glad to have ya. Did you introduce Meg to yer granddad yet?" she asked, arranging her shawl over the back of her chair. Although his mum was in her fifties, and carried a few extra pounds, she could still turn heads. She was a beautiful woman and Kade adored her, even if she did give him a hard time.

"No Mum, he left the church before I had a chance," Kade answered, looking around the room. "Is he here yet?"

"Not yet, love. Yer brother took all the boys to the sitter's. Pop went with him. They'll be here soon. Did you enjoy the service, Meg?" Norma asked.

Meg nodded enthusiastically, "yes, it was beautiful. I loved the bagpipes. The bride was lovely, and the groomsmen looked so handsome. I have to admit, there's something provocative about a man in a kilt."

"Aye, is there now?" Kade chuckled, suddenly glad he'd worn his own wools.

"Yes!" Meg grinned, drawing healthy laughter from Thom. "Is it true that Scots don't wear anything under their kilts?"

"Well, dear Meggie, you know what we say—," Kade paused, his grin promising a playful punchline.

"Uh-uh..."

"Good girls never ask, and bad girls find out for themselves..." he finished, brows raised.

Meg shook her head, and playfully rolled her eyes, but he could see a twinkle in them. A brief glimpse of curiosity, but it was there, he was certain of it.

"I had a tourist ask me once if anything was worn under the kilt, do you know what I told her," Kade's dad teased. Meg glanced around, sure by the smiles that his family had heard the joke a thousand times, but still found it endearing.

"What?"

"I said 'no my dear, it's all in good working order!'"

Meg groaned, but couldn't suppress her giggles, the punchline made even funnier by his thick Scottish brogue.

"Now that's funny!" She seemed pleased to be included in their family bantering.

Kade stood up, slipping his chair back with a screech, "well on that happy note, I'm going to the bar. Meggie, would you like to join me for a scotch?" Kade asked, holding out his hand to her.

"Nonsense, she'll stay with me so we can chat some more. Bring the lovely girl back a drink, my darling. And I'll have a Guinness," Norma insisted, wrapping her arm through Meg's. Meg looked up at him and shrugged, obviously pleased with the acceptance.

"Okay, okay, I seem to be outvoted. Dad? Can I bring you back something too?"

"I'll have a pint, lad. Thanks!"

Kade smiled, happy his parents were taking Meg under their wing, even if she was just pretending to be his girl. He hoped they liked her as much as he did. He sashayed over to the bar, stopping along the way to greet family and friends he hadn't seen for awhile. He was having the best time, he thought, his eyes landing on Meg from across the room. She was full out laughing, and he couldn't help but feel proud.

CHAPTER 13

Meg

Kade was dashing in his kilt. When he'd picked her up at her door earlier, she was gobsmacked by how handsome he looked; all cleaned up in a suit jacket, a red wool tartan, knee high socks, and where she was used to seeing a tool belt, a decorative sporran hanging loosely over his hips. She couldn't shake her longing. If it was meant to impress, it had worked.

His parents were exactly as she'd imagined, friendly, funny and not at all afraid to speak their minds. They were genuine, deep-souled, down-home folks, and it was clear they'd raised their children in their likeness. She liked them very much and was happy she'd agreed to come. It had been a long time since she'd felt so welcome, in spite of the fact that the event reminded her how alone she really was, and how much she missed her own family. Norma reminded Meg so much of her beloved Nana, it was no surprise she felt instantly at ease with her.

"So do ya plan on making Fort William your permanent home?" Thom asked, reaching for his wife's hand. Norma glanced at him, her smile softening her edges.The sweet gesture was not lost on Meg, and made her hopeful that one day she would find a mate that would still lovingly hold her hand, after more than thirty years of marriage! She'd heard tale of it, an urban legend, that there were actually men in the real world, that believed in loyalty and monogamy. She'd come across them in story books; there was no shortage of romantic men in the novels she loved to devour, she just never thought she would meet one face to face.

"I think so. My family on my father's side immigrated from Scotland. It feels like home. But you never know what the future holds," Meg replied warmly, her eyes scanning the room for Kade. She wasn't sure what he'd shared with his parents, and prayed they wouldn't ask anything too personal. She had a role to play that night, but she needed Kade's guidance. He'd finally made it to the bar, she saw, but was deep in a conversation with an older man.

"Well, we're pleased you came back home!" Norma gushed following Meg's eyes. "Oh look. Dad's here. Just in time for dinner. Typical Scot, not to miss a meal!" she laughed, waving them over.

"Is that Kade's grandfather?"Meg asked, noting the family resemblance. The old man ambled his way to the table, Kade draped over his shoulder, proudly guiding him, a tray of drinks in his free hand.

"Pop's here," Kade noted happily, placing the tray down. Meg looked up at the tall man, and was instantly drawn to his warm eyes. Aside from the well-earned crows feet, they were exactly like Kade's.

"Meggie, this is my granddad, Malcolm MacDonald. Pop, this is my friend Meg," he introduced, handing Meg a dram of scotch. She gratefully eased it from his fingers, setting it down before offering her hand to Malcolm. He eyed her up and down, with soft recognition, as though deciding if he'd seen her somewhere before, the way seniors often do.

"It's nice to meet you, sir," Meg greeted, allowing him to shake her hand.

"Please, call me Pop. No need to be formal. So you're the American keeping my grandson so busy. No wonder he hasn't been coming around," Malcolm teased, dropping into the chair beside her.

"Now Pop, you behave yerself," Kade scolded warmly, taking the chair beside him, the blush on his cheeks not unnoticed.

"Never ya mind. I'm pushing 80, I'll say and do whatever I damn well please," he insisted jovially, lifting the scotch out of Kade's hand and downing it in one swallow. He banged the empty glass on the table with flourish.

"Dad, you know yer not allowed to drink Scotch," Norma warned, half-heartedly. Meg got the sense that Malcolm would drink whatever the hell he pleased too.

"Keep your breath, daughter. I've been drinking scotch for over 60 years, and I'm still on the right side of the grass," he smirked, tossing Meg a winked. She raised her own glass and toasted him before swallowing down the warm, amber liquid, enjoying the burn as it coated her throat. She liked him already.

* * *

"Come on Meggie, dance with me." Kade slipped in behind her, placing a hand in the small of her back. She'd been schmoozing with the bride, complimenting her on the beautiful wedding, and turned to smile at him. "I promised you a turn on the dance floor, don't make me a liar."

"I can't," she insisted gently, suddenly nervous to be in his arms. She'd been enjoying herself so much, and felt so at ease with his family, she could almost imagine herself as Kade's girlfriend, and that made her way too vulnerable. "My feet hurt."

"I won't take no for an answer. Now take my hand, woman!" he insisted, his sexy grin hard to resist. She glanced warmly at the bride, as if to say, 'can you believe this guy?'

"I think you should go, Meg. You'll never win a battle of wills with a Scot," she insisted, gently urging her towards him. Meg shook her head and laughed, knowing she'd been outvoted.

"Fine," she drawled, stifling her giggles. Accepting his hand, she allowed Kade to lead her towards the dance floor. He gently spun her around before pulling her into his arms. Inhaling deeply, she swallowed his sexy scent. Not only did he look good, he smelled delicious too, spicy and dangerous. He twirled her around the room, keeping perfect time with the band.

"I can't recall the last time I've danced. I think I've forgotten how," Meg giggled, landing on his foot for the second time.

"Dinna worry, lass. I step on my feet too, although I prefer to walk on the bottoms."

"Ha ha, very funny," she giggled, poking him. "I never promised you I was a good dancer. I'm a hippo in heels!"

"Nonsense. You're doing fine," he assured, confidently spinning her into a dip. She smiled up at him, surprised with his graceful moves. She felt pretty, and feminine, and light as a feather.

"Well, for a carpenter you're not so bad yourself. How did you learn to dance?" she gushed. He raised her effortlessly, gingerly pulling her back into his arms.

"It just comes naturally, I guess," he smirked.

"You're just full of surprises, aren't you?"

"I suppose I am. I've plenty of tricks up my sleeve," he purred provocatively. She searched his eyes, foraging for a snappy comeback, but came up short, her mind flooded with naughty images of what those tricks might be. Chuckling softly, he swayed her to the music, until the very last note.

She pulled away, gathering herself. Her feet really were killing her. "I'm ready for a drink," she announced, clearing her throat, "coming?" After a brief segue, the band eased into another tune.

"One more Meggie, it's a slow one. I promise I'll go easy on you," he persuaded, his raised brows encouraging her. He looked so happy, so hopeful, she couldn't say no. Holding his thick shoulder for balance, she slipped off her shoes, tossing them to the side of the dance floor. Kade smiled, obviously pleased with the decision.

"There," she cooed, "that's better. Come on then, I'm ready." She melted into his arms, now several inches shorter, and stared up at his smiling face. He pulled her close, but not uncomfortably so. It was obvious he was respecting her space, although she could still feel his body heat through his cotton dress shirt. He softly sang the lyrics into her ear, his voice delightfully soothing. Another pleasant surprise. She relaxed into him, enjoying the tranquil sound of his voice, hypnotic and sexy.

"Are you enjoying yourself?" he asked warmly, meeting her gaze. "I know it must feel strange, being thrown into my clan this way, but you're fitting in well."

"It was a bit strange at first, only because I don't know anyone, but your family is wonderful..."

"They seem to like you too."

"Kade, I know you wanted me to come and pretend to be your girlfriend, but what exactly did you tell them?" she probed gently. He shrugged, unperturbed by the question.

"Nothing. I just told them you were crazy about me, and that you couldn't bare to be apart..."

"Kade!"

He ducked, avoiding her playful punch. "I'm teasing. No worries. I just told them I liked ya, is all, that we're good friends."

She raised her brows, not sure whether to believe him or not.

"I promise! They're just happy I'm not here alone. Don't worry," he assured, pulling her back into the rhythm of the song. "And to be honest, I'm happy too."

"Me too, otherwise I'd probably have been at home, absorbed in a trashy romance novel, already on my third glass of wine," she admitted, drunk on his cologne.

"Ah see? I'm saving you from being an alcoholic spinster. No need to thank me..."

"You goof-ball," she teased, her smile hidden against his shoulder.

"I resemble that remark," he chirped back, not insulted in the least.

CHAPTER 14

Kade

Kade parked the car in front of her house, engaging the hand break before turning towards her. She quickly reached for the handle, opening the passenger door, before he could say a word. He had a wonderful night with her and didn't want it to end, but wasn't sure she felt the same way. Did she want him to come inside? Would she think him too forward if he asked? It wasn't like him to be so nervous. He slipped the key out of the ignition and waited half a second before following her, easily catching up by the time she reached the front door. She seemed completely at ease; a good sign, he decided.

"I'm going to freshen up," Meg smiled, tossing her purse on the console table by the door. He dropped his keys beside it. "Help yourself to a drink. I'll be right back."

"Can I get you something?" he asked, his eyes following her down the hallway, certain her answer would offer some clue how the rest of the night would unfold.

"Surprise me."

He chuckled softly at her ambiguity. She never made it easy for him.

He walked through the house into the kitchen, unfazed by the dark. He knew the house well enough. Pulling two glasses from the cupboard, he opened the fridge. It offered water, orange juice, and wine. He stood there for a moment, leaning against the open door, contemplating his options. Would wine be too forward? Would it give her the wrong idea? And what was the wrong idea? That he wanted to see her naked? He laughed, trying to shake off his doubts.

Of course he wanted to see her naked. What man wouldn't? And yet, they didn't have that kind of relationship, did they? He was her contractor. Sure, they'd just had a great night together; she'd met his family; they'd danced most of the night, in spite of her gentle protests, but still—. Hadn't she only agreed to come as a favour to him?

"Don't be daft," he scolded, reaching for the chilled wine. They drank together all the time, it didn't mean anything. He filled the glasses and placed the bottle back, shutting the fridge door with a thud. Sitting down at the kitchen table he sipped his wine, gently fingering an old diary sitting on top of a pile of books. Was it hers? It seemed unlikely, given the age. He contemplated taking a peek inside, before her foot steps, padding down the hallway, made him think better of it.

"Sorry about that, I had to pee so bad," she smirked, dropping into the chair across from him.

"Wine?" he asked, casually sliding a glass across the table.

"Lovely." She swirled the liquid as though her thoughts were a million miles away, but did not drink. He wondered if he'd chosen wrong.

"Would you prefer water?"

"No," she smiled, taking a small sip.

"You seem tired," he observed, offering her an out if she wanted one. He hoped she didn't. She looked at him thoughtfully before answering.

"A little. You had me on my feet all night," she grinned. "But it was fun! I'm glad I went."

"It was fun seeing another side to ya."

She raised her brows. "Another side?"

"Aye. You're always working so hard. So determined. It was nice to see you let your hair down and cut loose."

"Hmmm," she smirked, as though processing the observation.

"I meant that in a good way, Meggie," he assured.

"I know you did. You always do."

He held her gaze, challenging her to read his mind. It was bold, for sure, but he had to know if she was thinking the same thing. Before he could get a read on them, she quickly dropped her eyes, but not before a blush stained her cheeks. This was where he normally threw caution to the wind, and offered a kiss, confident his advances would be echoed. But there was nothing normal about Meggie. She was a mystery. Her giggle made him glance up.

"What's on yer mind," he asked, clearing his throat.

"Nothing really, it's silly."

"No, tell me."

"Honestly? I was just thinking about what kind of car you might be," she offered playfully, shrugging her shoulders. He stared at her curiously, amused they were on such different pages.

"Car?"

"I told you it was silly," she blushed, waving off her embarrassment. "It's just a game my dad and I used to play. When we were people watching, we would guess what make of car someone was. We'd give them a make and model to match the way they carried themselves. My dad was a car guy, you know? I guess tonight's making me nostalgic."

Kade grinned, waiting for her to continue, suddenly curious which car she chose for him. "Well? What is it then?" he chuckled.

She paused for a moment, as though trying to decide whether or not to play.

"Come on, don't leave me hanging."

"Well, I'm trying to decide," she purred, taking a mouthful of wine. He liked the way her lips played with the edge of the glass, and found himself curiously distracted.

"You're either a 67 Ford Mustang Fastback, or Chevy Silverado."

He raised a brow, contemplating her choices. "Huh, well those are remarkably different," he grinned, "you can't settle on one?"

"I'm not sure. You see, the Silverado is tough. It can take a beating and keep on pushing, you know? Hard working, dependable, just as handsome as it is durable," she offered, carefully reading him. "But the mustang, now that's a confident car. It's fast and slick, maybe even a little reckless, but an old-school classic none the less."

"Yeah, I can see that," he smiled, pleased with both. They fit him well, if he did say so himself. "My turn—"

"Ok, what kind of car would I be?" she asked, suddenly more relaxed.

"That's easy—a fire engine-red, Ferrari Testarossa!" She looked at him like he'd lost his mind. Of course she was a Testarossa, he thought, sure of his answer. "Seriously," he chuckled, amused by her expression. "The Testarossa is not your average sports car. It's a little gem, designed with quirky surprises throughout. It's truly exotic, special, in a way that doesn't exist anymore."

Meg stared at him for a moment, her mouth gaping in surprise.

"Not to mention that you're both red headed beauties, with curves for days!" he added spontaneously. "It also has a wider rear end than most sports cars, but that's just part of it's charm. It just makes for a smoother ride—"

"Kade!" she squealed, scolding him playfully. His boisterous laughter rang through the room. There was nothing he enjoyed more than coaxing a rise out of her.

"What? You asked!" he grinned, pleased to see the twinkle in her eyes. "I like this game! When do we get to inspect under the hood?"

"Oh my god, you're a brat!" she giggled, brushing off the flirtation.

He knew he was riding the rails between lover and friend, and if he didn't make his intentions clear, he'd chug all the way to friendship town, a precarious place very few people escaped. God he wanted her! Their eyes connected again, and this time he was determined to make his intentions clear...

"Well, it's getting late," she offered, her words soft but certain. He held her gaze a moment longer, before returning her nod, hoping she might change her mind. Instead she rose from her chair, taking her glass with her. She rinsed it in the sink, daintily placing it in the rack. It seemed she was distracting herself, maybe shaking off her own arousal. Either way, he knew it his cue to say goodnight.

"It *is* late," he agreed, bringing her his glass. She took it gingerly, her hand brushing his own. Strangely, her touch was innocent, yet erotically charged all at once. Again he considered kissing her, hesitating a moment too long. She turned away and grabbed a tea towel, wiping away the evidence of their chemistry.

“I’ll walk you out,” she smiled, gesturing him to follow.

“Have a good sleep,” he offered quietly as they reached the door. Stalling, he slowly picked up his keys, not wanting the night to end. Cautiously, she opened the front door, gently resting her head against it.

“You too.”

Nodding he slipped by her, feeling the heat of her body as he passed, his heart pounding uncontrollably under his ribs. He felt like a sixteen year old, adrenalin coursing through his body. It was almost embarrassing. He just needed to go home and chug off, the sooner the better, he thought, navigating down the first few steps.

“Kade, wait—”

His heart leapt at the sound of his name. It was the invitation he’d been waiting for. Spinning quickly, he leapt up the stairs, returning to her. Pulling her into his arms he pressed his mouth against hers, desperate, urgent. It was as though he’d lost his damn mind.

Her quiet moans fuelled his need further and he held her against the open door, their bodies entwined, his hardness raising his kilt. God he’d never wanted anyone as much as he wanted her; this beautiful, quirky, American. She parted her lips, ever so slightly, inviting him to tease her with his tongue. It was warm, soft, and wet; as deliciously sweet and intoxicating as the wine she’d been sipping.

“Kade,” she whispered between kisses, gently pressing her hand against his chest. He pulled away with difficulty. His skin was flushed with excitement, his passion so intense he could barely focus. It took a few seconds to realize she was reigning him in. She looked at him perplexed, almost confused, before her eyes softened.

"I was going to ask you what time you'll be here for work tomorrow," she grinned, a playful note of humour under her breath. Kade's mouth dropped open, suddenly realizing how badly he'd misread the situation, his hands still resting in the small of her back, dangerously close to her curvy bottom.

"Oh, I'm not leavin' woman," he challenged, still dizzy with arousal.

"Oh," she breathed, their eyes locked. "I thought this was a pretend date?"

"Aye, dinna worry. It's only a pretend kiss." He kissed her again, this time with more control.

"Well then," she purred into his mouth, "I'll to pretend to invite you in."

"Aye?" he asked, making sure he'd heard correctly.

"*Aye*," she nodded, her smile affirming that his hearing was just fine.

CHAPTER 15

Meg

"My god, I'm too big to carry," Meg giggled, surprised to be swept off her feet.

"You're light as a feather," Kade assured, easily navigating his way to her bedroom. "Besides, this is the only way I can be certain you won't change yer mind."

"I won't change my mind," she promised, tightening her grip around his shoulders.

All night she'd forced herself to ignore her desires, to play it cool, but he was so frigging charming. In spite of the many months spent apart, she knew she was still messed up over Nathan, and there were days she still missed him, despite how difficult their relationship had been. It was stupid, and it frustrated the hell out of her. Kade was definitely the kind of man she could fall in love with, but not until she rid herself of Nathan's ghost. He deserved a woman who could offer her whole heart, and although she'd come a long way, hers was still mending. She was still in pieces.

But that kiss...

It was like she'd been wading through a lazy stream, carefully picking her way to the bank, when *WHAM*, a flash flood came rushing through the valley, recklessly sweeping her off her feet. His kiss surged through her like a bloody tidal wave before she could even process what was happening.

“God, I’ve been wantin’ ya for so long woman,” he growled, gently laying her on the mattress, his face inches from hers.

“You’ve only known me a short time,” she giggled, shifting her body to make room for him.

“Aye, and I’ve shown incredible restraint.”

He pinned his mouth against hers again, matching the passion he’d shared at the front door. She didn’t think it possible, but that kiss was even hotter than the first. Her body liquified beneath him. It had been more than six months since she’d been with a man, and even longer since she’d felt such need! She was completely at his mercy.

At first he was tentative, as though he couldn’t believe she was actually with him. It was endearing, but also maddening. She’d never been so turned on in her life, her body literally trembling from desire. His mouth explored her face and neck, softly, sensually; teasing desperate, lustful moans from her, his tongue tracing down her long neck, his hands carefully exploring her curves. His seduction was sweet and controlled, as though he thought her a timid little bird ready to fly off, spooked by sudden movements.

“Is this okay?” he asked, looking up from her cleavage. She regarded him curiously for a several seconds, surprised by the formality.

“It is,” she agreed, playfully adding, “but if you don’t get my clothes off soon, there’s a strong possibility I’ll internally combust.” He chuckled under his breath, his curls sweeping into his eyes.

“Ah, Meggie, don’t you know by now, I never rush anything? I want to explore every inch of your beautiful body."

"I appreciate the seduction, I do," she assured, squirming beneath him, her womb aching with need, "and I'm not opposed to romantic love-making sessions, but right now I just want you to get this damn dress off and fuck me! Yours too!"

He grinned impishly, his eyes pooled with amusement, before shifting to his knees. "Well, you're the boss," he quipped, wrapping his hands firmly under her knees. Assertively, he pulled her towards him, quickly hooking his fingers into her panties. "And it's not a dress, it's a kilt," he laughed, aggressively tearing the silky material away.

"Oh," she moaned, turned on by his intensity. Her wetness, suddenly exposed and vulnerable, only served to heat her further. God, she wanted him.

Grinning he lowered himself between her legs, burying his face in her puss. Her pleasure was instantaneous, every one of the thousands of nerves responding to his tongue. Her arousal was surprising, and if she was being honest, made her feel a little modest. She was unaccustomed to a man so greedily enjoying her. In the past, she'd always been made to feel like it was a chore, a means to an end, and her first reaction was to shy away. She could feel her knees closing of their own volition, wordlessly offering him permission to quit. But, Kade was having none of it.

"Oh no you don't Meggie," he mumbled into her mound, forcing her legs apart. "This is the best fucking part and I won't have you deny me."

He quickly retuned to his work, as if he couldn't wait even one more second to taste her again, his velvety tongue generously tracing her folds, eagerly lapping her spicy juices. God, he made her feel wild, impulsive and daring, his obvious enjoyment arousing her even further. So desperate was her need, as soon as he plunged two long fingers inside, she came with a fiery intensity that surprised them both. Moaning between her thighs, his approval was obvious, as he persisted in drinking every drop of her sweetness.

"I need to fuck you, woman," he insisted, raising himself to his knees, his cock raised under his wools. Cheekily, he wiped her juices from his chin before reaching down to unhook his kilt, exposing himself to her for the first time. Still drunk from her orgasm, she smiled gratefully, pleased by what she saw. His staff was full, thick, and proud, just like the Scot who wielded it. He shrugged his shoulders and grinned, as though knowing full well how impressive he was.

Within seconds he had the rest of his clothing removed and was working on unfastening her dress, fumbling with the zipper.

"It's stuck," Meg laughed, doing her best to help him. The zipper was not cooperating and she could see he was growing playfully impatient, both of them giggling at the absurdity of it. "Leave it," Meg snickered, feeling eager herself.

"How much do you love this dress?" he asked devilishly, his eyes challenging her. She fondly recalled how he dealt with her panties and shrugged.

"I don't love it—," she purred, the words barely passing her lips before he yanked the zipper apart, allowing the material to slip down her shoulders.

"Oh, Christ, that's better," he growled, helping her to stand, the defiled dress falling to the floor. He eyed her greedily, pleased with what he saw. Fuelling her confidence, she dropped to her knees, taking him into her mouth.

She hungrily licked and sucked his cock, taking long, deep pulls on the shaft, playfully flicking the tip with her tongue. His moans, deep and guttural, proved the pleasure was maddening. Holding steady against the wall, he used his free hand to guide her task. He stared down at her, silently begging her not to stop, but clearly struggling with control. Sensing his need made it even more exciting to please him. She grabbed his ass with both hands, guiding him deeper down her throat, her moans vibrating deliciously around his cock.

"God Meggie, you need to stop," he begged, unconvincingly. She knew he was torn between exploding down her throat, or finishing their long-awaited love-making inside her womb.

"Meggie, come here," he insisted, peeling her away. He wrapped his hands around her bottom, encouraging her to wrap her long legs around him, his angry cock pressing hard against her nakedness. He dropped them both to the bed, playfully.

Feeling safe under his weight, she stared at him, drinking him in with curious eyes. Breathless, his need was unmistakable. "Bed side table. Condoms," she instructed, pleased she had cause to use them.

Grinning, he reached into the drawer, tearing the colourful package with his teeth. Moments later he slipped his fullness into her, his reassuring eyes locking with hers. The sex was erotically charged, sinfully sensual, and she happily submitted to him, body and soul. Her doubts, for the moment, slipped graciously to the furthest corner of her mind.

CHAPTER 16

Katherine

July 18, 1961

Dear Diary,

I'm in love with Mack. There, I said it. I know we're young, but I don't care, and neither does he. We know how we feel. My parents fell in love at my age so I'm sure they'd understand. We've been dating incognito for many months, and to tell you the truth, I'm tired of hiding.

Since school let out for break, it's been much easier spending time together. Mum has been less and less nosy about my whereabouts. I think she's preoccupied. She and dad have been arguing a lot lately. They never do it in front of me, but I know there's tension between them. I think it might be about Dad's work. I overheard them talking about some sort of promotion. Mum doesn't seem happy about it. I wonder if she's worried about all the extra hours? I asked her if something was going on, but she told me not to fret. She said there was no point worrying on something that might never happen...whatever that means. She has a flair for dramatics.

I almost got caught fibbing last week. I told Mum I was going to be at Esme's, but when she and Dad went to the market, they saw Esme on the corner (without me). Thankfully Esme thinks quick on her feet, and can keep a straight face. She doesn't mind lying at all! She told them I was meeting her after the library. Thankfully Mum bought it. When I got home Esme called straight away and told me. She's such a good friend. I can count on her to watch my back! Anyway, no one was the wiser, but it got me thinking. I don't like lying and I don't want to sneak around anymore, and why should I? I'm almost a grown woman.

I think that Mack wants to get even closer. We've kissed, a lot, and there have been times that we've carried things even further than that. I must admit, it's been hard to stop at times, but I'm torn. I was raised to wait until marriage. I can handle God being disappointed in me, but my mother is another story! Mack has been so patient and understanding, although I know it's killing him. He looks so inviting when he's all worked up. I love that he wants me so! To be honest, it's kind of killing me too. I can't believe how much I want to be with him.

Mum and Dad are going to Edinburgh on Friday. Mum's cousin is getting married after finally finding the man of her dreams, at nearly 30! She's so old! They asked me to come along but I said I didn't want to. Mum was determined I go, insisting I was too young to be home alone overnight, but Dad told her to stop being a worry-wart, that I would be fine. I told them I would ask Esme to stay over, if that made them feel any better. Mum said it didn't, but I know she was (partially) joking. Anyway, they finally agreed that I could stay home. I'm so happy! Mack is coming over. He hasn't even been inside my house yet!

I've decided that when Mum and Dad get back, I'm going to tell them about Mack. It's time they meet the man I hope to marry!

* * *

"I'm so booorrred," Esme drawled loudly. Katherine held the phone away, trying to muffle the shrillness coming through the receiver. She'd pulled the phone from the hallway into her bedroom, stretching the long cord as far as it would go. It teetered precariously on her dressing table.

"Why don't you call Alec. I'm sure he'd love to go out with you tonight," Katherine soothed, squinting into the mirror, applying eyeshadow with her free hand.

"Alec is history. He dumped me yesterday."

"Oh? I'm sorry. Are you okay?" Katherine asked, surprised with the confession.

"Noooo. I really loved him. I thought he loved me too. How did you get so lucky with Mack? I want a boyfriend like him," Esme moaned, obviously miserable. Katherine couldn't help feeling proud, but knew better than to boast, especially to Esme. Especially now.

"What happened?" she asked instead, carefully selecting her tone.

"I went all the way with him, the prick. Obviously he's had his fill. Mairi saw him with Evelyn Murray earlier today, at Argyle's. They were holding hands and kissing!"

"That's terrible, Esme. I'm sorry."

"I know, it stinks. I'm coming over. I don't want to be alone," Esme insisted. "You don't mind, do you?" she added, after a brief hesitation.

"Normally I wouldn't, but you know Mack will be here soon, any minute, and I haven't even tidied up—"

"But this is important, Kat! Can't you tell him no?"

"Well—" she hesitated, unsure how to decline without upsetting her further. Esme rarely took no for an answer, especially from Kat.

"You owe me this, Kat! I've been such a good friend to you!"

"I know ya have, and I appreciate it, but tonight's not the best night. My parents are away and, well, this is the first time Mack has been to the house," Katherine wavered, desperately trying to be diplomatic. "I thought he might spend the night—"

"God, yer not gonna sleep with him, are ya?" Esme asked, not masking her disgust.

"I'm not sure," Katherine answered quietly, swallowing her irritation. Who was Esme to judge? The girl lost her virginity in eleventh grade.

"Don't do it, Kat. Seriously. Boys only want one thing, and once they get it, they treat you like shite. Trust me!"

"Mack's not like that. He would never—"

"They all do! It's true! They can't help themselves. They're dogs!" Esme spat, her words cutting through the receiver. Katherine sat with them for a moment, and gave pause to their meaning. Would Mack do that? Would he still respect her if she slept with him? She wanted to think so—

"Kat?"

"Yes?" she whispered, the sudden apprehension weighing on her. She really didn't have reason to doubt Esme, she had way more experience. And yet, Katherine was uneasy.

"Just listen to me. Call him and tell him no, I promise ya, it's for the best. He'll only hurt ya. I need to come over. If you're a true friend, you'll let me," Esme begged. If she meant to cause doubt, with an extra helping of guilt, it was working, and Katherine almost conceded—then the door bell chimed.

"Shite, he's already here!" Katherine jumped, knocking the phone off her dressing table. She scrambled to her feet, the phone cord curled around her legs, making her drop the receiver. Her heart beating inside her chest, she quickly retrieved it. "Hello? You still there?"

"—be there in twenty minutes."

"Esme, no. He's ringing the bell. I'm sorry but I have to go. I will call you in the morning."

"Kaaattttt—"

Despising conflict, Katherine winced. "I'm hanging up. Don't be mad." She flipped the phone over with her foot and dropped the receiver into its cradle, before Esme could utter another word. She hated being a bad friend, but what choice did she have? She couldn't send Mack home now! The doorbell chimed for a third time, prompting her to hustle. She took one last look in the mirror, her fingers combing hastily through her hair, before skipping down the stairs.

Mack stood rigidly on her porch, looking as nervous as she felt, a rustic bouquet of heather in his hand, a twine bow holding the stems.

"Is everything okay," he asked, astutely reading her body language. Katherine nodded, straightening her pretty summer dress, before stepping aside.

"Yes, sorry. I was talking to Esme. Come in," she assured, closing the door behind him. "Excuse the mess."

"Mess?" he asked, glancing around. She knew the house wasn't that bad, but demonstrating modesty was a habit she'd picked up from her mother, and sometimes apples didn't fall far from trees, as much as she hated to admit.

"Would you like something to drink? Maybe a sandwich or some biscuits?" she offered tightly, hoping the formality would ease her nerves.

Mack shook his head and chuckled, handing her the flowers, their sweetness perfuming the air between them. She breathed them in, grateful for the pause.

"Lovely," she approved, pleased her tone was somewhat back to normal, in spite of her butterflies. Why was she so nervous? This was Mack. Her Mack, she thought, Esme's warnings still echoing in her head.

He boyishly slipped off his shoes without unlacing them, respectful as ever.

"Follow me," she gestured, leading him to the living room. She sat down on the chesterfield, patting the cushion beside her, before setting the flowers down on the coffee table. He offered her a sweet kiss before dropping into the sofa beside her. They'd kissed many times before, but each time their lips connected, it felt like the first time. She smiled at him coyly.

"What?" he asked, noticing the expression. She couldn't admit what was on her mind. Her thoughts were a mash of pure giddiness, vulnerability, and an unmapped desire, reserved solely for virgins. How could she articulate that without totally embarrassing herself?

"Nothing. I'm just glad you're here. It feels weird though—"

"What does?"

"Having you here, in my house. But it's good," she assured, resting her hand on his knee. Smiling, his eyes dropped to her hand. She knew her touch stirred him, just as much as his kisses affected her.

"—and your parents won't be home for awhile?"

"No, not until morning."

Mack slowly leaned in, cupping her chin in his hand, and raised her mouth for another kiss. She couldn't deny him. He was the one.

Mack

"Take me upstairs," she whispered. It wasn't his first time being intimate with someone, he'd done it before, but for some reason, he couldn't shake his nerves. Kat was not like any other woman. She was precious, but as anxious as he was to make love to her, he didn't want to disappoint her.

"Are ya sure?"

"I think so."

"You have to be sure," he insisted, his voice deep with desire.

"I am. I'm sure. Do ya not want to?" she asked searching his face. He grinned, charmed by the question.

"Of course I do, don't be silly," he chuckled, pressing his mouth into hers. He grabbed her hand, gesturing her to follow.

Her bedroom was the first door at the top of the stairs. It was warm and feminine and smelled distinctively like her. He was certain the scent would ingrain in his brain forever, innocently sweet, with a just a hint of sexy muskiness. It was intoxicating.

"This is it," Katherine giggled, critically looking around her childhood bedroom.

"It's a fine room, Kat," he assured, unsure how to respond. He was just grateful to be there, quite frankly. He sat down on her bed, holding his hand out to her. She sashayed over, tentatively perching beside him. Lacing his fingers through her hair, he kissed her again, playfully teasing her with his tongue, paying close attention to any unspoken signals she might offer. He didn't want to do anything to offend her. She sighed quietly.

"Are you okay?"

"No, it's fine. I just…nothing," she replied, dropping her chin.

"It's not nothing. What's wrong?"

"Well, it's something Esme said. I can't get it out of my mind," she shrugged, refusing to look at him. Esme was a silly girl and Mack wasn't a fan. It was obvious that whatever she'd shared was troubling Kat.

"Go on then—"

"She said that boys only want one thing, that once they get it they move on. I want to be with ya, Mack, but I don't want to lose ya," Katherine confessed, still avoiding his eyes.

"Look at me, Kat," Mack whispered, raising her chin. "Some boys might feel that way, but not when they're in love. I'm no going anywhere."

"I'm just being stupid—," she pouted, easing her chin out of his grasp. He reached for her cheek, refusing to let her off the hook, and pulled her in for another sweet kiss.

"You're not," he breathed, "but if you want to change yer mind, it's okay, I promise. I'm ready when you are. I don't even mind waiting till your wedding night."

She leaned back and grinned at him. "Wedding?"

"Aye. Hopefully I'll be the groom, but either way—," he teased, offering a charming smile. It was so like her to worry, but he'd always be there to set her mind at ease. To comfort her.

"You're incorrigible."

"How many times have I told you not to use big words. You know how randy it makes me," he flirted.

"Aye? You don't say," she winked. "You are a presumptuous, incorrigible beast."

"That sounds like me," he growled, his kisses smothering her giggles.

She allowed him to ease her into the mattress, as trusting as she was vulnerable. Although he wanted her more than anything, he knew he had to pace himself, for both their sakes. Katherine meant the world to him. The truth was, she was above his station, and he knew it. She was intelligent, certainly more than he, and would be going on to University. He knew she wanted to be a doctor one day, and she could do it too. Although he was smart in other ways, he'd likely follow in his father's footsteps, working construction. His dad already began teaching him the trades since school let out. There was *never* any discussion about University for him. Even if he did have the grades and the aptitude, there was no money for it, so no one ever encouraged him to dream. If he were to make his millions, it would be through pure grit, and a determined spirit.

Kat came from money. Her folks weren't rich, by any means, but certainly they had enough to offer their daughter whatever she needed to succeed. They had high expectations for Kat, and rightly so. He'd be lying if he said he'd never wondered whether he could meet those expectations, or even come close. It was unlikely. He'd have to win them over with his charm.

"I almost forgot, I brought ya another present." Katherine sat up on her elbows, watching him reach into his pocket.

"Ah, I was wondering if you had something in your trousers, or if you were just happy to see me," she purred, pleased by her wit.

He handed her the box and winked. "Maybe it was both."

"What is it?"

"Open it and you'll see, silly."

Blushing, Katherine opened the box. "Oh, Mack, it's precious."

"I know it's not much, but I swear one day I'll buy you something finer—," he shrugged, confident he could keep his word. One day he would be the man she deserved.

"It's perfect."

"Will you wear it?"

"Aye, just as soon as I tell my parents about us."

Mack nodded. He looked forward to the day they could proudly show their love, but something told him they might have a difficult road ahead. He couldn't shake his doubt.

"Thank you," she said, delicately closing the box. She set it on the bedside table before turning back to him. "Now where were we?"

"I think we were right about here," he growled, lacing his fingers through her soft, coppery mane. He gently eased her head back, posing her for a proper kiss. "I love you, Kat," he whispered, his breath warm against her lips. She closed her eyes, accepting the promise of his kiss.

Then he made love to her, as slowly, patiently, and lovingly as any eighteen year old could; respecting that her first taste of sensuality was something she might never forget. Her pleasure was his responsibility, and when she reminisced about their first time, and every time after, he wanted it to be with applause.

CHAPTER 17

Lorna

Kade kissed that American bitch at her door, then followed her inside. There was no question what they were doing, and it pissed Lorna off. She'd befriended Meg, and made it clear that Kade was hands off, but apparently that wasn't enough. Lorna hated playing second fiddle. She wouldn't stand for it. She didn't lose, especially to someone like Meg. The woman wasn't even hot!

She took one last drag off her ciggy and tossed it out the driver's side window. She'd been waiting more than an hour for Kade to reemerge from Meg's doorway, but there was still no sign of him. She'd fully expected him by now. It was uncharacteristic for Kade to hang around after shagging. He liked sleeping in his own bed. That was a fact. So where was he?

She'd followed them from the wedding. A mutual friend had tipped her off that Kade was at the reception with Meg. Apparently they were cozy on the dance floor, too. Lorna knew she couldn't confront him in front of everyone, so she trailed them to Meg's place, assuming that Kade would just drop her off. Admittedly, it annoyed her when he first followed her in, but then he came back out and Lorna watched them kiss! It nearly made her head explode when they went *back inside!* How dare that

Yank cut in on her man, especially since Lorna had been so clear!

She'd spent the better part of the hour stewing in her own rage, stung by the betrayal. Kade and she were meant to be together. Their bodies fit perfectly. They loved each other. Yes, she'd made mistakes, they both had, but hadn't she apologized? As far as she was concerned, Kade was finally making his way back to her—at least until that Yankee bitch came along. Who the fuck was she, anyway? What did Kade know about her? What kind of woman picked up and moved across the globe, all alone? What exactly was Meg Miller running from, she wondered.

Lots and lots of questions, and if she had any chance of getting Kade back, she needed the answers. She needed to know what she was up against. She picked up her mobile and opened the browser, thumbing Meg's name into the search bar, followed with *Virginia, USA*. She scrolled down, opening several links, unsatisfied with the results. She tried a different approach, clicking on 'images' instead. Her eyes opened wide.

"There you are," she smirked, caressing the image on the screen with a polished thumb, "and who is this with you?"

CHAPTER 18

Kade

"Why are you eating?" Kade stopped in his tracks. The sunlight, reflecting off dust particles through the little kitchen window, appeared like fairies dancing on a beam. It seemed no coincidence that the ray fell gracefully over Meggie's crown, making her silky, red mane seem on fire. It was dazzling.

Smirking, Meg glanced over her laptop, chewing a mouthful of jam smeared scone, washing it down with a sip of coffee. "Well, mainly to stay alive," she responded dryly.

"Ha-ha, very funny. I mean, why are you eating right now? I told you last night I wanted to take you out for breakfast," Kade smiled, stooping for a kiss.

"Sorry, I didn't know you were serious. I thought you were just saying that so I'd put out. I'm not sure if you've clued in yet, but I'm pretty much a sure thing."

It had been almost two weeks since his cousins wedding, and Kade had slept over several nights since. They'd not yet talked about what that meant, but to him it felt completely organic, natural, how their relationship was blooming. They ebbed and flowed so smoothly, working diligently all day, determined to plow through the renovations, then playing hard at night. He was exhausted, but in the best way possible. He'd never felt so exhilarated, so fulfilled. He was happy, doing what he loved... and who. He might be falling in love with her, his sweet, beautiful, smart-assed Meg.

"Aye, and for that I'm grateful, but can't a gentleman take his lady out for eggs in the morning?" Kade asked, dropping into the chair beside her. He picked up her coffee cup and took a swallow.

"Yes, of course, but you sir, are no gentleman," Meg winked, stealing her mug back, "if last night was proof."

"Hmm, yes," he chuckled, "but if last night is our baseline, then I'm using the term lady rather loosely."

Meg laughed wholeheartedly, sweeping the plate of scones towards him. "Fair enough. I'll try and act more lady like."

"Don't ya dare! I'm no complaining!"

She leaned in for another kiss. "I knew there was a reason I liked you."

"Only one reason?" he sassed, playfully denying her.

"Well, you also look better in a skirt than I do..."

"You're itching for a smacked bottom."

"You're on to me," she agreed, her lips brushing his with a feather touch. "So, what's on the agenda today?"

"I'm re-installing the kitchen cabinets. The stain should already be dry. Then tomorrow the new granite counter is being delivered and installed. If you want to start priming your shop, I can help finish with the painting when I'm done," he suggested, leaning back in his seat. "It'll be nice when the kitchen is put back together. Then I can make you breakfast before you even get out of bed."

"Promises, promises. I'm sure once this honeymoon phase is over, I'll be scrounging for my own scraps," she goaded, only partially hiding her cynicism.

"What makes you think the honeymoon will ever be over," he asked innocently, reflecting on the long love affair his parents enjoyed.

Jaded, Meg shrugged, her own experiences much different. They'd never really talked about her ex. He must have done a real number on her, he thought, not to mention the choices her mother had made.

"I can't believe we're almost finished. I can finally see light at the end of the tunnel. Once the kitchen is complete, and the shop is painted, your work here is pretty much done. And just in time too, I'm nearly bankrupt," she smirked, curiously dodging the subject.

Kade sat straighter, reaching for an earlier offered scone. Over the past few months he'd learned to read her signals, and she clearly wanted the subject changed. Meg had definitely invited him closer over the past few weeks, but she still had some very thick walls. It made him more determined to earn her trust, and he was optimistic she'd eventually invite him inside.

"I'm practically working for slave labour," he retorted, "and lately I'm working for sexual favours, it seems. I'll be the one bankrupt soon."

"Ah, poor baby..."

"Aye, that I am. Now, if you'll excuse me, I have to get back to work before my boss has me heid," he chirped. "If you need any help getting set up in the shop, just give me a holler."

"I'll be fine. What do you say we break at noon and you can buy me lunch at The Coo?"

"Now that sounds like a plan," he agreed, inching out of the kitchen, glancing back with a smile.

Meg

Meg studied him as he left, a curious grin on her face. The last few weeks had been a dream. Kade was a great match, on almost every level. Their love-making was surreal, equal parts wild and romantic, both of them pushing their sexual boundaries. The way he made her feel, so desirable and confident, it was easy to stretch her comfort zone. But she wouldn't read too much into it. She'd done that once before and refused to subscribe to the fairytale again.

This time she was determined to have fun, and she was certain Kade wanted the same. She wouldn't ruin a good thing by doing something stupid, like falling in love, especially since she wasn't completely certain he was over Lorna. Her encounter with Kade's ex kept playing in her mind. *Kade always came crawling back.* Maybe it wasn't a matter of if, but when. If she refused to fall in love, she might avoid the heartbreak when it ended.

The morning flew by quickly. Meg finished priming all but one wall by the time Kade poked his head into the shop. His nod of a approval wasn't necessary, but it made her proud none the less. She worked meticulously hard, and it was cool that he noticed.

"Not bad, Meggie. If your wee book shop falls through you can always come work for me," Kade teased, helping her down off the ladder.

"I'll pass. I prefer being the one in charge," she declined, wiping a paint splattered hand across her damp forehead.

"Yes, I should know better," Kade chuckled. He pulled a hanky from his back pocket, wiping the primer off her face. "Are you ready for a bite to eat?"

"I'm famished! You might even talk me into some of Isla's sticky toffee pudding!"

They walked the half kilometre to The Coo, allowing the fresh air to revive them. The pub was already bustling when they arrived, forcing them to grab stools at the bar. As soon as they sat down, Isla greeted them with a grimace, gesturing to a table across the room.

Meg casually turned around, hoping to be subtle. Lorna was sitting with friends, her eyes burning into the back of Kade's head. Catching Meg's eye, she offered a terse nod before looking away. Meg knew bumping into Lorna was inevitable It wasn't a matter of if, but when, and she'd been dreading it. It was clear Lorna wasn't over Kade, and wouldn't back down without a fight. That woman was feisty.

"Don't look now, but it appears your crazy ex is coming this way," Isla spat, handing them a menu with the lunch specials.

"Hello Kade, Meg—," Lorna greeted, her tone as sweet as pie.

Meg spun her stool around to offer a proper hello. She was pleased to be met with a smile, and felt a pang of shame for thinking the worst. In spite of everything, Lorna had been kind to her, and if anyone was on the wrong side of the circumstances, it was probably herself.

"Hi Lorna. It's good to see you," Meg greeted, hoping to ease the tension.

"Is it?" Lorna asked, her smug eyes landing on Kade. A dry smirk was his only response, but it didn't seem to phase Lorna in the least. "How are your renovations coming along?" she asked, addressing Meg.

"Quite well! We're almost finished," Meg replied, hoping she sounded less uptight than she felt.

"So, you'll be moving on then, Kade," Lorna smirked. "On to something else?"

"I suppose," he shrugged, either ignoring the double meaning, or oblivious to it. It was clear to Meg that Lorna meant the message for her, maybe even as a warning. Uncomfortable, she suddenly wished she were anywhere else, but between the two ex-lovers. It was too confusing.

"You must be enjoying yourself, Meg?" Lorna asked, tipping her head innocently.

"Enjoying myself?"

"Yes, you're quite handy with tools, aren't you? I saw that you were heavily involved with Habitat for Humanity back home, in Virginia."

"Um, yes, that's true—," Meg choked. It didn't surprise her that Lorna 'Googled' her. She might have done the same thing, had tables been turned, but it didn't make her less uncomfortable. The opposite in fact. She glanced up slowly, stunned by the forged empathy masking the woman's face. *What else had she uncovered?*

As though reading her mind, Lorna offered a curious smile, patting her hand. "Well that must have been so rewarding, helping people less fortunate than yourself. You're such a generous person, well thought of in your community too."

Although Lorna's words were complimentary, their meaning was not. She wanted Meg to know she'd spent time trolling her, that she knew things about her. That her past was not unpublished.

Isla interrupted, her patience waning. "Can I get you something, Lorna?"

"No, no. I just wanted to say hello," she replied, tossing Meg a subtle wink. "I was just leaving. Well, good luck to you then."

Confused, Meg narrowed her eyes. "Good luck?"

"Aye. Good luck—with the rest of the renovations. Bye Kade. Let's catch up soon?"

He managed a terse goodbye before Lorna turned her back. Then she left, leaving nothing but the ghost of her floral perfume behind. The sweet scent turned Meg's stomach. Emotions churning, she no longer had an appetite.

"*That funt is a toilet-headed cumsplat*," Isla blurted indelicately, wiping the bar forcefully, as though mopping away the entire encounter. Scots had the most creative insults.

"I know you don't like her, Isla, but don't let her get to you. She'll only use it against you. You know it's best to ignore her," Kade advised, offering a reassuring smile.

Isla, shook her head, still not convinced. "She's a trouble maker. Why does she still have her hooks in you?"

Good question, Meg thought, too polite to ask.

"Does she?" Kade shrugged, looking down at his menu. "What's fresh today?" he asked, quickly changing the subject.

"It's all fresh, you wee bugger," Isla scoffed, respectfully backing down.

"I'll have the curry. What about you, Meggie?" Kade looked at Meg for the first time since the strange encounter, his eyes pooled with guilt. She sensed his reluctance, his shame. *What did that mean?*

"I'm actually not as hungry as I thought. I might just go home."

Alarmed, Kade took her hand, squeezing it tenderly. "It's fine, Meg. Stay and have lunch. Isla, pour us a dram—"

"You got it," Isla agreed, reaching for the good scotch.

"Not for me, Isla," Meg interjected, slipping her purse over her shoulder. The exchange had upset her in ways she never expected, and it wasn't just about Lorna and Kade. The woman had churned her memories like a bear stirring a nest of angry bees, desperate to steal the honey. It might have been her intention.

She was flooded with thoughts of Nathan, and their life together. The bad times and the good. She and Nathan, volunteering together back home in Virginia, when they were happy; when she was proud to be his girlfriend. She'd been reminded of everything she'd left behind, her job, her family, her old life. It was disconcerting, to say the least.

"I'm actually feeling unwell. But you should stay, Kade. I'll meet you back at the house."

He eyed her curiously, hoping to gauge her feelings, looking for reassurance. She wanted to offer it, but in that moment, she couldn't summon enough empathy for them both. It was all so troubling. Instead she offered him a quick peck on the cheek, and left the pub, grateful he didn't follow her.

CHAPTER 19

Kade

When Kade returned to the house, Meg was sitting on the front porch, wrapped in a lambswool blanket, the little red diary in her hands. A cup of tea rested on the arm of the chair. He knew her well enough to understand that reading was meditation for her, comforting and grounding. Something had upset her at the pub, and as difficult as it was not to follow her, he'd sensed she needed space.

"Hi," she greeted, looking up.

"Hello. I brought soup."

"That was kind of you," she smiled, gesturing for him to sit in the chair beside her. The air was chilly, and he wanted nothing more than to go inside and warm up, but there was something pressing on her mind.

"It might get cold," he warned, placing the take out bag on the small, wicker table between them.

"That's okay. I'll warm it up in the microwave," she said, picking up her tea. He watched the steam curl around her face, wistfully caressing her as though it loved her, and wanted to bring her peace. She took a sip, her eyes staring off into the distance.

"Are you alright?" he asked, cautiously touching her knee. Although she nodded, he still didn't believe her. "What's on yer mind?"

"I'll be fine. I just needed a moment to unwind. I don't want to trouble you, Kade. We're having too much fun to taint it with my shit," she insisted lightly, punctuating her words with an unconvincing smile. It almost offended him. Did she think him so shallow that he wouldn't care about her feelings? Did she not want him to? Had he not shown her that his affection was sincere?

"No, Meg," he swallowed, "I can see you're upset. Just tell me what happened...at the pub. Was it Lorna? Did she upset you?"

Meg was silent for a moment, her eyes searching his, as though she wordlessly hoped to find some answers herself. To what questions, he didn't know. He allowed her silence, hoping she'd extract what she needed to trust him. He didn't want to push her; he hated when people did that to him.

"No. It wasn't just her. It was the whole scene. Everything about it made me feel vulnerable...nostalgic...unglued. It's hard for me to explain without going into detail about my past—"

"—so give me the details, tell me. If you're upset, I want to know why? I want to help," Kade interrupted, hoping sincerity would crack her open. She shifted her eyes back to the horizon, as though considering his offer, and he was hopeful, until her shoulders dropped definitively.

"I know your natural inclination is to fix things Kade, to make them better, but I have to do this on my own. I don't want our friendship built on some sort of codependent proclivity. It may work for a short time, but ultimately it's a foundation for resentment. I don't need rescuing. I'm quite capable of rescuing myself," she pronounced, her eyes not returning to his. "Understand?"

He shifted uncomfortably in his seat, letting the words sink in. *Did he understand?*

"Well first of all, although I consider myself a bright guy, I have no idea what proclivity means, and B, I'm not trying to fix you, I'm just trying to understand who you are," he began, holding his emotions in check, the word *friendship* still ringing in his ears. Whatever she'd gone through in her past, it had been difficult. She'd been triggered that afternoon, there was no doubt in his mind. "I just want to know you Meggie. I care about ya."

Her face softening she chuckled quietly, finally meeting his gaze. "Proclivity...it means something we have a predisposition to. My past relationship was codependent to the extreme. It nearly broke me." Meg bit her lip and inhaled deeply, as though she'd said too much. "Look at me being all melodramatic. What kind of soup did you bring me?"

What the hell? "Soup?" Kade asked, confused by the sudden shift. "Meggie..."

"Stop worrying, Kade. I'm fine. Sometimes we all need an hour to reboot, don't we? Why don't we go inside and warm up. Thanks for bringing me lunch. That really was thoughtful."

Without waiting, she stood up, the blanket still cradling her shoulders, the diary tucked loosely under her arm. She picked up the soup and went inside, without looking back. Kade sat for a moment, processing what just happened, his emotions quietly kicking him from the inside out. He was falling for Meggie, but suddenly wondered if his feelings were reciprocated. Was he inflating their relationship? Making assumptions?

Not since Lorna had he allowed himself to love a woman. They were children when they'd met, and truth be told, they never learned how to communicate. The last few months with Meg made it clear to him that his relationship with Lorna ended because they never evolved beyond the high-school sweetheart stage, and he'd needed more than that. Because they were so young, their relationship bar had been set intolerably low, and when they tried to raise it, it came crashing back down. That's why he could never go back, and maybe that's why Lorna ultimately cheated on him.

But with Meggie, it was different. There was no bar. She made him want to be better, to reach hire, to love harder. With her, things were different, and he loved being with her. A man of few words, they were always honest. Although he hadn't told her these things outright, he thought she knew. He'd definitely tried to show her through the little things he did for her, and of course, in the bedroom. She'd used the word *friendship*, and that stung. He wasn't sure about America, but in Scotland, that meant the brakes were on. Had she gone as far as she was capable of going?

"Coming?" she called from inside.

Standing, he picked up her mug and pensively followed her call, still grasping for answers, for reassurance.

Meg

Meg swallowed the last spoonful of the soup, appreciating the warm comfort filling her belly. She loved the little things he did to make her smile. There was no doubt that he was a good man, and she wished she could trust in that, but she still worried about Lorna.

What did Isla say, *Why does she still have her hooks in you?* Meg had seen it too. It was subtle, but it was there. Kade seemed guarded when Lorna was around, sullen, maybe even uncomfortable. If he wasn't working through his feelings for her, why the uneasiness?

And Lorna. Meg had her own mixed feeling about the woman. She was pleasant enough, but it was obvious that Lorna was territorial when it came to Kade. They may not have been dating, but there were definitely still cords attached, healthy or not! Lorna was still in love. Was Kade?

Kade took a long swallow of coffee, patiently waiting for her to finish. She knew he wanted to continue their conversation, she could tell from his body language, but she was afraid. If she did ask the questions she was curious about, he would be completely honest. That was his way, and she wasn't sure she was ready to hear the answers. They had a good thing going; great sex, a warm friendship, a solid working relationship; if she asked for the truth about Lorna, if he admitted that he still had feelings for her, it would change everything. Maybe she was selfish, but she liked the simplicity of their relationship, especially after everything she'd left behind.

She sensed that Kade was ready to know more too. She respected that, she did, but what could she tell him? That although there were thousands of miles between her and Nathan, in some ways he still had his hooks in her too? Maybe not in the same way; not by his physical presence, but certainly emotionally. That in spite of the tumultuous relationship they had, she was still trying to shake him? Nathan had so much control over her when they were together, and in some ways he still did. Because of him, she still questioned herself daily, almost every thought, every deed.

That was the legacy he left her with. Nathan had been her oxygen. He'd pulled her underwater so deeply, so far below, she was convinced she couldn't breath without him. Although things were better since moving to Scotland, she was still fighting to breach the surface. It was shameful to admit, and she wasn't ready to confess that. She liked who she was with Kade. It was the closest she'd come to herself in years and she wanted things to stay that way. What they had was so easy, playful. Why complicate it?

"Meggie?"

Meg looked up and nodded, bracing herself. He smiled warmly before continuing. "Why so quiet? What's on yer mind?"

"Truthfully?" she paused, knowing her answer would pivot their relationship one way or another. "I was just thinking—"

He leaned in closer. "About?"

"Maybe we could take the rest of the day off?" she suggested, forcing a smile. "Play hooky?"

He sat back, his brows raised. "Hooky?"

"Why not? We've both been working so hard. Let's just chill out." She knew she was avoiding his questions. And she knew he knew. He regarded her curiously, releasing the softest of sighs before offering her a smile. She was buying them both more time. Maybe she was wrong, but she sensed he was grateful too.

"What did you have in mind?" he asked provocatively, reaching for her hand.

"Probably the same thing as you—," she purred, standing up. She gently nudged him back into the chair before straddling him, easing her full, round bottom onto his lap.

"Aye, you read my mind—," he managed to choke, right before she pressed her lips against his.

There was no shortage of passion between them, and Kade heated quickly, his erection filling the space between them. His hardness pressed against her clit, coaxing her arousal to the surface. She shamelessly grooved against him, allowing her pleasure to build. He cradled her ass with his strong hands, rocking her hips back and forth to tease out her orgasm, his teeth gently biting her sensitive neck. His laboured breath burned passionately on her flesh, pushing her over the edge. The wave radiate from her core, sending explosive tingles through her, momentarily seizing every cell in her body, suspending every fear, every doubt. She gripped his shoulders, burying her face into the crease of his neck, her satisfied moans escaping her lips. He stiffened beneath her, inspiring her with naughty encouragements.

"Jesus woman, you're so damn hot. You'll make me cum just listening to ya."

"I want you to cum," she gasped, raising her face to look at him. Although glazed over, he couldn't take his eyes off her. He released her hips, raising his hands to her face, drawing her in for a sensual kiss. She was utterly consumed by him, her insecurities suddenly quiet.

"Fuck me, Kade. Take me to bed."

"No, I'll have you right here, Meggie."

He raised her off his lap, standing her on shaking legs, before hastily clearing the dishes from the table. They crashed to the planks below, smashing against the newly refurbished hardwood. Meg giggled, completely unfazed, his urgency arousing her further. He turned with a grin, easily lifting her onto the sturdy chrome table. Convinced a modern table could never hold the weight of unbridled passion, she was suddenly grateful she'd never replaced it. She'd never be able to part with it now, she thought, giggling to herself.

Fumbling with his jeans, he slipped them past his hips. "Raise yer arse, woman," he ordered playfully. She gladly obeyed, raising her bottom so he could easily remove her pants. He discarded her clothing to the floor, ignoring the socks, and raised her legs onto the table, shifting her as close to the edge as possible.

"You'll forgive the lack of foreplay Meggie, but I need to take you right now," he panted, entering her unapologetically. She took no offence, excited by his lack of self control. It was a side of him she hadn't seen since the night he'd ripped apart her dress. She hoped it wouldn't be the last.

She held him tightly while he ravaged her, certain their fucking was a release for him, just as it was for her; a way to connect physically, where emotionally she was impotent. His closeness was both exciting and reassuring, and was all she was capable of receiving in that moment.

She needed to want him. She just didn't want to need him.

He kissed her hard while he came, wordlessly, almost angrily. His intensity was infectious and urged her towards another screaming orgasm. Wrapping her legs around his hips, she shuddered wildly through every spasm. Moments later he collapsed, exhausted, spent from exertion, his forearms holding the brunt of his weight. With his thickness softening inside her, his hot essence pooled down her thighs. The sensation was surprisingly intimate, and one she'd never experienced before. No man had ever been inside her without a condom.

"Well, that was a pleasant turn of events," he choked, finally able to catch his breath.

"And not unwelcome," Meg agreed, shifting uncomfortably on the cold surface. She didn't want to move, enjoying the closeness of him, but the unforgiving formica made her spine grumpy. Sensing her discomfort, Kade hoisted himself away, offering his hand. Gratefully, she sat forward, her legs dangling off the table, watching him return his pants over his perfectly fine ass.

"I may take a bath," she suggested cautiously. "Would you like to join me in that sexy tub?"

He nodded, helping her down. "Aye. And what's on the agenda for the rest of the day?"

"Maybe a lazy walk, music, some food...more of this?"

"Okay," he agreed, retrieving her clothes from the floor, "and maybe some conversation?”

She knew what he meant, but played coy anyway. “If you can talk with your mouth full,” she teased, urging him towards the bathroom.

“Aww, that’s how it will be then, is it?” he gauged back lightly, his eyes conveying something altogether different.

“For now,” she offered honestly. “Okay?”

He nodded, but she knew she was only biding time. She knew he deserved more. and like a true Scot, it was killing him to hold his tongue.

CHAPTER 20

Katherine

August 6, 1961

Dear Diary,

Today's the big day! Mack is finally meeting Mum and Dad. We're both nervous, but Mack more than I. He admitted he's worried they won't approve, in particular because he's not Catholic. I know Mum won't like that very much, but she's just going to have to come around. I adore Mack. He's so thoughtful and kind, everything I ever wanted. Who cares what religion he is?

We've only made love a few times, but each time we're together he makes me feel so special. He's so sweet, and takes his time with me. I won't go into details, but let's just say, that boy knows what he's doing! It makes me blush just thinking about it. I'd like to be intimate more often, but we don't have privacy. Mack is also terrified I might get pregnant, even with rubbers. When we're married, we can make love as often as we like.

He hasn't "officially" asked me to marry him, but we've talked about the possibility when I turn 18. I'll be in university but we can make it work. If there's a will there's a way. Because Dad teaches at the U of E, my tuition is covered, and I get first year of residence paid for, too. It's a benefit for full time faculty. It's a good thing, because even though Dad makes a decent living, I'm not sure they could afford undergraduate studies <u>and</u> med school for me. I'm registered to start this September. I suggested that Mack can get a small apartment near campus, *and work in Edinburgh. Then we can spend our free time together. There are so many opportunities for him in the city. He suggested we wait until schools over, but that's so far away! I reminded him that once I have my undergrad degree, it's off to med school, so really, I won't be finished school until I'm at least 26 or 27. No way can I wait that long to marry him. I asked him what difference it made when we tied the knot? We're going to be together forever, anyway. He seemed to think this was reasonable, but still, I can tell he's worried.*

As much as I love Mum and Dad, I'm excited to be on my own. I'm ready to be independent, and truthfully, I think it's best for Mum and Dad too. They aren't fighting as much anymore, but I still sense tension. I talked to mum about this, but whenever I bring up school, she changes the subject. I know she'll really miss me, but I feel like the time apart will be good for us. She still sees me as a child and that won't change until I leave home.

So anyway, I finally told my parents about Mack. Mum gave me the third degree, asking me every question under the sun. I think I handled it well, and of course I was very discreet. She doesn't need to know everything. I told her we met through friends and that we're quite fond of each other, but not much else. I told her Mack insisted on meeting them to ask their blessing to date me. (This is a wee exaggeration, but I knew it would score him few brownie points with Mum.) She hemmed and hawed a little, but in the end, Dad convinced her that it would do no harm. Dad is wise. It's not like they can keep us apart or lock me in a tower, for heaven's sake!

I am hoping it all goes well. I would rather have their support, but even if they don't like him, it won't change a thing. Not at all. He'll be coming for dinner so I have to make some shortbread. It's his favourite. I'll keep you posted!

* * *

"How could she be so rude?" Katherine cried, her body trembling in Mack's arms. They'd found themselves sitting in the park, desperate to escape the after dinner tension.

"She's your mum. She cares about you, is all," he soothed, tenderly kissing her crown. "Besides, I wouldn't say she was rude, just really direct."

"I know her better than you Mack, and trust me, she was acting so cold towards ya. And why would she ask ya all those questions about your Dad? I'm not dating your father!"

"I think she's just looking out for ya. She wants to make sure I'm good enough for her little girl. I can't say I blame her. You deserve to live yer best life, Kat."

"And I'll have one! With you. Did ya see her scowl when you told her you'd be apprenticing with your father? Learning how to build houses and such? Like there was no honour in that? I wanted to reach across the table and slap her. I'm sorry she made you feel bad. You don't deserve that. I know ya so well, Mack, and I know that you'll be great at whatever you put yer mind to!" Katherine insisted, hoping to reassure him. Mack was a respectful boy, and it worried her that he'd take Mary's words to heart.

"I appreciate that. Honestly, I think yer being too hard on her. I didn't take as much offence as you. The truth is, yer parents have such high hopes for ya. They know yer ambitious, that school is important to ya. It's understandable they worry I'll be a distraction."

"I like being distracted by you," Katherine blushed, raising her mouth for a kiss. Mack was only happy to oblige. She pulled back, just enough to meet his eyes. "I hope you know how much I love you, Mack. It doesn't matter whether my parents accept that or not. We know what we want, right?"

"I love you too, Kat, more than anything."

She sighed deeply, comforted by his words. Her mother *was* cold to Mack, from the moment he'd walked in, and didn't let up until he said goodnight, yet he handled it with such grace. Kat was sure her Dad was impressed with Mack's manners, but her Mum was too busy grilling him to appreciate how respectful he was. It was frustrating to say the least. Would Mary ever approve of anyone she brought home? It was unlikely, she thought.

In spite of the challenging night, Kat was determined to stay positive. She and Mack would figure things out. She would be old enough to marry in eight months, surely her parents understood that? Heck, they married before they were even twenty.

Her mother was a war bride. She'd met Katherine's father in 1942, while he was on a short military leave. The way Mary told it, she was visiting a dance hall with friends, and Douglas jumped in to defended her honour. Another solider (an Irish fella, with no manners) insisted Mary dance with him, harassing her to the point of tears, refusing to take no for an answer. Douglas stepped in and kindly asked the young solider to move on. When diplomacy didn't work, he put the Irish bloke in a head lock and shoved him out the door.

Katherine's mum said it was love at first sight. They spent the next four days together, followed by a quick ceremony at city hall. Then Douglas returned to the front. He came back about a year later and they had a proper Catholic wedding, at the insistence of Mary's mother. Nine months later, Katherine was born and Douglas started University. Tic Tac Toe. The story was so romantic, but what stood out the most for Katherine, was her certainty that Mary never asked *her* parents for permission to marry her solider.

So why the hypocrisy?

"What do you say, shall I walk you home? It's getting late and I don't want to give your folks cause to worry," Mack urged, his tone thick with concern.

"I suppose, but I'll be going right to my room. I'm too upset to talk to my parents right now."

"Be patient with them, mo ghràdh, they're good people at heart."

"I know, but yer dad's been so kind to me. I just hoped the same for you," Kat sighed, recalling the lovely visits she had with Mack's father. "He's so welcoming."

"Well, I suppose he has less to lose," he shrugged.

"What does *that* mean?"

"Let's face it, he thinks you're a step up for me. A smart, ambitious, beautiful woman from a good family; going to University in the fall? You'll have so many opportunities. Someone like you raises his status—"

"Mack, what are you saying?" she interrupted. "That my parents think the otherwise? That somehow yer not good enough for me, for our family?"

Always the diplomat, Mack smiled warmly. "I'm saying they've more to lose, is all."

"Don't be daft," she sighed, brushing him off. "They just don't know how much you mean to me. But once they understand, I'm sure they'll back down. I'll insist on it."

"Ah Kat, yer such a sweetheart," he smiled, taking his feet. "Now, come on, let's get moving."

"Okay, but kiss me first," she purred, allowing him to raise her from the bench.

His kiss was short and sweet. Kat sensed he was holding back. "Do you trust me?" she whispered, wrapping her hands around his cheeks. "I'll do what it takes for us to be together. I promise ya."

"I know ya will," he answered softly.

* * *

"Katherine, is that you?"

Kat poked her head in the living room on her way past. "Aye Mum, it's me."

"Come sit with us, Dad and I have to tell you something," Mary insisted, stern eyes warning her daughter not to challenge her.

"Mum, I'm tired. I'm going to bed," she shrugged, not particularly interested in anything her mother had to say. It worried her to see Mack so disheartened.

"Katherine, please listen to your mum. This is important," Douglas intervened. Kat threw her father a helpless look, begging him to rescue her. Unmoved, he patted the couch beside him, inviting her to join them. Kat sensed something was wrong. Her parents were uncharacteristically calm. Had someone died?

"There's something yer father and I have been meaning to discuss with ya," Mary began, pausing only long enough for Kat to take a seat beside her father.

"Okay? What's is it? Is something wrong?" Kat asked. Her parents stared at each other. Had they discovered that she and Mack were sleeping together? That things were more serious than Katherine lead them to believe? Had her mother found her diary?

"Nothing's wrong," Douglas assured. "In fact, it's good news for our family."

Kat raised her eyes to Mary, to see if she agreed. Although she found her Dad hard to gauge, her Mum was an open book—and her face read anxious.

"Mum?"

"Well, it will be good news, in time. We're moving to America. Yer Dad accepted a transfer to teach at Duke University. It's a ten year contract," Mary offered reluctantly.

"It's a great opportunity for me, sweetheart. Certainly better money," Douglas assured. "The University is offering a relocation package, plus other benefits I can't turn down. It's commencing at the beginning of the fall semester."

"I know it's a lot to take in, Katherine. It wasn't easy for me either, all things considered. The thought of leaving my friends and starting over is difficult, but once I realized how beneficial this was for our family, I got behind yer father."

"Wait, is this what you and Dad have been fighting about?" she asked, trying to process what she heard.

Mary sat forward, surprised by the observation. "Well, I wouldn't call it fighting," she offered tersely. "We've just been discussing, trying to make the right decision."

"Duke's a good school, very well respected, and North Carolina is a fine place to live," Douglas interjected, as though he'd memorized exactly what he wanted to say to his daughter. Katherine regarded him cynically, allowing his words to sink in.

"Live? Us?" Kat murmured, searching for clarity. "You think I should go *with* ya?"

Douglas nodded enthusiastically. "Aye! Duke has one of the best undergraduate science programs in the United States, following that, the Duke University of Medicine. It's fully covered, your tuition. You'll have everything you need, Katherine!"

"But Dad, I don't want to move. I thought we had it all planned out. I'm going to Edinburgh. I already picked my courses! I don't understand?"

"If Dad takes this job at Duke, Katherine, you're education will be fully covered. Our new home is only blocks from campus. You won't need to live in residence. You'll be able to walk—"

Kat shook her head and cried, "but I want to live in residence—"

"This is for the best, daughter. We want the finest education for ya, and if we stay in Scotland, I'm afraid I can't pay for yer medical school. Besides, I've always wanted to teach abroad. I've been praying for this opportunity a long time. It's a win for all of us," Douglas explained calmly, hoping, if not to convince her, at least to soothe her.

"Dad, no. I don't want to go," Katherine sobbed. She couldn't leave Mack. Never. Moving to the states was out of the question. "I won't go. I don't need to go to medical school! I'll choose something else."

"Don't be daft, Katherine! You've always wanted to be a doctor. I know this is a big change, and I know it's scary, but stop and think about what yer saying, girl! Have ya lost yer mind?" Mary scolded. Katherine looked at her mother and scowled, suddenly more angry than upset. Of course she was losing her mind! They were turning her life upside-down!

"I won't go!" Katherine panicked, her mind grasping for alternative options. She could live with Esme until school started; get part time work to help with expenses; and then as soon as she could marry without permission, she and Mack would live together, in Edinburgh. Maybe she would go to business school instead, take a job as a secretary. "I won't leave Mack. We're in love!" she blurted.

Mary opened her mouth in rebuttal, but was quickly silenced by her husband's calmly raised hand. "Aye, you will go," he affirmed, his tone clear, his word final. "You cannot stay here. Your opportunities are abroad."

"But Da—"

"It's decided," he insisted, meeting his wife's stare. Katherine's mouth dropped open, as if to speak again, but she knew he was done. Although her father was a patient man, once he'd made a decision, he wouldn't be budged.

"This is not fair. What about what I want?" she implored her mother, certain her tearful pleas wouldn't help.

"Wheesht, I know yer upset, Katherine, but I promise ya, once we've settled you'll see it's for the best," Mary gently chided, taking her husband's side. "We'll start packing our things. You'll need to sort through yer room and start giving things away that aren't essential. I'll be taking donations to the church for charity. Pack wisely, daughter."

Unwilling to hear another word, Katherine stood up and left the room, leaving her parents to whisper behind her back. There had to be another way. She had to talk to Mack, she thought, turning towards the front door.

"Katherine? You'll not leave the house!" her mother shouted from the living room. "Go straight to yer room, we'll talk more in the morning."

Katherine held the door handle, wanting more than anything to defy her mum, to storm out of the house so they would understand how angry she was, but wisdom prevailed. No, she needed to handle things properly. Acting like a spoiled child wouldn't serve anyone. She needed time to think things through. She would speak with Mack tomorrow, she thought, he would know what to do.

CHAPTER 21

Kade

"Well, what do you think? It's pretty sweet in here!" Kade stood in the middle of the shop, his arms crossed proudly. I think it's time to unpack those books and get yer wee shop set up! It won't be long now before yer open for business!"

"I think you're right. It turned out exactly as I hoped. The book shelves look even better than expected." Meg slowly spun around, taking in the entire space. "You might be a wizard. Where do you keep your magic wand?"

"You know exactly where I keep it, Lass. Now what do you say I use a little of my magic on you?" He halted her mid-twirl, pulling her in for a kiss, pleased with himself.

"You already have me under your spell, Scotsman. You should know that by now?"

"Do I?" he flirted, offering another peck. "Then what do you say we make things official. Be my girl."

"I thought I was?" Meg chirped, playfully easing away. Kade was all too familiar with her avoidance techniques.

"No, we're lovers. I'm talking about more."

Meg's smile faded. "More?"

"Yes more. I'm a patient man, Meggie. I don't want to pressure you to do anything yer not ready for, nor to talk about things ya still don't want to share, but I think it's time to figure out what this is, between you and I, don't you?"

It had been nearly a week since their awkward encounter with his ex, and while they seemed to have passed through unscathed, he was ready to have a heart to heart. They'd been pussy footing around long enough.

"What *this* is?" she asked nervously, twirling her locket between unsteady fingers.

"Aye. We've spent most every day together for months, and many nights too, and I've been loving every minute with you. Do you not know how much I care for ya?"

"I care about you too, Kade," she whispered, dropping her eyes.

He gently raised her chin, greeting her with a curious smile. "Well?"

"I'm not sure...I...um...there are things I'm still trying to figure out—," she sighed, tearing her eyes away. Kade dropped his hand and inhaled slowly, hoping his frustration was well hidden.

"What's to figure out? We're great together," he pressed. He needed answers.

"For how long Kade?" she snapped, clearly frustrated.

"How long?"

"Yes, how long will I be enough? How long will I hold your interest? How long until you work your way back to Lorna?" she asked, her eyes misting.

He shook his head slowly, confused with her outburst. "Lorna?"

"Yes, Lorna. I know you two have a complex history, she told me. I see how you are around her, she clearly gets under your skin. She has this...hold on you. Even Isla mentioned it," she choked, visibly shaken.

This was completely expected. He thought her reluctance was due to her own past, her own insecurities, even issues with her ex. When the hell did Lorna speak with her?

"She said that? When?" Kade asked. "What exactly did she say?"

"Awhile back. She happened upon me at the park, enjoying a quiet Sunday. We actually had a pleasant visit, and she even introduced me to some friends. She told me that you and she were close, that you had a complicated relationship. She said that you've broken up many times and that you always find your way back to each other—"

"Wait, what?"

"Yes, that's what she said. I've been nervous to bring it up because...I don't know...I guess I was afraid it might be true. We're having a great time together, it's been so refreshing. Honestly? I guess I didn't want to complicate things. I just wanted to enjoy *this* while it lasts," she admitted, gesturing between them. She sighed deeply, gathering her thoughts. "I've done *complicated* Kade, and I'm still recovering."

Kade dropped his shoulders, trying to process her words. Had he known Lorna would sabotage him, he would've been forthcoming about his past sooner. He hated that Meg had been carrying such a heavy burden. No wonder she'd been resisting him.

"She told you I always go back to her?" he asked, uncomfortably recalling the toxic grip Lorna had on him. *HAD. Past tense.*

"Her exact words were that you would come crawling back with your tail tucked between your legs."

"Is that right?" he smirked, his face tight. "My tail tucked—"

"—between your legs," Meg finished, returning his grin.

Kade took her hands in his, and considered all that transpired. Lorna's manipulation was surprising, but at the same time, not unexpected. "Can I buy you a drink? I think this conversation needs some anesthesia. It's a wee bit painful," he chuckled softly, his eyes begging her to accept. "It's hard for me to talk about, Meggie, but I'd like to, if yer willing to listen."

Meg nodded, a rogue tear escaped down her cheek. He gently swiped it away with his thumb. "Come on, let's go."

Meg

Isla set their drinks in front of them, along with a plate of smokies, a delicious smoked salmon appy that Meg was acquiring a taste for. She picked up her whiskey and downed it, gesturing for another. Kade winked and followed suit.

"Make that two, Isla," he grinned, taking Meg's hand.

Isla picked up the empty glasses. "Celebrating something, are we?"

"We're drinking, my friend, that's all you need to know," Kade smirked, offering her a knowing look.

"Aye, say no more. I'll bring over the bottle."

"This is why I love you Iz," Kade called after her.

"It's quiet in here," Meg observed. Although the whiskey helped, she was still trying to settle her nerves. She didn't meant to unload on Kade. She'd been struggling with her feelings for the better part of the week, ever since their encounter with Lorna. The climate around the woman, and her concerns that Kade still might love her, were only part of it. She'd finally come to the conclusion that Kade deserved to know the truth, of why she was so guarded.

“It’s still early. I’m actually glad it’s not busy yet.” He was uncharacteristically nervous, and Meg suddenly felt bad for him. It was even more reason to be honest with him. He wasn’t the only one with ghosts. She knew she had to come clean about Nathan. It was time.

“What an interesting turn of events,” Meg offered lightly. “Here I was thinking this would be a nondescript day—”

“Aye, but it’s been coming for awhile,” Kade shrugged, taking her hand. “I’m sorry that you’ve been worrying about this for so long. I had no idea.”

“I didn’t want to make assumptions, Kade. We’re having a good time together, but I wasn’t sure what that meant, especially given the circumstances. To be honest, it never seemed appropriate to question you about it. I didn’t want to pry.”

“I know. I’ve had the same hesitations. I’ve been wanting to know more about your story too, but I’ve also been reluctant to press. I didn’t want you to withdraw,” he confessed. “My relationship with Lorna failed because we didn’t know how to communicate, at least in part. But you and I? We have the potential for something really special, Meggie, I don’t want it to break down before we even discover what it could be. Maybe it’s time we trust each other.”

“Maybe it is.” Meg patiently waited as Kade searched for his words. There was so much she wanted to know, but she didn’t want to bombard him with questions, and possibly influence what he needed to share.

“Lorna was a big part of my life, and at one time, I thought we might get married,” he began. “We had a pretty decent run, while we were young. We started dating when we were still in high school. Christ, I was 17 when we met. It was fun, for a while. We even talked about living together, but my parents convinced me to live on my own. They thought I'd regret not having the experience, and honestly, I'm grateful they insisted."

Meg nodded. Living alone for the first time, in her quaint Scottish cottage, had been the best experience of her life. She'd moved in with Nathan from her father's house, bypassing the whole independent thing. She wondered if things might have been different had she lived on her own first; she might have fought harder for her needs, wants, and wishes to be met. She'd always thought Nathan might have been less controlling if she'd been more assertive. She'd learned over the past few months that what she thought was weakness, was simply a lack of confidence.

She should have done it sooner, but she'd been so afraid to fail. She never wanted to move back home, and put her dad in that position. There would have been too much shame in that. After her father died, and things went off the rails with Nathan, Meg knew she had no choice but to take care of herself.

"The thing is," Kade continued, "while I was evolving, gaining my independence, working at building my business, Lorna was just happy to enjoy the status quo. It was like her emotional maturity landed on eighteen and just stayed there, even as we were pushing through our twenties. She still wanted to party, stay out late, and act like we were kids. Being the eldest of the four brothers, I had a first-hand view of their lives. They were getting married and having babies, and building their families. I was suppose to be their role-model, but instead they became mine. I wanted the same things."

"That was my first impression of you, Kade," Meg admitted, recalling the first time Kade had opened up about his family.

"*First* impression?"

"Yes, but then, when I asked if you ever wanted to marry, you seemed completely put off by the idea. It made me second guess myself."

Kade regarded her thoughtfully, trying to recall the conversation. "Aye, I did do that. It wasn't my intention to lead you astray, Meggie. I suppose when ya asked, I'd been thinking about Lorna. I'd come to the conclusion that she and I would never wed, but I didn't mean that I was opposed to marriage. Just the opposite, I want a wife."

Meg met his eyes, drawn in by his sincerity. Taking her hand once more, he smiled sweetly, allowing her witness to his vulnerability. Her heart skipped a beat, and she swallowed hard, desperate to compose herself. "I see," was all she managed to choke, interrupted by Isla returning to the table.

"Sorry it took me so long. Someone called in for supper take-out. It's an order for twelve and they want it in a half-hour. Jay-sus! Some people are so doaty. A little notice wouldn't kill em," Isla grumbled, setting a bottle of scotch between them. "You don't like the smokies?" she asked, noticing the untouched plate. She set down two glasses, filling them halfway.

"No, they're perfect," Meg assured, popping one into her mouth. The smoky flavour, mixed with the perfect amount of seasoning, melted on her tongue. They paired perfectly with scotch, Meg thought, chasing the appetizer with a mouthful of the smooth, rich whiskey. "Mmmm," she moaned.

"Aye, Red. I love yer passion...for my cooking," Isla flirted, offering Kade a cheeky wink. "Ya better tie this one down, before I do."

Meg giggled, blaming her blush on the whiskey, although the flirting didn't hurt. "Thanks Isla," she chirped flirtatiously, "if only I wasn't straight."

"No one's perfect, love," Isla smirked, leaving the two of them alone.

Kade grinned. "Hmmm, now that's an interesting image."

"I'm sure it is. Don't think it's never crossed my mind—," Meg teased, knowing the image would make him squirm. She loved talking dirty with Kade, and smiled, appreciating how daring she felt with him.

"Yer killin' me woman."

"Well, maybe we can talk about it later, in more detail—"

"You can be sure of it!" He took a deep swallow of scotch, his naughty smile making her laugh.

"That's the sound I like to hear. You have the greatest laugh. It makes me happy. I think that's why I work so hard to make it happen," Kade confessed, his words warming her faster than the scotch had. "When I think on it, I realize that's what was missing from my life."

"How so?"

"I worked hard to please Lorna, but it wasn't the same. Her expectations were so high. She wanted me to please her, to give way to her, with little regard for what I needed. I tried to make her happy, but the truth was, it wasn't because the effort was reciprocated; it was because if I didn't, she'd make me feel inadequate…guilty. She had this way of manipulating me…it doesn't make me proud to admit it—," he trailed off.

Meg understood that all too well. At times, it had been the same for her and Nathan.

"I suppose I found it easier to keep the peace rather than deal with a scene. She wasn't afraid to make one in public either," he said, his mind drifting uncomfortably to the past. "Anyway, I make it all seem bad. She was my girlfriend a long time, so I suppose we had good times, too. She could also be quite dynamic. It was confusing, to say the least."

Meg nodded, encouraging him to go on.

"We finally did move in together a few years ago, and early on, things were fine. I guess I hoped that once we moved in, she would settle. Unfortunately, after a few months, I realized that things were not to be that way. We fought, a lot. She wasn't stable. Meggie. I don't say that to make excuses. It's the truth. I won't go into it, out of respect for her, but her mind games were too much to bear. I just wanted to be happy, to have a peaceful home, but Lorna seemed to thrive on chaos. We separated for a few months, and yes, I did see other people, as did she, but for one reason or another, we ended up back together. She moved back in, and we tried again. Then it started all over. We couldn't seem to develop our relationship, it was the same damn patterns over and over. God, I hate admitting this..." he shrugged, pausing to take a breath. Meg could see how hard it was for him to talk about, how much shame he had. She took his hand, hoping to offer him solace.

"Honestly, I felt this deep, internal pressure to make things work and I just kept trying. We'd invested a lot of time, and I felt it the right thing to do. I was wrong about that. I should have ended things years earlier, but sometimes life's lessons are hard to learn. We were stuck in a cycle together, and I knew I'd never progress as long as she and I stayed together."

"So what happened," Meg asked, surprised by their parallels.

"She cheated on me. That was the straw that broke the camel's back. It was earlier this year, end of January. To be truthful, things were winding down anyway, but we were still together. I walked in on her banging some bloke. I don't know who he was, and I really didn't care. I wanted her out."

"That must have been awful," Meg comforted. Kade was such a positive person, so animated and full of life. She could hardly imagine what it was like for him to bear such chaos. It actually hurt her heart to think about it.

"It was. It took some time to process everything, but I finally recognized that I was better off without her."

"But Lorna seems so confident that you and she will reunite?" Meg questioned, recalling the woman's revelation. "She was pretty clear about that."

"Aye, she can be very convincing. Now you see why I was so entangled in the manipulation? She's very good at spinning the truth to her liking, and she'll twist your words, and then use them to gain the upper hand. Christ, she could force the Pope question his truth."

Meg nodded, hesitant to speak. She sat quietly, allowing his story to settle in, until he broke the silence between them.

"I have to be up front about something, Meg..." He refused to meet her eyes.

"Go on," she urged.

"We did have a moment, Lorna and I, a few months back. It was before I met you, on my thirtieth birthday. My mates threw a bit of a bash for me, here at the pub. Lorna showed up with a few mates. I dunno, I suppose I was lonely. I told ya how charming she could be when she wanted, and I suppose after a few pints, I found myself thinking about the good times. I admit, for a drunken split second, I even questioned why we weren't together. I suppose part of me will always feel affection for her on some level..." he paused, long enough to look at her.

Meg tried to express empathy, but his confession stung a little, despite that fact that she completely related. In many ways it was how she felt about Nathan, the difference being, he was on the other side of the ocean. She was grateful she didn't have to face him on a regular basis. She went to extreme measures to separate herself because she didn't trust herself not to fall under his spell again.

"I now understand that affection is not the same as loving someone. Lorna was my first love, but she won't be my last," he professed, leaning in closer. "I'm certain of it."

"What makes you so sure, Kade?" she asked, desperate to ease her own uncertainties.

"Because in the few months I've known you, Meggie, I've been happier than in all the years I ever spent with Lorna. I feel content with you, peaceful. I can be myself without any worry it won't be enough. You've offered me hope again."

Meg briefly closed her eyes, allowing his words to really touch her. Was he in *love* with her? Was that what he meant? She struggled with doubt, her old insecurities choking her. Could she move past them and love him back? She wanted to.

Timidly, she glanced up, opening her mouth to speak, but as her eyes landed behind him, the words caught in her throat.

"Meggie?" Kade asked, his face pained.

"Nathan?" she choked. It was all she could manage. Kade turned slowly, following the trail of her eyes. It was Lorna, standing in the doorway, with a man she thought she'd never see again.

CHAPTER 22

Katherine

August 11, 1961

Dear Diary,

I want to die. I'm suppose to be packing but I can't move. Even writing this entry is excruciating. I can't stop sobbing. I've been crying for days. Mum keeps checking on me, talking in a cheerful voice, saying everything will be fine. She has no idea what she's talking about. Now when she comes by my room, I just pretend to be napping. I can't even look at her, nor Dad.

It's taken me a few days to write about this whole mess. Maybe I was hoping it was all just a bad dream I would wake from. How can a person go from being on top of the world, to THIS, literally overnight? How?

Mack doesn't want me. It's over.

I'm still going over our last conversation, trying to make sense of it. It's on a loop inside my brain, replaying again and again, and I still have so many questions. I feel sick inside.

I told him what my parents want to do, moving to North Carolina for Dad's transfer, and how they enrolled me in classes at Duke. At first he seemed as shocked as I, and I thought for sure he would insist I don't leave, for us to be together, maybe even marry so that they'd have no choice but to leave me behind.

I explained how the University in Edinburgh was no longer an option, unless I paid for it myself, but how I was willing to change direction. I would do anything to be with him, and I told him so, even taking business courses so I could find a job as a girl-Friday, or a secretary. I took shorthand and typing in high-school, and I was pretty fast. When he went quiet, I thought he was brainstorming with me, considering how to make it work—but then he shocked me and said I should move to America!

He said something I'll never forget, or forgive, as long as I'm breathing. I asked him how he could let the woman he loved move so far away and he replied 'How could I not?' I said 'Mack, if you love me, you'll ask me to stay!', and he said 'No Kat, yer wrong.'

Wrong, he said. I thought he wanted me to be his wife? Did he not love me?

I tried to press him. I begged, cried, and pleaded for answers, but he kept saying 'I can't', over and over. Finally, when I realized he was not willing to fight for me, I told him there was a chance he'd never see me again. He put his head down and let me walk away. It broke my heart.

He hasn't called on me since. No visit or phone call. I even left a message with his Dad, but nothing. I cried to Esme a few nights back. (She seemed more upset about me leaving than Mack did!) She said she warned me about him, but I wouldn't listen. She said she knew he would hurt me. I showed her the gift he gave me, but she shrugged and said it was meaningless now. Maybe she's right. I want to throw it in the trash.

(Dad just popped his head in my room and told me that he's arranged passage on a ship to take us to America. He said we leave a week Saturday. He's bloody oblivious to my misery.)

I can't believe it's going to end this way. As disappointed as I am with Mack, I will ever stop loving him. We're soul mates, I'm sure of it. If I knew he wanted me too, I'd do whatever it took to be with him. Anything.

* * *

Sitting at her dressing table, Katherine held Mack's gift in the palm of her hand. She caressed it delicately with her fingertips, as though it was as fragile as the love he'd shared, wistfully dreaming of a future that would never be. Grieving, she'd passed through denial, and depression was now the hapless frontrunner. Although she didn't want reminders of Mack, she coulnever part with the only thing he'd ever given her. It was the only evidence she had that she wasn't crazy, that she'd not imagined the whole ill-fated love-affair.

"Katherine?" her mother called out, her footsteps echoing up the stairs.

Panicking, Kat quickly hid the gift, worried her mother would see it, and convince her to return it.

"Are you almost ready? The movers will be here in an hour to load the crates. We'll be getting new furniture when we arrive in North Carolina, are you sure you want that old dressing table?" Mary asked. She waited cautiously at the bedroom door, as though crossing the threshold would only start another fight.

"Aye," Kat whispered, refusing to turn around. "If I change my mind, I'll sell it."

"I'm not sure who'd want to buy it, but okay," she treaded softly. "And you've packed all the clothes and books you want to ship? I'm taking the last load of donations to the church. The heavy stuff will be picked up by volunteers tomorrow. I've left a key with our agent—"

"Yes, mother! Please!" Kat cried. "You've asked me a million times. It's done."

"I'm sorry, Katherine," her mother frowned, inching towards her, "I don't mean to nag. I know how unhappy you are, and I suppose I don't know how to make things better—"

"You can't!" Kat interrupted, trying to hold her temper. The truth was, she knew her Mum was as unsettled with the move as she was, but Kat wasn't ready to pardon her. She was too numb.

"I know, Lamb. For what's it's worth, I know how you feel."

"You don't, Mum. You've no idea what I'm going through," Katherine spat, wishing she would leave her be.

Mary looked at her daughter, her eyes filled with regret. "Yer friend Esme is waiting at the door to say good-bye. Shall I send her up?"

Katherine shrugged, refusing mercy. "Aye."

Mary offered her daughter a mournful look, and sadly left the room. Moments later, Esme poked her head through the open doorway. "Is it safe to come in?" she smirked, holding her hand up in a gesture of peace.

"No, but come in anyway."

"It seems so empty in here," Esme observed solemnly, scoping the room. She flopped down on the bare mattress.

"It's not the only thing."

"Kat, I don't know why yer so devastated! I'd give anything to be in yer shoes! America! That's where Elvis lives! And Marilyn! It's such a progressive country—"

"But Mack lives here," Kat shrugged, irritated by her friend's enthusiasm.

"As do I, don't forget," Esme shrugged, trying to hide a grimace. Kat caught the look, but ignored it all the same. Esme hated Mack, for whatever reason, and Kat had no interest in rehashing it, not that day.

"And you," Kat sighed, joining her friend on the bed. She gave her a hug, afraid the tears would start flowing again. "I'm glad yer here. I'm just upset that Mack didn't bother to say good-bye."

"True—," Esme hesitated for a moment, pouting. "But—"

"It's going to be terrible."

"Aye, for a short time. But think of the adventures ahead. You'll get to go to University. Not every one is so lucky," Esme scolded. Kat nodded, regretting her insensitivity. Esme was right, it was just difficult to see the forest through the trees when she was feeling so pitiful.

"I'm going to miss you," Katherine admitted, patting her friends hand. "You're such a good friend to me."

Esme opened her mouth to speak, but quickly dropped her eyes, offering nothing. It was as though she couldn't find the words. Kat pulled her in for another embrace, smiling through the pain.

"Katherine, the men from the ship are here," her mother's voice trilled up the stairs.

Esme stood, "I better go—"

"Wait!" Kat blurted. She lifted the mattress, slipping her hand beneath, searching for something. "Take this."

"What? Yer diary?" Esme asked, her brows raised.

"Aye."

"But why?"

"I can't bring it. It's filled with memories of Mack and I don't want to read them again and again. I don't need reminders. If I take it with me, I won't be able to help myself and it'll only torture me. Burn it," Kat cried, pressing the diary into Esme's hands. "Please, I'm begging you. I don't want it."

Esme nodded, tucking the wee book into her purse.

The girls mournfully walked down the stairs, hand in hand, neither of them speaking. Mary nodded warmly at Esme, reserving her usual disdain. That irritated Kat even more.

"Write to me?" Kat asked, offering a final hug.

"Of course. You as well?"

"I promise," Katherine assured sadly. "Don't forget me."

CHAPTER 23

Meg

"Hello Meg, fancy meeting you here! We were grabbing a quick bite before heading over to the Sealladh to see you. Nathan's flight just arrived. I picked him up in Glasgow! He said he was starvin'," Lorna chirped, oozing confidence, as though she and Meg were the best of friends. "I wanted to surprise ya!".

Speechless, Meg peeled her eyes off Nathan long enough to acknowledge the woman, confused with their connection. *How did they know each other?*

Lorna tossed her a cheeky wink, hooking her arm through Nathan's. "It's been a long time, you must be overcome with emotion?"

"I know I am," Nathan smiled, his eyes shifting curiously between Meg and her companion. He extended a hand towards Kade. "I'm Nathan Forrester. Nate."

"Kade...Campbell," Kade offered, bewildered. Accepting Nathan's greeting, he looked at Meg for assistance, but she still couldn't find her voice. The entire lower half of her body had liquified beneath the table, making escape impossible. She wasn't sure whether to laugh or cry.

"Pleasure." Nathan pumped Kade's hand, entirely too long.

Lorna hesitated for a moment, as though waiting for Meg to chime in. When it wasn't coming, she trilled, "Nathan's a dear old friend of Meg's. A boyfriend, right?"

"R...right," Meg stuttered, struggling for air. *What the hell was he doing here?* A small part of her was pleased to see him; the part she wanted to kick in the ass. He looked...different...composed...content almost.

Kade pulled back, unable to hide his surprise. "Really?"

"Ex." Nathan laughed, raising his hands, as though proving he was no threat. Meg knew differently.

"I don't understand..." she said, alternating her gaze between the new arrivals. She couldn't bear to meet Kade's eyes.

"May we join ya?" Lorna asked, dropping in the booth beside Meg, without invitation.

Nathan waited for Kade to slide over before taking his place beside him. "It's good to see you, Meg. It's been too long," he offered sincerely. "Miss me?"

Smirking at her silence, he continued, "I was surprised to hear you were in Scotland. You disappeared without a forwarding address, and of course, no one told me where you went. Had I not received an email from this lovely lady, I might never have found you."

"You weren't meant to," Meg said, glaring at Lorna. "Why did you come?"

"Maybe we could talk about that later? Alone?" Nathan smiled dryly, lacing his fingers on the table in front of him.

"Uh-uh," Meg denied. She took a deep breath, desperate to fill her lungs. "Tell me now."

"I came to apologize," he replied flatly. Nathan hated appearing vulnerable, that much hadn't changed. "I've had time to think things through over the past few months. I know I made mistakes. I see that now."

Meg's eyes landed on Kade. He still looked confused, maybe even a little heartbroken, and she couldn't bear it. She pulled her eyes away, forcing them back on Nathan. He smiled sweetly, wordlessly begging her to understand. Her heart, hammering beneath her shirt, refused to slow down. Adrenalin seize her senses. It was surreal, the scene playing out in front of her. She could barely breathe, or blink.

"Wait," Kade interrupted, glaring at Lorna. "You wrote this man an email? Why? How do you know him?"

"I don't know him," Lorna laughed nervously. "I was researching Meg online and I happened to come across an article on the two of them. When I realized that they were a couple, I wrote Nathan to see what he could tell me. Honestly, I just wanted to understand more about her and why she was here, to make sure she was right for ya Kade. I was just looking out for ya...really."

Kade glared at her cynically, not buying a word. "Researching? More like spying on her."

"Call it what you like, I didn't have bad intentions," she insisted innocently. "And neither does Nathan. He poured his heart out to me, telling me how much Meg meant to him." Her eyes shifted to Meg. "How much he missed you. He begged me to tell him where you were, so he could at least tell you as much. You know me, I can't resist a good love story. I thought you'd be pleased Meg? The man is madly in love with ya. What girl wouldn't swoon over a fella travelling half way around the world for her?"

Meg picked up the bottle of whiskey and poured herself a shot. Without a word, she downed the smokey amber in one nervous swallow.

Amused, Nathan held out his hand for her glass. “May I? I could use one of those.” Meg dropped the empty glass in his hand and shrugged.

“Knock yourself out.”

“When did you start drinking scotch?” he asked lightly. “You’ve always been a lightweight?”

“Things change,” Meg shrugged, wondering if his words carried a double meaning. They almost always did.

“I suppose they do,” he mused, filling his glass. He held the bottle up, offering a splash to Kade.

Kade shook his head, and eased back into the seat, his arms crossed securely across his chest. He looked like he wished the floor would open up and swallow him whole. Meg didn’t blame him.

“Maybe we should give these two some alone time, Kade. They deserve a private reunion. It sounds like they have some catching up to do,” Lorna urged, her smile unfading, as though she truly believed she’d saved the day. Meg wanted to slap her, and by the look on Kade’s face, he felt the same way.

“I would appreciate that,” Nathan agreed cautiously. “Do you mind Kade? I promise I’m not here to cause trouble.”

It was so like him to be charming, reassuring. As a cop, he was trained well in the art of diplomacy, and knew how to diffuse a threat. Managing Kade was easy for him. Meg battled her feelings, torn about the choices. While she dreaded speaking with Nathan, part of her wanted to hear him out, to find out what inspired him make such a grand gesture, traveling all the way to Scotland to see her. She also didn’t want Kade to leave, he offered such comfort. At the same time, she couldn’t bear seeing him upset.

Concerned, Kade looked her way. Meg held his gaze, silently begging him to understand, before reluctantly nodding. He dropped his shoulders, defeated. Meg wished she could hold him, reassure him that everything would be okay, but she wasn't convinced herself. She wasn't sure of anything.

"Great!" Lorna blurted, a little too loudly. She hugged Meg awkwardly before sliding out of the booth, a gesture Meg found insincere, and given the circumstances, highly inappropriate.

"Nathan, you have my mobile. Text me if you need anything. I can drive you to your hotel later—," she stopped suddenly and giggled. "I mean, unless you don't need me to."

"Lorna, that's enough," Kade said, his tone subdued. He shared a look with Nathan, a wordless warning between men. After a brief pause, Nathan extended a reassuring handshake, before allowing him out of the booth, his polite smile, unreciprocated.

Lorna urged Kade to the bar, but he resisted, heading towards the exit instead.

"I'll be right back," Meg said, unapologetically excusing herself. She raced to Kade, ignoring Lorna's disapproving scowls.

"Kade wait—"

"Meg, it's fine. Do what you need to do," he offered flatly.

"I'm sorry. Don't be upset," she pleaded, taking his hand. "I don't know what to do."

He squeezed her fingers, hedging, as though gathering his thoughts. "Then you need to figure that out, Meggie," he urged. "I knew you had a past, and I suspected it wasn't easy. I'm the one who's sorry. You didn't deserve to have this thrust on you this way."

"You were so honest with me tonight, and I need you to know how much I appreciate it. There was so much I wanted to share with you, too...obviously," she dropped her eyes, overcome by the dilemma. She wanted nothing more than to take his hand and lead him out of the pub, away from Nathan, and the chaos Lorna conjured. The woman was more manipulative than Meg imagined, and she finally understood how difficult things must have been for him.

But Nathan was waiting for her. No matter the circumstances, her ghost had been summoned, and maybe it was time to stop hiding in the shadows. Doubts had plagued her for months, keeping her guarded and wary, blocking her from loving Kade, maybe from loving anyone. If she didn't audit them, once and for all, she might always be shackled to them. She had to know if she still loved Nathan, and if nothing else, why she couldn't shake him. She owed it to herself, and to Kade. He deserved that much.

"I need to go, Meggie." Kade frowned, his brow furrowing.

"Will I see you later?"

"I think it best I go home."

"Kade?"

"I'm fine. I'm just leaving, I'm not leaving you," he choked, pulling her in for a hug. He softly rested his forehead against hers, a simple gesture more intimate than a kiss. It was reassuring.

"I'll call you later," she promised, as Kade slipped out the exit.

Meg slowly made her way back to Nathan, gauging his expression, his body language. It was something she did without thinking, something she'd always done. He appeared calm, and relaxed, completely unfazed by the intimacy he'd witnessed. It was out of character, and not at all what she expected. The Nathan she'd left in Virginia would have been cold and expressionless, jealousy seething beneath a cool demeanour. Instead, he greeted her with a smile. A genuine smile.

"It looks like Lorna followed him," Nathan observed, gesturing towards the door. "Strange woman..."

"You think?" Meg scoffed, settling into the booth. "You don't think it strange that a woman you've never met sent you an email? Creeping me?"

"Of course I did, but I'm an opportunist, Meg," he smiled. "You know that. Like I said, I really wanted to find you. You've been on my mind."

"How did she get your email?" Meg asked, trying to hide her cynicism.

"She emailed 'general inquiries' at my precinct. She asked for me specifically saying she had information about you, and to contact her if I was interested."

"She's resourceful, I'll give her that."

"Seems that way," he shrugged, waving over a server. Isla cautiously approached the table. Meg summoned a smile, if only to reassure her friend.

"Hi Red, what can I get for ya?"

"We'll have some menus..." Nathan paused mid-sentence, looking at Meg warmly, "Is that okay, Meg, can we eat?"

She nodded, astonished he'd asked for her input. Nathan rarely asked her what she wanted, and certainly never asked permission.

"...Menus...and wine?" he questioned again, casually slipping off his jacket.

"Sure," Meg agreed, handing Isla the empty glasses from the table. Nathan nodded and raised two fingers, wordlessly indicating his approval.

"Are you finished with the Smokies? Shall I pack them up?" Isla questioned, wiping the table.

"No need, we're finished," Meg replied, thinking it best to start fresh.

"And the scotch?"

"You can take that too. Put everything on my tab."

Isla cleared the table. Balancing the dishes, she smiled faintly at Meg, "I'll be back with yer drinks."

"Nice woman. Do you know her well?" Nathan asked, settling back into his seat.

"We've become friends. She owns the place."

"It's...quaint. So, Scotland? Why?" he asked, guarding his tone.

Meg shrugged, "I'm not sure. I guess I've always been curious about my roots. You knew my family heritage was here."

"I recall you mentioning it. I never considered you might leave the country. Imagine my surprise when I found out," he drawled. "Has it been hard to adapt?"

"Not as much as you might think."

"You've made friends...and possibly an enemy too?"

"Lorna is Kade's ex, if you haven't figured that out already. To be honest, I hadn't considered her an enemy until today," Meg admitted curtly, still stinging from the betrayal.

"You've always been too trusting."

"Have I?" she smirked, considering the observation.

"That's not a bad thing, Meg," he backtracked, returning her grin. "So tell me about Kade—"

"I'd rather not."

He stared at her like a man gauging a mine field. "Fair enough," he shrugged, unwilling to navigate through.

Isla returned with two glasses of wine, filled to the brim, of course. Setting them on the table, she handed them each a menu.

"We'll take the special, Isla," Meg asserted, waving it off. Normally she wouldn't have ordered for Nathan, or for anyone, but she had something to prove. Maybe she was testing him.

Nathan smirked, as though appreciating her moxie. "You haven't even heard the special? What if it's terrible?"

"Bite yer tongue, Lad. Nothing I make is crap," Isla scolded, commandeering his menu. "The special tonight is mash and lamb shank, with jellied mint and smashed peas on the side."

"I meant no offence," he laughed.

"Trust me," Meg chuckled, enjoying the lashing he was getting, "you'll love it." She adored the way Isla could call people on their shit, and still leave them smiling. It was her superpower.

"Maybe I'll bring ya some Haggis and Neeps," Isla teased, "or some blood pudding?"

"The lamb is fine," Nathan assured, wise to agree.

After twenty minutes, and minimal small talk, Isla delivered food to the table. It wasn't fancy, but it smelled delicious, and the serving was plentiful.

"Wow, this is good," Nathan praised, pausing between healthy bites. "I haven't had a decent meal since yesterday. Adjusting to the time difference is getting to me. I might have a bit of jet lag."

"Did you sleep on the plane?"

"Here and there, for a few minutes. I am tired, I admit. I probably should have gone straight to the hotel for some sleep, but Lorna convinced me to eat first. It was just a happy coincidence that we ran into you."

"Not as coincidental as you think. It was a safe bet I'd be here, I often drop in after work. She could have taken you anywhere, but she brought you to my neighbourhood pub," Meg scoffed, taking a swallow of wine. "Maybe you should go to your hotel right after dinner. We can catch up when you're feeling fresher."

"No," Nathan insisted, "I've missed you. I came a long way to see you."

Meg stole a moment to consider his words, slowly nodding her head. "Since you mention it," she began, "what do you say we forgo the small talk and get to the heart of the matter. I think we owe each other that much."

Nathan cocked his head, regarding her carefully, his tired eyes twinkling with curiosity. "There's something different about you, Meg. You seem...more self-assured...confident."

"Is that a bad thing?" she asked, bracing for conflict. Nathan had a way of pulling the rug out, a critical punchline, right after a compliment. She was prepared.

"Not at all," he soothed, raising his hand defensively. "It's refreshing. I wasn't sure what to expect when we finally reunited. I understand you might feel guarded, I get it. I've had a lot of time to consider things while you were gone. I admit, I was pissed off at first. I felt sucker punched when you left, completely blind sided. One day we're a happy couple, and the next day you're gone, with only a note to say goodbye."

"We'd not been a happy couple for a long time, Nathan. The fact that you thought so, is paramount to why I left."

"I know. I see that now. Our relationship was imbalanced. You thought I was a jerk—"

"That's an understatement."

Nathan inhaled slowly, pausing at her words. Admittedly, she was poking him, pushing his buttons. If he'd changed the way he claimed, she wanted proof. The old Nate rarely tolerated scrutiny, or being interrupted. He considered it disrespectful and had no problem correcting her.

"That's fair," he agreed, strangely calm. "I never appreciated how loving you were, Meg. I took you for granted. You deserved better."

"Oh?" she questioned, humbled by his response. Intrigued, she sat forward, returning his gaze. "You said I seem more confident and self-assured. Do you think this is new? Because it isn't," she paused, gathering her grit. "I'm starting to see it's always been there, but in the years you and I were a couple, my confidence never served you, Nathan. Having a strong woman by your side was not something you valued."

"You're right..."

"Why do *you* think that was?" she asked curiously.

He gently set his fork down, offering his full attention. "I'm not sure," he admitted, "maybe I didn't know that's what I wanted."

"Or," she continued, "maybe it was intimidating?"

"I was selfish," he shrugged, leaving Meg to interpret his response. She considered it for a moment. Co-dependant Meg would have let him off the hook, accepting his reply at face value, not press him. She'd have believed him. But that wasn't enough anymore.

"Selfish?" she coaxed, unafraid.

"I suppose," he agreed, "but in all fairness, You never said anything to me. I didn't know it bothered you so much."

He was right. She'd never said anything, at least not after awhile. She'd adapted, blended in, kept the peace. She just wanted him to be happy, more than she needed her own way. And for awhile, it worked. Over time, they became complacent in their roles. Changing the status quo would have meant conflict. Maybe they weren't even capable! It's human nature to resist change, complacency can be so seductive. Could she place all the blame on him, for the break down of the relationship? Hadn't she played a part? Would have asserting herself made the difference? Who could say. The fact was, Nathan was sitting in front of her now, hopeful, vulnerable. That had to mean something.

"That's on me," she nodded. "Maybe we both could've worked on our short-comings."

He smiled. "Yeah, I think that's fair."

"But a lot of time has passed; a lot of water under the bridge. Maybe that was best for both of us," Meg surmised, her thoughts drifting to Kade.

Nathan shook his head apprehensively, sensing her shift. "No Meg, I love you. I always have. All I'm asking for is a chance," he persuaded. He reached for her hand. She looked down at their entwined fingers, recalling their chemistry from the early days; when they were filled with the unblemished hope that new couples share, naively excited about their future and the magic it promised.

Meg glanced nervously around the room. The pub was bustling with customers, but ironically, the activity offered them more privacy. She was grateful for that.

"At one time, I loved you. More than anything in the world," she confessed, just managing to control her tears, "but things have changed. I may have real feelings for Kade—"

"Meg, you loved me before, and I know if you trust me, just give me a chance to prove that I was worthy of that love, that I still am..." he paused, forcing her to meet his eyes, "you may fall in love again."

He seemed so earnest, so compelling. At one time, Meg would have done anything to hear him say such things. She'd prayed for it.

Thoughts spun chaotically through her mind, flustering her. Seduced by his words, his pleas, his confession, she whispered, "I don't know—"

"I know it's overwhelming. I feel the same way. You can't imagine how tortured I felt on the plane, terrified you'd turn your back on me. It takes a lot for me to be vulnerable, to lay out my feelings, you know that, but I did it for you." He pressed on. "Just one week. That's all I ask. Spend one week with me, with no distractions, just the two of us. After, if you want to part ways, I'll go. I won't fight you. But maybe, just maybe, you will see how much I've changed. How sincere I am. I want to marry you, Meg."

"But...Kade—"

"I know what I'm asking is unfair to him, and I'm sorry, but I think we deserve a chance to see this through. If he cares for you, I think he'd want that for you as well."

Meg felt herself drawn in, in spite of her reservations. God, she'd loved him, desperately, but they'd gotten it so wrong. What if they did things right? Approached things differently. Would things be better? Could they rebuild?

"Please, Meg. Just one week."

"Okay, Nathan," she sighed, enticed his hopeful smile, "but four days only."

"Four days?"

"Yes," she asserted, "and no sex."

"But I came all this way..." he smirked, squeezing her fingers seductively.

Meg eased her hand away. "You said *no distractions*. I can't think of anything more distracting," she smiled.

"Okay, okay, but I stay at your place."

"Or, you stay at your hotel—this isn't a negotiation."

"Okay, Meg, you win this round," he winked. "But I'm going woo you so hard, you won't be able to resist me."

"One more thing," she hesitated, "I have to talk to Kade."

"Of course," Nathan shrugged, his smile waning, "but let's finish our meal."

CHAPTER 24

Kade

Kade paced uneasily from one room to the next, tidying up, nervously waiting for Meg to arrive. She'd texted a half hour earlier, asking if she could drop in. It was the first time she was visiting his home, and given the circumstances, he wanted to make a good impression. The entire evening had tried his patience. Lorna made a mess of things, and worse, claimed she did it for him, trying to normalize it. It was typical of the crazy shite she pulled, over and over, while they were together.

After he'd left the pub, Lorna followed, insisting she walk him home. In spite of his protests, she escorted him anyway, trying to justify her actions, and plant seeds of doubt. She insisted Meg was an outsider, and at the end of the day, she would stick with her roots and choose Nathan. She was certain of it. She was convinced that Meg could never love him the way he deserved. No one would love him as much as Lorna did, and that somehow, the whole scheme was some grand gesture she'd made to prove it. He pointed out, not so politely, that if her scheme was proof of how much she loved him, and what he deserved, then she didn't think much of him. It was ballsy, to be sure, but certainly not loving. She insisted it was for love, and that they belonged together. It infuriated him that she wasn't listening, and when she tried to kiss him, he pushed her away and told her that no matter what happened with Meg, he would never take her back. If the evening proved nothing else, he was certain of that. He didn't want to be an asshole, but he needed to be clear. It was over.

And then there was Nathan. There was something about him that rubbed Kade the wrong way. Sure, most of it was jealousy. How could he not feel threatened? The man flew over an ocean to collect his woman. No matter how you looked at it, it sent a clear message. Kade knew nothing about the man, aside from the fact that he was once heavily meshed in Meg's life. What they'd had was serious, but to what extent? Why did they part? Meg moved to Scotland to put a great distance between them for a reason. Nathan had hurt her, but how, Kade still didn't know. That was the hard part. At this point, it was all guessing.

Nathan seemed too confident. Maybe that's what irritated Kade the most. The man just dropped out of the blue, without any thought that Meg might have someone in her life, and with no concern whatsoever that Kade might have something to say about it.

And his timing couldn't have been any worse. He swooped in literally minutes before Kade could tell Meg how he felt about her, how much he cared for her. They were at a pivotal point, finally opening up to each other, and instead they were forced apart by Nathan's untimely visit, with too many questions left unanswered. The way Kade saw it, no matter how you sliced it, he was the underdog.

What the hell was Nathan doing? Did he come to take her home? Would Meg drop everything and go, after all the blood, sweat, and tears she'd invested in renovating her home, her life? He liked to think she was too smart for that, but the truth was, he didn't know anything about their history, or the influence Nathan had on her. It drove him crazy thinking about it.

When the doorbell finally chimed, Kade jumped, startled by the noise. “Be cool, man,” he chided, feeling ridiculous. He took a deep breath and opened the door, greeting the beautiful red head with a smile. She fell into his arms, and embraced him tightly, as though they hadn’t seen each other in months. Kade chuckled softly, until he realized she was softly sobbing.

“Hey, what’s wrong?” he asked, raising her chin. She could barely look him in the eye. “Meg?”

“Sorry to come so late,” she choked, unwinding herself from him.

“It’s not that late. It’s not past ten yet,” he assured, taking her coat. “Come in. Can I get you a drink?”

“Maybe some water. My stomach’s been upset since dinner.”

“Tea?” he suggested, fondly remembering how his father made tea for his mum when she was unwell.

“Okay,” Meg agreed listlessly, following him into the kitchen. “It’s nice in here,” she observed quietly, sitting at the small table that anchored the room.

“Thanks, I’m proud of it. I wanted it to be a show kitchen. The appliances are top of the line,” he boasted. Filling the kettle, he set it over the flame before turning back to her.

“Makes sense, since you spend so much time cooking gourmet meals, and all,” she teased warmly.

“Tis true, it’s wasted on me. I was more less thinking of resale. Kitchens and bathrooms sell homes, after all. I bought this place to flip but I liked it so much I ended up staying. Chamomile?" he asked, opening a cupboard. A passive nod answered for her.

Guarded, Kade set a mug on the counter, dropping a tea bag into it. “I’m glad you came by,” he admitted. She dropped her eyes. “What is it, Meggie? Is everything alright?”

"I…I wanted to apologize for earlier. I can't imagine this was easy for you." She crossed her arms protectively over her midsection. He could tell she was nervous.

"It wasn't yer fault. How could you know there'd be such a crazy plot twist? I should be the one apologizing…for Lorna's behaviour."

Frowning, Meg shook her head, as though she still couldn't believe it. "Did she talk to you about it? What ever possessed her to do such a thing?"

"Rational thought alludes her. She has no regard for consequences," he shrugged, irritation bubbling to the surface all over again. "If it's any consolation, I read her the riot act, although I'm not sure it did any good."

"You're not her keeper, Kade. I don't hold you responsible…" she assured, her voice trailing off. Kade sensed she was holding back.

"Maybe so, but it was her jealousy that motivated her. And she is my ex," he concluded, pouring the boiled water into the cup. He handed her the mug, joining her at the table.

Raising it to her lips, she mindlessly blew the steam away, recklessly taking a sip. "Careful," Kade warned, "it'll burn you."

Sadly, she set the mug down, opening her lips to speak. When another reluctant sigh passed her lips, Kade's instincts started firing.

"Nathan…" he whispered. She nodded, ever so slowly, her hands wrapped tightly around the scorching mug. Perhaps the sting was her penance.

"He had a lot to say," she confessed, pausing to gather her thoughts. "I'm not going to sugar coat it, he wants me back in his life."

Kade swallowed hard. "Is that right?" he replied, sounding calmer than he felt. "And how do you feel?"

"Good question, I was hoping it would come a little later—"

"You know I'm not one to pussy foot around," he shrugged, hiding his frustration.

"He asked me to spend some time with him. I don't know how I feel, exactly. I wish it was a simple matter," she answered, visibly torn.

"Is it not?" Had she not left Nathan for a reason? And what of him? Did the past few months have any meaning?

As though reading his mind, she reached for his hand, entwining her warmed fingers through his. "Kade, it's no surprise that I've been sorting through my feelings, even before Nathan arrived."

"Aye..."

"I left for so many reasons. I was grieving the loss of my dad, and very confused. I wanted so much more from Nathan, and he wasn't capable of meeting my needs. He could be self-centred, at times. I blamed it on his job. It isn't easy being a cop. They have to shut out much of their emotion, for self-preservation. They train themselves to be indifferent, to cut through the messy stuff, so they can problem solve quickly and effectively. For their partner, it can be difficult when those same strategies are applied at home," she explained, her thoughts drifting backwards.

"I never knew how Nathan truly felt. He was not good at expressing his feelings. When he came home at the end of the day, the last thing he wanted was to work though our issues, my issues. He needed things to be calm. He needed to control his environment, because so much of his day was chaos," she continued, desperate for him understand. "I felt a responsibility to keep the peace, even when my emotions were in turmoil. After my dad died, holding it all in became too much of a burden."

"I can understand that," Kade commiserated. It was hard for him to imagine Meggie sacrificing so much of herself for Nathan, for dismissing her feelings. She was such a passionate woman. And yet, had he not done it himself?

"Nathan was a stubborn man, but at times I saw glimpses of kindness, vulnerability. It kept me hopeful that one day, maybe things would get better. In the beginning, he really tried to make me happy. He needed love and companionship, but he wasn't capable of true intimacy. Whether he knew it or not, he held me at arms length. Over time, it was as though his arms grew longer, and when my dad...he had no idea how to deal with my grief. Although my detachment wasn't personal, he took it as such. It was almost insulting to him..." she frowned, her brows knit with emotion.

Moved by her sadness, Kade wanted to take her in his arms and kiss away her sorrow. Instead, he resisted his instincts and waited for her story to unfold, hesitant to interrupt.

"Things became strained between us, his insecurity gave way to anger, his frustration pushed him to blame. He was angry most of the time, and I'm certain he felt things slipping out of his control. The more distant I became, the more insensitive he grew, and still he denied anything was wrong. Our relationship had broken down, and I couldn't bear carrying the blame anymore. I still loved him, I did, but one day I woke up and realized I had nothing left to offer. I was completely hollow inside."

"So you came here?"

"Yes. You have to understand, Nathan is a natural born influencer, and he could've easily convinced me to see things his way, to minimize the problem, to stay. I know he loved me, and in spite of his deficits, he could be rather charming and persuasive. I knew if I didn't leave, I might not have the strength to stay away, no matter how dysfunctional things were. At the time, I knew I needed to fill my cup, and it couldn't come from him. I had to find my way home, to myself."

Kade nodded supportively. "You did the right thing."

Forcing a smile, Meg nodded, "I think so too, but that didn't stop me from missing him. Maybe this is something you don't want to hear, but I still struggle with those feelings, Kade. They've kept me from moving forward, from truly allowing me to open up to you. When Nathan showed up, it became clear to me that those feelings needed investigating. Part of me worries what will happen, or won't, if they remain unexplored. Does that sound stupid?"

"No, I understand," Kade reassured, tightening his grip around her hand, though it battled his ego to do so. Part of him wanted to dismiss her feelings, to convince her that leopards can't change their spots, that Nathan came to collect what was his, and nothing more. He had a hunch things weren't what they seemed, and he was ready to tell her that, but by denying her feelings, was he no better than Nathan? He cared for Meggie, and wanted her in his life, but the true test was in his response. Were her feelings less valid, less important, than his own? And if he did convince her, and she swallowed those feeling down, would they not still be inside her, eating her from the inside out? Would she ever truly be free?

"You do?" she asked, failing to mask her relief. Kade smiled warmly, doing his best to convince her, and maybe himself.

"Aye, I do. I've been in yer shoes, Meggie. Maybe not to the same extent, but I understand what it's like to miss someone you shouldn't, to know something's not right for ya, but wanting it anyway."

"It doesn't make sense—," she pouted, searching his face for answers.

"No, the heart doesn't always make sense, and rarely explains itself. Sometimes we just have to see things through, wait until our heart catches up with our head."

"I feel so torn. The last thing I want is to hurt you, Kade. I care about you. You've been my rock these past few months, breathed fresh life into me. I can't tell you how ashamed I feel—"

"Nonsense. You don't need to feel bad. Meg, I care about you. Of course I want you in my life, to see where this could go, but I'll no stand in the way of yer happiness. I have no claim on you," he assured, more confident than he felt. "If yer heart leads you back to Nathan, back to America, then it's meant to be. If you choose to stay, then at least it's with an open heart." Meg let out a grateful sigh. Her comfort offered him solace.

"Do you mean that Kade?"

"Aye," he whispered, dropping his eyes, afraid they would reveal what he truly felt..

"I don't expect your patience...I mean...I couldn't ask you...I don't want to be selfish..." she stammered. "God, you deserve better."

"No more than you, Meggie," he yielded. "I want you to be happy."

"What's next?" she asked, chewing her lip.

You stay with me, in my bed. Let me love on you, is what he wanted to say. "I don't know. What *is* next?"

"Nathan asked me for some time and I offered him a few days. He feels I owe it to him, to ourselves, to figure things out," she confessed, pushing through her discomfort.

"You don't owe a thing, Meggie, but to yourself," Kade insisted, annoyed by Nathan's entitlement.

"I suppose that's true," she hedged, perhaps needing more from him. He wasn't sure what else to say, afraid that if he offered more, he'd lose his resolve. He knew he was doing right by her, but he was aching inside.

They were quiet for several minutes, both of them lost in thought, sorting through emotions neither of them were willing to share.

"Will you walk me out?" she asked reluctantly, uncurling her fingers from his.

"Sure," he agreed, raising from his chair. Walking her to the door was excruciating, like leading her to the lion's den. His instinct was to rescue her, save her from the battle she needed to fight, spare her the pain; but in doing so, she might never come to the conclusions she needed. He had to let her go.

"I'll call you in a few days," she promised, pulling him into an embrace. He held her stiffly, afraid his body would betray him.

"That's fine, Meggie," he nodded, easing apart. "Do what ya must. I've been meaning to spend time with Pop anyway. He's been after me for a visit."

"To Glencoe?"

"Aye. A visit will do us both good."

She smiled faintly, reaching for the door. "Okay...and Kade... thank you."

He returned her smile, if nothing but to mask his sadness. "Don't thank me, Meggie. I've done nothing."

She paused briefly, as though hoping for more, then turned and walked out the door.

"Fuck," he muttered under his breath, closing the door behind her.

CHAPTER 25

Meg

"Wow, you sure went crazy with the colour," Nathan chuckled, following her through the cottage. Meg spun around, a smirk her only reply. She knew he'd comment on her decorating decisions, and it secretly pleased her. Like it or not, the cottage was a reflection of who she was, who she'd hid from him for so many years, and she was proud to show it off. "It's nice," he added, returning her cheeky grin.

"You hate it, admit it," she taunted, opening the bathroom door. She flipped on the light, momentarily blinding them with the brilliant yellow walls. His shock made her laugh.

"No, I don't hate it," he insisted, "It's...creative. I'm just thinking about resale. All these colours have narrowed down potential buyers. Not everyone has your...eclectic taste."

It never dawned on Meg to decorate for anyone but herself. She never considered selling her home, but perhaps he had a point. If they were to reunite, she would have to move back to Virginia. She would have to sell. Most of her inheritance was tied up in the small Scotland property, in the renovations. Perhaps she could rent it, she thought, saddened by the thought of someone else enjoying her home; but if she returned to Nathan, she wouldn't do it penniless.

"I suppose," she conceded wistfully, inviting him to follow her to the next room. "These two rooms near the shop are unfinished," she continued, "after a short break, I plan on maybe renovate them for a bed & breakfast. See how they share a Jack and Jill bathroom? They're small but functional. At one time, they were rented out, but overtime the past owner let everything fall to neglect."

"I see," Nathan acknowledged, swiping away the cobweb dangling over his head. "Not sure how safe it is for a single woman to invite strangers into her home. Maybe a hostel is not the best idea you've ever had."

"It's not a hostel, Nathan. You make it sound so unsavoury," she chided cautiously. "Fort William is a quaint little town over looking a beautiful loch. It attracts thousands of visitors from all over the world. I'm trying to capitalize on an opportunity. My shop will bring in the tourists, but it's not enough to earn a good living. I could charge 80 pounds a night per room. Besides, I assure you, it's much safer here than in the U.S."

"It's not safe anywhere Meg. I'm sure U.K. cops have seen their share of violent crimes too," he frowned tightly. "It's concern, nothing more."

"You don't need to be concerned," she shrugged, anxious to change the subject. She wasn't prepared to defend her choices.

"Anyway, it's neither here nor there. If you move home, it'll be someone else's problem," Nathan concluded, backing out of the room.

"I suppose," Meg sighed, turning off the switch. She closed the door behind her, hiding her dreams in the dark, out of Nathan's reach.

Things had been going unexpectedly well since Nathan's return.

Admittedly, she'd kept one foot on the dock, half expecting the boat to sink, but to her surprise, she was enjoying his company. He seemed genuinely happy to be with her, grateful even. Accommodating and respectful, and more conversational than usual, it was like he was a different man, changed significantly by consequence and regret. It seemed no matter what Meg threw at him, he took it in stride, even when she challenged him. Although no closer to making a decision, she couldn't deny feeling optimistic. Was he finally the man she'd always hoped for?

They were on day three, and Meg reluctantly invited Nathan to her home. He seemed pleased that she'd asked, as though an important step forward in building her trust. Maybe it was. It wasn't easy sharing her space with him, the space Kade made beautiful. Each room, all four corners, every nook and cranny, reminded her of Kade; a special moment, a shared joke, a sexy seduction. He was never far from her mind, but more so when she was at home. It pained her so, the thought of never seeing him again.

"What does Sea-Lad mean?" Nathan asked, pulling her out of her thoughts. "The sign out front?"

"It's pronounced Shoo-lad" she giggled with fondness, considering the Gaelic moniker bestowed on her cottage. "The Sealladh...it means 'The View'."

"Then why don't they spell it the way it sounds," he scoffed, "or better yet, just call it the view?"

"I don't know, I suppose the area is heavily influenced by Gaelic culture. I find it charming," she shrugged. "Now let's go to the kitchen, I'll make you something special."

"Aren't you forgetting something?" he asked flirtatiously, snuggling up to her. It was the first time he moved on her since his arrival, and while it caught her by surprise, she was curiously flattered.

"Forgetting something?" she asked, allowing him to embrace her. It was strange how quickly her body recalled his touch, responded to his heat and scent.

"You skipped your bedroom…"

"Ah, I suppose I did," she agreed, not ready to share that with him, the room Kade so lovingly restored, so she could feel nurtured in her new home. A safe space in a foreign land. The room that became their intimate refuge after a long day of work.

"Well, let me see it," he coaxed, his breath hot against her neck. The intimate gesture should've enticed her, but instead made her anxious. She wanted to want him, but she wasn't ready. Whatever the reason, it didn't seem the right time, or place.

"Maybe later," she offered politely, peddling softly. She pressed her hand against his chest, gently inviting him to step back "I'm starving."

"So am I," he growled, kissing her neck, playfully ignoring her signals. Meg felt a familiar twist in her gut, an unmistakeable nod to her discomfort. In the past, she would have shrugged it off, swallowed her unease in an effort to keep Nathan happy, but things had changed. She'd changed.

"I'm serious, Nathan, not right now," she asserted calmly, wiggling out of his grip. His eyes glazed over, and for a split second, seemed agitated; but when he smiled, she quickly shook off the notion. She was being overly sensitive, she thought, her emotions in a twist. He kissed her playfully on the nose before releasing her.

"Sorry, you're right," he apologized, raising his hands in defeat. "I shouldn't have been so forward."

"No, it's okay," she placated, suddenly ashamed. Of course he wanted to kiss her, it wasn't unexpected. He'd made his intentions clear, why he was there. It was only a matter of time before he would make a pass at her, especially since she'd invited him home. She was the one holding back, not him.

"Let's go eat," he suggested, delicately brushing the hair from her eyes. She sombrely nodded, appreciating the tender gesture.

"Would you like a drink?" she asked, as they made their way to the kitchen.

"Sure, I think we both need it," he laughed. He lead her through the hallway, his hand lingering provocatively on the small of her back.

CHAPTER 26

Kade

Kade poured his granddad a scotch, neat, the way he liked it, joining him on the porch with the bottle in hand. It was a rare, balmy night for October and they were outside, enjoying the fresh air, watching the sun set over the neighbourhood. Kade had been there a few days, helping his Pop with some of the heavier yard work, preparing his home for the coming winter. Staying busy was the best way to keep his mind off Meggie. While he hoped for the best possible outcome, he couldn't help but worry she might be persuaded to leave, and fly back home to America. It left him with a sick feeling that even whisky couldn't cure.

Malcolm took a generous sip, exhaling boldly, "Ahhh, I like my whisky old, and my women young! Do you know who said that, grandson?"

Kade shook his head and chuckled, always amused with the old man. "Errol Flynn. You've told me once or twice."

"Aye, it bears repeating."

"Would you even know what to do with a young woman, Pop?" Kade teased, offering a cheeky air toast with his own dram.

"Ya wee smart ass, I think I could give it a go, although it's been a long time," Malcolm sat back in his seat, crossing one crooked knee over the other.

"Do you miss Gramma?"

"Aye, there are days. She was a good woman, always looking out for me."

"I miss her too. She always made the best scones, especially the ones with the dried fruit," Kade nodded, wishing he had some right then and there.

"Always thinking about yer stomach. So grandson, when are you going to tell me what's troubling ya?" Pop asked, his glassy eyes twinkling with insight.

Kade laughed inwardly, shaking his head.

"Go on now. Do you think I don't know when my favourite grandchild is upset?"

"I'm not yer favourite, Pop," he chuckled.

"Well, yer in the top ten. Now spill it," Malcolm insisted, unwilling to let him off the hook.

"It's nothing—"

"Bull-shite, it's about yer woman."

"How do you know?" Kade scoffed, feigning annoyance. He could never be upset with the old man.

"When a man looks the way you do, it's always about a woman," Pop pressed, standing firm. He leaned forward to punctuate his point. "It's written all over yer face. Yer heart is aching."

"Yer right," Kade sighed, swallowing down the remainder of scotch. "It is a woman."

"Is it Meg, the one I like? Or the other one, the crazy, wee harpy?"

"Gee Pop, don't hold back."

"I won't. So which is it?"

"The one you like. Lorna is history. She has been for awhile," Kade admitted, certain his granddad would be pleased. Malcolm never liked Lorna, not at all. No matter how 'nice' she treated him, he could see right past it.

"So what's the problem?" Pop asked, handing Kade the bottle. Kade waved him off. One shot was enough, besides, he was still hung over from the night before. His granddad drank him under the table. How the man had woken up fresh as a daisy was beyond Kade's comprehension.

"Her ex-boyfriend flew in from the U.S., he wants to make amends. He wants her back," Kade admitted flatly. It sounded worse out-loud.

"And?"

Kade snorted, "what do you mean *and*? That's a lot!"

"She's *yer* girlfriend Kade, he's an ex. Ex means past. Ancient history," Pop decreed, as a matter of fact.

"Well, that's the thing...we never made it official."

"What do you mean, *official*? You and Meg looked pretty cozy at the wedding."

"I guess we did. The truth is, we were taking things slow. It's complicated," Kade shrugged, wishing he could explain it better. He wasn't sure he understood it himself.

Malcolm shook his head, "sounds like yer complicating it. Is he with her right now?"

"Yeah."

"And yer here? With an old man? What the hell for?"

Kade eyed his granddad closely, wondering where he was leading him. "I don't know. I thought I should give her space. Seemed the right thing to do."

"That seemed right to ya, lad? Giving space to a woman that doesn't know where ya stand? Holding the door open for a man not afraid to tell her where he does?" Malcolm goaded, not unkindly, cutting right through the bullshit.

Despondent, Kade stared at his Pop, allowing his wise words to sink in. He swallowed hard, forcing their significance past the lump in his throat.

"I've circled around this big blue ball more years than I care to admit, Kade. I've leaned a lot about life, and loss. Sometimes life throws up roadblocks...as a test...to see if we're deserving. To determine whether or not we truly value what we're wantin', you see?" Malcolm continued. "Do you love her?"

Kade sat back, thinking about Meggie, and how dismal he felt without her. Christ even the few days they'd spent apart left him empty. She'd become such a huge part of his life.

"It's a simple yes or no," Malcolm gently pressed.

Kade nodded, certain of nothing more. "Yes."

His grandfather smiled, as though he completely understood. "Good. Let an old man tutor you, then. You have to fight for her. If you don't, you'll regret it forever, I promise ya," he lectured, waving a demanding, bony finger at Kade. "Don't make the same mistakes I did."

Curious, Kade raised his brows, wondering what mistakes his grandfather could have made. The man had been married to the same woman for 43 years. As far as he knew, they were thick as thieves until his gramma died, 10 years earlier.

"I know what yer thinkin'," Malcolm paused, refilling his cup.

"You do?"

"Aye, yer thinking this old man can't relate. Maybe it's no the same thing, but trust me, I know what it's like to let a woman like Meg slip away."

"I suppose I was thinking that. You and gramma were married a long time. You seemed so in love," Kade agreed, picturing his patriarch as a young man. He'd heard tales of his grandfather's exploits, an untamed man at heart.

"I did love her...and she loved me, but things were different back then. It wasn't always easy for us, but once you got married you stuck it out, made it work, and I'm glad we did. I can't imagine it was easy for Fae to be married to me. I think she always knew a piece of my heart belonged to another..." he trailed off, his eyes wet with memories.

"What are you saying, Pops?" Kade asked, startled by the admission.

"Your grandmother and I met when I was only 21. She was the daughter of my boss. My father was teaching me carpentry and I was meant to take over the business, but then he suddenly died. A good friend of his took me under his wing and continued my training. I suppose it was meant to be, meeting Fae. She was a proud woman, strong, wise, and kind. I knew she'd be a good wife, and she proved me right. She gave me five amazing kids, yer mother included. We had a solid marriage..." he paused, choosing his next words carefully. "She was my best friend, and she cared for me. Don't get me wrong, I was a good husband, and a good father, but I had regrets, Kade. As much as I loved my wife, and my family, I never stopped thinking about the one I let go."

"Wow, I had no idea," Kade consoled, patting his grandfather's hand.

The old man quietly accepted the comfort, nodding his head regrettably. They stayed that way for a few minutes, Kade respecting his need for stillness. Finally, Malcolm broke the spell.

“Go get yer woman, Kade.”

“I promised her a few days, Pop, besides I want to know more of your story—”

“If you wait you’ll be a day late, and a dollar short,” he insisted, urging Kade to go. “I’ll share more another time, you have my word.”

Everything his Pop said made sense. Right or wrong, bad timing or no, he needed Meg to understand how he felt, if he had half a chance of winning her heart. If she moved back with Nathan without knowing the truth, he’d never forgive himself. Whatever her choice, he’d go down fighting.

“You’re right, I’ll go, but can I help you inside first?” Kade offered, raising from his seat.

“No Lad, I can take myself to bed. Besides, it's a braw, bricht moonlicht nicht the nicht. I’ll stay and enjoy it. I might not have many left.”

CHAPTER 27

Meg

"Do you recall that little restaurant on Pine Street?" Nathan smirked.

"The one with all the clowns?" Meg laughed, remembering how they'd dropped in for dinner one night, prepared to have a romantic evening, only to discover the place was decorated with wall to wall clowns; pictures, statues, knickknacks, even the table cloths were printed with creepy marionettes. They couldn't stop giggling the entire night, even after many disapproving glances from the staff. It was one of her favourite memories of Nathan, the night ending with a sexy romp in the back of his car. Laughing was such an aphrodisiac.

"Yes! Even funnier that my captain recommended it, telling me it was the perfect spot to celebrate our anniversary," Nathan howled, his eyes twinkling with humour. *God how she loved his laugh.* "... And he was serious! Such a redneck!"

"Ha! But so loveable. How is Bill?" Meg asked thoughtfully, grateful the awkwardness from earlier was behind them. It felt good reminiscing, conjuring up some of the happier memories they'd shared.

"He's doing well, I think. Retired now," he answered, pouring the last of the merlot into his glass. "Any more wine?"

"We've already poured through two bottles. How about some coffee?" she suggested, carefully standing up. Feeling quite tipsy, she stabilized herself with the table, certain she didn't need any more alcohol.

Nathan offered her a derisive look, masked by a crooked smile. "There she is, *Square Peg Meg,*" he mocked playfully, "showing up just when the fun's about to start."

Baffled, she pulled back, thrown by the taunting. She wasn't prepared for it. She used to hate when he called her that. Although it was just his way of teasing her, it was a sore spot, especially when he used it to exploit her. Realizing he'd over stepped, he reached for her hand. "Don't hold back on me," he charmed, "we have no where to go, and we're having such a nice night together." He smiled sweetly, seductively massaging her fingers.

"Okay, you're right," she conceded, pardoning the misstep, "I'll open another, but promise me you'll never call me that again."

"Your right, my love," he reversed, a sheepish look on his face. I'm sorry. I was trying to be cute." Meg exhaled slowly, feeling silly for being triggered.

Smiling thinly, she nodded her head in forgiveness. "Let me just clear the table."

"I'll do that, you cooked," he volunteered, gathering the dishes.

"Really?" she chuckled, surprised by the offer. In the whole time they were together, she'd never seen Nathan clear a dish.

"Don't act so surprised, who do you think did my dishes when you bailed?" he slurred, carelessly stacking the plates, dangerously close to chipping them. Meg's smile faded, again struck by his choice of words. "I mean, you'd be proud of me Meg, I really pulled it together," he added, softening his tone.

"You always liked a tidy home," she shrugged, shaking it off. "I'm going to the storage room to grab the wine. Think you can handle things?" she quipped, watching him juggle the dishes on his way to the sink. He set them down carefully before turning back to her.

"Oh, I can handle it," he purred, pulling her towards him. He eased her into his embrace, cradling her. It was actually nice, the hug, and she slipped her arms around his waist, resting her tipsy head against his shoulder. "You smell good," he flattered, breathing in her scent.

"So do you," she agreed warmly. It was one more thing she'd always found hard resist. He wore a hint of *Dior Homme Intense*. That, and his own musky pheromones, were usually enough to make her putty in his hands. His scent was nostalgically arousing, and instantly took her back to a better time. She raised her eyes, pleased to be greeted with his smile. His was arousal evident, as he grew hard against her. As tempted as she was, it was definitely too soon. They weren't ready. Intimacy was never their problem, and she was certain that sex would only confuse them both.

"I'll get the wine," she repeated, peeling herself away.

"Forget the wine," he ordered, tightening his grip, "we're having a moment here."

"Yes, a moment that could dangerously morph into something neither of us is ready for," she cautioned modestly. It was a tone she'd adopted over time, worried she might offend him, and trigger a tantrum. The fact that she was using it again actually pissed her off. She didn't have to filter herself anymore, not for him, so why was she doing it?

"Speak for yourself, baby," he growled, raising her chin for a kiss.

"I am, Nathan," she mumbled, his mouth pressing against hers.

She dropped her head back, out of reach.

"Come on, Meg, stop teasing. I have been patient all night, but you're driving me crazy," he grinned, dropping his hands to her ass. "Maybe you've been fucking your way through town, but I haven't been laid in months."

Shocked, she tried to push him away, anger flaming her cheeks. She didn't care if it was the liquor talking, he was completely out of line. "Take your hands off me!" she yelled, squirming out of his hold. He held her firm, refusing to set her free.

"Not this time," he growled. "I came a long way to see you, and it's time I show you how much I want you."

"No, not like this," she cried, suddenly frightened. "I don't want this!"

His eyes grew cold, blank. "*Yes*, you do. You invited me to your home. You made me my favourite dinner. The wine? What else was this little seduction about?" he accused, restraining her against the counter, his cock hard against her groin.

"Nathan, stop!" she screamed, unable to move. He wrapped a hand through her hair, forcefully pressing his mouth on hers, his stale breath choking her. She came dangerously close to vomiting, her fear derailing her. Tears rolled down her cheeks, in silent protest. With his free hand he greedily raised her skirt, violently pulling at her panties. He was intent on taking what he wanted, and there was nothing she could do to stop him.

"Get the fuck off her!"

CHAPTER 28

Kade

Kade stood on Meg's front porch for several minutes, debating whether or not to ring the bell. He was certain she was home, the cottage warm and well lit, delicious cooking smells wafting through the draughty front door.

It had been a short, thirty minute drive between his grandfather's house and hers, but it was long enough to shake his confidence, his bravado dissipating with every kilometre travelled. It wasn't that he'd changed his mind about professing his love, quite the contrary. He just wanted the timing to be right. What if she didn't appreciate him barging in, if his enthusiasm wasn't returned? And yet, he didn't hate the idea of interrupting a romantic evening with Nathan. He was torn, to be sure.

Finally he made up his mind, chastising himself for being so impetuous. He would have his time with her, but he would do it his way. He couldn't risk being turned away, not with Nathan looking on. He was about to walk away when he heard Meg's distressed scream from inside. It took him less than a second to make a decision, concerned for her well being. He pushed passed the unlocked door, following the sound of a scuffle in the kitchen.

"Get the fuck off her!" he hollered, grabbing the bastard by his collar, forgetting momentarily that Nathan was a cop, well trained in combat. Caught off guard, Nathan lost his balance and dropped to the floor, a surprised look on his smug face. Driven by rage, Kade dropped to his knees, punching him several times in the jaw.

"Stop," Nathan snarled, kicking Kade away. In a split second both men were back on their feet, throwing punches and shoving each other, dishes crashing to the floor. Ignoring the impact of a solid strike, Kade moved in, pressing the rapist against the counter, wrapping his arm around Nathan's neck.

"What the fuck do you think yer doing?" he grunted, his forearm wedged tightly against Nathan's throat, blinded by insane rage. "You piece of shite! I could fucking kill ya!" Nathan clawed at Kade's grip, desperate to draw air into his lungs.

"Kade stop!" Meg cried, yanking on his belt, her words jerking him back to his senses. "Stop…he's not worth it. Please…"

He nodded, cautiously releasing pressure. "Yer going to get yer shite and leave, is that understood?" he spat, his anger hot in Nathan's ear. Before receiving a response, he squeezed his throat again. "Ya hear me?"

Nathan nodded curtly, dropping his hands, wordlessly imploring Kade to release him. Finally, Kade shoved him aside.

"Easy," Nathan croaked, raising his hands. He stared at Meg with forced regret, challenging her to come to his defence.

"Get out," she dismissed, her arms protectively covering her chest.

"Meg…"

"She said fuck off, ya bastard," Kade screamed, shoving Nathan again. "I'll show you the door."

Meg

Grateful Nathan left without further incident, Meg sank to the floor, adrenalin coursing through her body. Shamed by stupidity, she wept freely, gasping for each sorrowful breath.

Worried, Kade raced to her side, dropping to his knees. "Meggie, are ya hurt?"

"N..no," she sobbed, allowing him to comfort her. He held her gently, stroking her hair, until she caught her breath, and her sobs gave over to whimpers. When she finally calmed down, she looked up at him, shocked by what she saw. His face was swollen and covered in blood, the bruising already visible.

"Oh God, your face—"

"I faired better than he did," Kade scoffed, brushing off her concern. "Are ya sure yer okay?"

"Yes. Just shook up. If you hadn't arrived when you did, the outcome would have been much worse."

"Aye, you seemed on the losing side of that situation," he agreed, his voice still tight with anger.

"I'm sorry, Kade. I'm so sorry—"

He shook his head, pulling her closer. "You've got nothing to be sorry for. Ya did nothing wrong."

"But you're hurt, and it's my fault," she frowned, gently touching his bruised flesh. He pulled away, sucking in his breath, her feather touch stinging him. "Let me help you," she begged, "I need to clean these wounds."

He followed her to the bathroom, and patiently sat on the toilet while she dabbed his face with a cool cloth, wincing each time she grazed an open wound. His lip was cut open, but she was confident it would heal quickly, and the gashes on his cheek and eyebrow were superficial. No need for stitches. Thankfully, he looked worse than probably he felt.

"You'll have a black eye, I'm afraid. We should get a steak on that," Meg advised, her voice barely a whisper. She leaned in, inspecting the damage.

"I'll no waste a good steak on that," Kade chuckled, wrapping an arm around her back. "An icepack will do."

Meg eased in closer, circling her arms around him, resting her cheek on his crown. They quietly held each other, neither of them feeling the need to speak; just a moment to collect themselves, and recover from the trauma.

"Why don't you go lay down," Meg urged, kissing his forehead sweetly. "I'll get you some ice and clean up the damage."

"I'll help you," he insisted, softly cupping her bottom.

"Oh no you won't! You need to rest. Besides, it's the least I can do for my hero!"

"Yer hero, eh?" he chucked, in no hurry to relocate his hand. Meg didn't mind.

"I'll join you when I'm done. That is, if you want to spend the night?"

"I can't think of anywhere else I'd rather be," he promised, accepting her cautious kiss. "Ach—"

"Oh, god, sorry!" she cried, worried she'd hurt him. He smiled at her puckishly, earning a playful cuff to the side of his head.

"Ya wee beast..." he called after her, as she made her way out the door.

CHAPTER 29

Kade

"Meggie, are you awake?" Kade asked, sidling up to her, adjusting the covers around them. He pulled her close, wrapping around her, ignoring his aches and pains. It was early morning, the sun just rising above the horizon.

"Mmm, that's nice," she purred, spooning her bottom closer. If he hadn't been so sore, he might have capitalized on the moment, but he was in no condition to make love. His stubborn cock had other ideas, stiffening against her back side.

"It is nice, he agreed, nuzzling her neck. His sleep had been fitful, but he didn't mind, knowing Meggie was safe beside him.

"Are you having trouble sleeping?" she asked, rolling over to face him. He shifted to give her space, cloaking her with his arm.

"Yes."

"Are you in pain?" she asked, gently touching his face.

"Not much. I guess I have a lot on my mind," he assured.

"Me too."

"Are you worried about Nathan? About him returning?" he

asked, frowning in the dark.

“No. It’s unlikely. He’s a vain man. If I had to guess, I’d say he’ll be on a plane before the end of today.”

“Good riddance.” He hoped she was right.

Quietly contemplating, Meg whispered, “Kade?”

“Ya?”

“Thank you for...for saving me.”

“I’m just grateful I was here. I wasn’t planning on it,” he admitted.

“Divine timing?”

“Maybe.”

“Why did you come?” she asked, resting her head on his shoulder. He sighed deeply, recalling his conversation with Pop.

“I came to fight for you,” he chuckled, “I just didn’t know it would be so literal.”

“You came back to fight for me?”

“Aye, I did,” he said, embracing her a little tighter. He exhaled slowly, wishing he’d told how he felt sooner. Maybe he could have spared her.

“What are you saying, Kade?” Meg asked quietly, her voice barely a whisper.

“I suppose I’m saying I love you,” he confessed, kissing the top of her head.

“Even after...everything?”

“Everything?”

“Yes. The indecisiveness, the confusion, my insecurities. All of it," she volunteered, sounding dangerously close to tears.

Lips tight, Kade held them against her crown, considering her question. Was she really worried about all that? He'd never thought for a moment she deserved anything less than his support and patience, no matter how difficult it had been for him. No one understood more than he, the demons she was battling. Had Nathan not shown up when he had, he would have told her so.

"Meggie, I think true love is unconditional, at least it should be. I know that now, more than ever. I admit, I didn't want you to spend time with Nathan, but I knew it was important for you, even necessary. But then I realized, being apart from you, that it was equally important for you to know how I felt...how much I love you. That's why I came back. It only seemed right that you had all the facts before making a choice."

Meg rolled over, resting against his chest, her eyes searching his in the pale morning light. "You are, by far, the most generous man I have ever met."

"Let's not get carried away," he teased, curling his fingers through her disheveled hair.

"No, I mean it. Spending time with...with him...made me realize how special you are. I never have to censor myself for fear of offending you. I don't have to walk on egg shells, or try to decipher your words, like they're some cryptic code. When you say something, I know you mean it. Do you know how rare that is?" she asked, her words insistent, sincere.

Touched, Kade smiled modestly. "Well, it's not that rare where I come from."

"I'm being serious," she pressed. "I also realized that you can miss someone and not want them back. My past relationship was a chapter in my life, but it wasn't my whole story, and I don't want it to be! It was an important chapter, I admit. The truth is, I wouldn't be here today without that experience. Maybe I wouldn't even recognize how amazing you really are. I don't like who I am around Nathan, and that became crystal clear over the past few days. I never realized how small I need to shrink myself to make space for him."

"A crying shame," Kade grinned.

"See? You say things like that!"

Kade pulled her in for a tender kiss, mindful of his fat lip. Hearing her confession was music to his ears, and he couldn't recall feeling happier.

Meg eased away, smiling. "I love you too."

"Say it again," Kade urged playfully.

"I love you. I love you. I love you."

"But do ya love me?" he teased, kissing her forehead.

"There's something you need to know," Meg giggled, snuggling against his chest.

"What's that?"

"I would have come to my senses. I would've chosen you, even if you didn't storm in with guns a-blazing," she grinned.

"Oh, I know," he smirked.

"Now who's being the beast?" she giggled, tickling his ribs.

"Ah, don't...tickle me...I...can't...take it!" he laughed, squirming beneath her.

"Oh, have I found your kryptonite, sir? Is this the one thing that will drop you to your knees?" she laughed, her fingers creeping dangerously towards his armpits.

"It's not the only thing I'll kneel for," he growled, flipping her on her back. He raised her arms over her head and kissed her again, his tongue lingering in her warm mouth.

“Mmm, you don’t say,” she moaned beneath his kiss. Kade grinned at her, his eyes twinkling with mischief, before sliding down her body.

“I’ll also beg for pussy.”

CHAPTER 30

Meg

Meg was in her shop, the nasty Nathan business behind her. She hadn't thought of him in weeks, and was grateful for it. She was finally free. It was a damn miracle.

She was busy unpacking an order that arrived that morning; a box of delicate, silver, antiqued holiday ornaments. They would be a big seller, she was sure of it! It was mid-October and she'd been up and running for over a week, excited to capitalize on Christmas sales. She was pleased to see many of the locals supporting her business, stopping in to browse the little shop. They were excited by the changes she'd made, complimenting the renovations. Of course, it was a great opportunity to hand out Kade's business cards, and she did, often. He'd already been offered several jobs by folks admiring his excellent craftsmanship.

The little chime rang, signalling a customer. Meg glanced up, pleased to see someone she recognized.

"Mr. MacDonald! What brings you here?" she greeted, walking around the counter to meet him.

"No need to be formal. I told you at the wedding, call me Pop," he scolded cordially, accepting her hug. "Kade told me he was finished with the renovations and encouraged me to stop by. I hope you don't mind?"

"Of course not! I'm happy you're here!" Meg welcomed, wrapping her arm through his. "I was just putting on the kettle. Can I offer you some tea?"

"No, no, don't bother. I'll just look around," Malcolm declined, patting her hand warmly.

"Your grandson did a wonderful job," she boasted, leading him back to the counter.

"I'm proud of the lad. He's a hard worker," he praised, running an approving hand across the refurbished wood. Smiling, he paused to admire the old cash register. "Very fine. He has the skill of his old granddad."

"Yes, Kade told me you were a carpenter," Meg smiled, twirling the chain around her neck. "He's quite proud of you, too."

"Did ya know this place once belonged to someone I knew?" Pop recounted, admiring her necklace.

"Really? Was it the old man who recently died?" Meg asked curiously. She'd been wanting to learn more of the cottage's history, and planned on a trip to the historical society in a few weeks, once she had more time. It thrilled her to know that Pop might have some intel.

"No, it was before him. It was a long time ago," he explained, his tone thick with melancholy. "Belonged to a girl I was acquainted with. Her mum remarried and they moved to Inverness."

"Interesting! Do you know when the cottage was built?"

Leaning on the counter, Pop nodded, "aye, the early 1900's, you can tell by the architecture," he explained. "Around the time when they used granite stones for facing. It's beautiful, isn't it?"

"Yes, it's what I loved most about the house...and the view of course," she sighed, proud of her cozy cottage. "So, the girl who lived here, how well did you know her?"

"I knew her well enough. We met when we were teenagers," he confessed. "I haven't always been such an ugly, old man."

"Nonsense! You're still handsome. Not many men have a thick head of hair at your age. I'm certain you still turn heads," she flattered. Kade had the look, and demeanour of his grandfather. It was like peering forty years into the future.

"Oh, sure," Malcolm laughed, "the old chickens still scratch at the barn door, especially since my wife died, but I'm no interested—"

"Oh, why not?" Meg asked kindly, noting his sadness.

"Do ya mind if we sit down?" he asked, ignoring the question.

"Of course, where are my manners," she blurted, gesturing him to a cozy corner. She'd set up a reading nook to encourage customers to lounge, enjoying the books for as long as they wanted. They sat down, the old man grunting as his bottom dropped into the chair.

"That's better, being off our feet," he grinned, focusing on her necklace once more. "May I ask, Meg, where did you get that?"

"The locket?" she asked, unconsciously raising her hand to it. "Actually, I found it when I was moving. I've never seen it before. It might belong to my Nana, but I'm not sure."

"May I?" he asked, holding out his shaking palm.

"Of course." She unlatched it, gingerly placing it in his hand.

"Have you opened it?" he questioned, holding it up for closer examination.

"No, I couldn't figure out how. I think it's broken," she explained, watching him fiddle with the clasp. He turned it sideways before rotating the clasp, easily popping it open.

"There's a knack to it," he murmured, retrieving his reading glasses from his shirt pocket.

"How did you do that so easily?" Meg gasped, anxious to see inside.

"Because," he smiled, looking up at her willfully, "I bought it."

Meg returned his smile, not sure whether he was pulling her leg, or not. He tenderly fingered the photograph inside, a nostalgic, almost regretful look on his withered face.

"Pop?"

"You say this might be your Nana's? Is this her?" he asked, returning the trinket. Meg dropped her glasses from the top of her head, and slipped them in place, raising the locket for a closer look. Inside was a tiny, black and white photograph of a young woman, her hair tied back, the sweetest smile on her face. There was no way of knowing for sure if it was her grandmother, but there was no mistaking who was in the photo beside. It was Malcolm, looking just like Kade!

Astonished, Meg offered the locket back. "Is this you?"

"It is," he assured, slowly nodding his head. "What was your grandmother's name?"

"Margie. Actually, I'm named after her," she offered proudly. "The woman in the locket? Is it her?"

"Perhaps not. *That* woman's name was Katherine," Pop shrugged, his smile fading.

"Wait!" Meg grinned. She jumped from her chair so quickly, she startled the poor man. "Katherine...Margaret?"

Malcolm leaned forward, cautiously optimistic. "Aye?"

"I'll be right back!"

Meg raced through the house, retrieving the old diary from her bedroom, quickly returning to the shop.

"The girl, that lived here, in this house, was it Katherine?" she panted, waving the diary in front of him, excited with her discovery.

"No, it was her friend, Esme Mitchell. Katherine lived a few blocks from here—"

"I found this diary when I first moved in! It was in one of the boxes piled up in this very corner. It belonged to a girl named Katherine Margaret!" she chirped, opening the pages. "She talks about Esme, and her parents, and moving to America...do you think this could have belonged to my grandmother?"

"Aye, it could very well be," he nodded, infected by her enthusiasm.

"She was in love..." Meg paused. Her jaw dropped, suddenly struck by the correlation. "With Mack?"

"Aye, Mack," he agreed, smiling ironically. "Otherwise known as Malcolm MacDonald. I have a story to tell, if yer willing to hear it."

Mack

Malcolm, leaned forward, still stroking the locket. He couldn't believe what he was seeing. After nearly 60 years, for it to resurface, was nothing short of a miracle. He raised his eyes, regarding Meg with affection.

"I was in love with Katherine...Kat. She was the smartest, sweetest woman I'd ever known. I wanted to marry her," he confessed, reluctantly returning the locket to Meg.

"What happened?" she asked, filled with empathy. "In her last entry she said that Mack...you...never came back for her, that she wanted to stay behind to be with you..."

"Aye, that's true," he sighed, dropping his eyes once more. "Perhaps I'll read what she wrote, afterwards, if ya don't object?"

"Of course!" Meg agreed, tucking the diary beside her.

Malcolm longed to read her words, to revisit the past where his lover waited for him. If only he could jump through the pages to comfort her. To say he had regrets was an understatement, and yet, had he not met Fae, he wouldn't have his beloved children, or his grand-kids. It was bitter-sweet, to be sure.

"I wanted her to stay with me, but you have to understand Meg, I had nothing. My mother died when I was a child, and it was just me and my father. We struggled for every pound. I had nothing to offer her, my Kat..." he stalled, his fingers tapping nervously against his thigh. It caused him great pain to remember how mournful she'd looked that day, pouring her heart out, begging him for answers. God how he'd wanted to pull her into his arms and tell her not to fret, that everything would be fine, but he couldn't. He just couldn't see a happy ending for them, not with what little he had. If only they'd had more time to build a life together, for him to established himself.

"She was so bright, and she had great ambition. That was uncommon for women back then. Her parents were strict, but they loved her, and they had the means to help her reach her goals," he continued. He glanced at Meg, again struck by how much she resembled Kat. He saw it the first time he'd met her, at his granddaughter's wedding. It nearly took his breath away. "Everything would have been fine, for she and I, had her parents not moved to the States. Her dad was a professor—"

Meg nodded, "yes, she wrote about that too. The transfer..."

"It seemed so sudden, their decision, and I completely understood Kat's desperation. I felt it too, but I also couldn't stand in her way. You see? She talked about giving up her dream to be a doctor, to work as a secretary or some such nonsense," he frowned, pausing once again. Meg was courteous enough to wait on an old man gathering his thoughts, and he was grateful for it.

"It made no sense to me. How could I ever forgive myself if I asked her to give up her dreams? I feared that once she came to her senses, she'd resent me."

"Then this must be her! My Nana *was* a Doctor. A general practitioner. She practiced for nearly forty years," Meg insisted. Pleased their sacrifice was not in vain, he acknowledged the revelation with a proud nod.

"Oh, how she loved you," Meg consoled, reaching for him. He gazed at his hand cradled in hers, stunned by the sharp contrast of their flesh. He'd gotten so old. How had so much time passed?

"And, I loved her, that's why I had to let her go," her breathed, his throat tightening. He was sentimentally quiet for a moment, recalling Kat's caresses as though they'd happened only yesterday. Quietly, he asked, "did she marry well?"

"Yes, I think so, but her husband died when my dad was just a boy, only ten years old. He spoke highly of him though," Meg recounted, sensitive to Malcolm's feelings. "Nana never remarried. She was too dedicated to her work, and her patients. When my own mother left, she brought us to live with her, to help dad raise me."

"What a generous thing to do…" he praised, his words trailing off. There was so much he wanted to know, yet it broke his heart, the telling of Kat's story that carried on without him. "I wrote her a letter—"

"A letter?"

"A love note. I knew she was leaving and though I'd no intention of stopping her, I needed her to know how much I loved her, and why I had to let her go," he confessed, his eyes landing on the diary. "Did she not mention it? In her diary?"

"No, her last entry was about leaving...and losing you. I found it strange that she wrote nothing else," Meg explained, reaching for it once more. "Doesn't it seem odd that she didn't take her diary with her? Something so personal? How did it end up here, in a box of old books?"

"Perhaps Esme acquired it?" he shrugged. "I gave the letter to Esme. I begged her to deliver it to Kat before she set sail. I had to let her know how I felt, but I knew I couldn't see her myself. In the letter I told Kat that if we were meant to be together, fate would find a way. I suggested that once she was settled in America, and registered for school, to send for me. I would come to her, if she still wanted me."

"Really?" Meg smiled, pulling the diary closer to her heart.

"Aye, I did," he sighed, "but she never wrote. I waited two years for word from her, but nothing came. I assumed she'd forgotten me."

Meg shook her head, "no, that makes no sense," she cried, flipping through the delicate pages. "She loved you! The last line of her diary says so." She cleared her throat to read the passage. *"We're soul mates, I'm sure of it. If I knew he wanted me too, I'd do whatever it took to be with him. Anything."*

Malcolm raised his eyes, gazing through a haze tears. Meg was right, it didn't make sense. *What happened to change her mind? Had he broken her heart beyond repair?*

"Your Nana, what year did she marry?"

"Sorry. I'm not certain. My father was born in '67 though, so certainly it was before that. She did tell me that she'd given birth right before her medical internship. She said she regretted missing his early years, even for such a worthy cause, but she'd worked too hard to quit. Apparently it was my grandfather who stepped in, allowing her to continue her studies. It actually made me proud that she pioneered the women's movement, and that her husband was so supportive."

"Aye, that sounds like Kat," Malcolm grinned proudly. "I see much of her in you."

"Thank-you," she blushed, obviously touched by the compliment.

"Yer Grandmother, is she no longer with you, then?" he asked sadly, wringing his hands in his lap.

"Hmm? No, she's alive and well! She still lives in North Carolina," Meg assured, patting his hand. "How stupid of me! I should have said so sooner!"

Malcolm sat forward, his old heart pounding nervously beneath his shirt. "If she is my Kat, do ya think she'd like to know about… all of this?"

"Well," Meg smiled warmly, "there's only one way to find out!"

"Will ya call, then?" he asked, struggling to leave his chair.

Meg jumped up first, offering him a hand. "Of course! We can call together."

Malcolm shook his head. "Oh no! You must speak to her yerself. What if it's her—and if she doesn't wish to hear from me? I don't think my heart could bear the rejection."

"Pop, I'm sure she won't reject you. There has to be an explanation why she didn't reach out, don't you think?"

"Perhaps, but I'll leave it with you to find out, Meg," he insisted, "that way you can soften the blow in the retelling."

"Ok," she soothed, walking with him. "I'll call her tonight."

Malcolm made his way to the door, nervously gripping Meg's arm, equally sated with hope, and apprehension.

"Oh, I forgot the diary!" Meg stammered, turning back. "You wanted to read it!"

"No, dear. I changed my mind," he declined, waving her off. "If Kat and I are meant to cross paths, she can tell me herself what her heart feels."

CHAPTER 31

Meg

"Wow, this is beyond coincidental," Kade insisted, flipping through the pages of the small diary. "It's actually extraordinary."

They were relaxing at the kitchen table, enjoying dessert and coffee, Meg anxiously watching the time. Considering the five hour time difference, she needed to phone her grandmother just past eleven, reaching her before her evening Zumba class. She tore her eyes from the clock to acknowledge Kade's observation.

"I know. I'm still trying to wrap my brain around it. I read the diary over again, after Pop left, certain I'd missed something. It still seems strange to me that a young woman would leave her diary behind. It's just not something we do. In spite of all the coincidences, I'm refraining from making an assumption. Until I hear it from Nana, I don't want to get my hopes up....for your grandfather's sake, and hers."

Kade raised his brows. "But the locket?"

"Yes, that's true. I did find it in her old dressing table. It *must* belong to her, right?" Meg grinned, reaching for the pendant. She fondled it affectionately, her thoughts drifting back to the diary, and Malcolm's story.

"Pretty weird that you found a locket with my granddad's picture in it. I still can't get over it...hold on...did you see this?" Kade asked, laying the open diary flat against the table.

"Careful, you'll break the binding," Meg warned, sucking in her breath. Books were sacred treasures to her, always handled with great care. She leaned over, at first, not really seeing what he saw. "I'm not sure what I'm looking at..."

"This hump, inside the back cover. It's not natural," he insisted, edging it closer to her. He was right, it was strange. Curious, she pressed her fingers against the bulge.

"You're right. It looks like the inside cover may have been peeled back and re-glued. Do you see how it doesn't line up perfectly?"

"Do ya mind if I check?" Kade asked, fumbling for the pocket knife he carried in his jeans. "I can make a slit and we can look in behind?"

"Do it!" she encouraged, wondering if it was another clue from the past. Kade made the incision, careful not to cut too closely.

"I'll need yer small fingers to fish it out."

Meg worked her fingers inside, carefully pulling out a folded envelope. In faded ink was one word, *KAT*.

"Holy shite," Kade blurted, "open it!"

"It looks like it already was," Meg observed, opening the flap. She quickly perused the page, reading down to the bottom. "It's from your grandfather. He signed it, *Forever yours, Mack.*"

"May I?" Kade asked, holding out his hand. He handled the letter as though it might disintegrate without warning. "This is amazing. Well, at least we know that Kat read his confession. Perhaps she did choose to move on with her life—"

"Maybe..." Meg agreed cautiously, "but it still doesn't add up. She wrote how she would do anything to be with him, if only she knew he wanted her. This letter tells her how Mack felt, without any doubt...so why didn't she reach out to him?"

"I guess there's only one person who knows," Kade speculated.

"Nana," she sighed passively. She was quiet for a moment, contemplating the significance of the letter. "What if there's a deeper purpose I came to Scotland, Kade?"

"Yes..."

"Would it be wrong of me *not* to tell her about this over the phone?" Meg reasoned, turning the letter over in her hands.

"Meaning?"

She continued, smiling tentatively. "What if I asked her to come here? So they could reunite face to face?"

"And if the diary isn't hers?" Kade cautioned, glancing down at the scarred book.

"True," she paused, her jaw tight. "Besides, what could I say to get her to come?"

"I have an idea..." he grinned, matter-of -factly. "You could invite her to our wedding."

Meg gasped, startled by his suggestion. "Wedding?"

Kade nodded, reaching into his pocket. He fumbled for a moment, retrieving a small velvet box. Meg stared at him in disbelief, lips parted, speechless. He dropped to a knee in front of her.

"Meggie, I've been waiting my whole life to meet a woman who would complete me. Who could've known she was on the other side of the world, waiting for the same thing? You've changed my world, mo ghaol, and I want to spend the rest of my life loving you. I want you to be my friend and partner, my lover, and god-willing, the mother of my children. I desperately want you for my wife. Will ya marry me?" he proposed. He flipped open the tiny box, revealing his promise.

"What?" she giggled, tears welling in her eyes. She could barely catch her breath. "We've only been together a few months!"

"True, but when you know, you know. There's not a doubt in my mind we're meant to spend our lives together. Sometimes love takes many years to bloom, but sometimes it just sneaks up on ya, and hits you with a hammer. My parents knew each other barely a month before they tied the knot, and they've been together forever. Thirty-two years and four boys later, they still act like honeymooners."

Meg cocked her head and grinned, "I think you may have lost your mind."

"Is that a yes?" He scooped up her hand earnestly.

She nodded through her tears, watching him slip the exquisite ruby over her finger. She'd never imagined, in a million years, that she would find a man like Kade. No one had ever loved her so purely, passionately…so perfectly.

"You've just made me the happiest man alive," he professed, pulling her into his arms. He kissed her tenderly, sealing the significance of the moment. "I promise you a happy ending."

"I can't believe this," she whispered, admiring the unique ring. "I had no idea."

"Ya must have had some idea," he smirked, kissing her again. "I'm hanging around all the time."

"Like a stray tom-cat. I knew I shouldn't have fed you," she goaded playfully, her giggles smothered with kisses.

"Aye, your mistake. Now you'll never be rid of me."

"I wouldn't want it any other way."

"So it's settled then, we'll marry in a few weeks. Then you can invite yer Nana, and she'll be none the wiser."

"How do you expect to pull off a wedding in just a few weeks? How's that even possible?"

"Don't fret, my red-headed beauty, I have connections. Leave it with me to figure things out. I'm sure Isla will help, you know she loves me. You just find yerself a pretty dress," he assured, kissing her forehead.

"She'll kick your ass! And...what about the guests? It's such short notice!" she stammered, her eyes following him back to his seat. Kade flopped in the chair, slouching like a man who didn't have a care in the word. *How could he be so calm!*

"We do things differently in Scotland, Meggie. No muss, no fuss. I promise ya, anyone who wants to be there, will be there."

"If you can pull this off, Kade, I'll worship the ground you walk on," she chuckled, shaking her head.

"Aye, you'll do that anyway, once yer my wife," he teased.

She threw a spoon at him, just missing his noggin. "Oh, you think so, Scotsman?"

Laughing, he ducked just in time. "I'm kidding!"

Meg leaned forward on her elbows, her smile fading. "In all seriousness, this is a *crazy* plan," she sighed.

"Crazy enough to work. There's just one thing...how do we get confirmation that your Nana is our Kat, without spilling the beans?"

Meg considered the dilemma for a moment. Didn't Malcolm mention that Kat's friend Esme lived in the very house they were sitting in? "I may have an idea..." she hinted, her eyes beaming confidence.

CHAPTER 32

Meg

"Meg, it's good to hear from you. How are your renovations coming along?" her grandmother chirped, delightfully surprised with the call.

"It's good to hear your voice too, Nana," Meg echoed, suddenly missing her. "Things are great. The renos are pretty much finished. I'm still working on the front bedrooms for the B&B, but I've had so much on my plate!"

"And the shop? Is it up and running?"

"It is!" she trilled, "I'm thinking of calling it, 'The Sealladh Bed and Bookery'. I'm working on the new website soon. I thought I'd play up the whole 'bed time story' theme!"

"How charming, dear. I'm sure it will be fantastic. You're so creative with things like that." Margie praised, putting a smile on Meg's face.

"Thanks, Nana. I've been doing some research on the house. I thought it would be interesting for visitors to read about it's history. The cottage was built in the early 1900's, by Eve and William Mitchell, who willed it to their son John," Meg explained cautiously.

"Apparently it stayed in the family until the mid-60's, before it sold to the man who purchased it before me. I was curious if you'd ever met the family? The Mitchell's? On Hill Road?" she pressed, hoping to trigger a response. Her grandmother remained silent, allowing a long moment to pass. Long enough for Meg's doubt to blossom.

"Yes...I *did* know the family. John, the son, walked out on his wife and daughter. It was quite the scandal! The daughter, Esme...she was my best friend all through school," Margie recalled reverently. "I haven't thought about her in years. Last I heard, she'd passed away. Poor dear, died from cirrhosis. After your grandfather passed away, I was anxious to reach out to her, but she never responded to my letters."

"Oh?" Meg questioned nonchalantly, curbing her excitement. It was her! *She was their Kat!*

"Yes. My, what a small world. Imagine the odds?"

"Image," Meg grinned, barely able to stifle her secret.

"I always loved her home. It was delightfully quaint," Nana continued, "you should email me some pictures, dear. I would love to see what you've done with the place."

"Actually," Meg drawled, "what would you say to a visit?"

"Oh," Margie sighed.

"Nana?"

"It's been so long since I've traveled..."

Meg sensed her grandmother's reluctance and wondered if it was because of the long journey, or something more. "Maybe it's because you've had no reason. I have something surprising to share. I'm getting married!" she gushed, hoping to persuade her with exciting news. Everything depended on it.

"Married? That's wonderful! Is it the young man you told me about? The one helping you fix the house?"

"Yes. I know it's quick, but I love him!" she gushed. "I think I knew Kade was my soul mate the moment we met. I just had to get the hell out of my own way!"

"I'm happy for you, Peanut. I'm so glad I encouraged you to take this leap of faith. I knew something magical would happen. Does he know how lucky he is?"

"I'm the lucky one. I think when you meet him, you'll understand," Meg assured, knowing how much Kade took after the man her grandmother once loved. "I want you here, Nana, at my wedding. I need my family with me."

"Oh, Meg…I want to be there to support you, but…" Margie paused, her wavering breath the only audible sound.

"Please?" She held her breath.

"Of course," her Nana sighed, email me all the details and I'll book a flight. I wouldn't miss it for the world."

"Thank-you! I can't begin to tell you how happy this makes me," Meg erupted, unable to mask her relief.

"I look forward to it, my darling. I can't believe I'm going to see my beloved Scotland again."

And your beloved Mack, Meg smiled secretively. Pleased, she sat back in her chair, gingerly slipping her glasses off. The plan was in motion.

The plan was in motion…

She exhaled slowly, astonished by absurdity she found herself in. It was like she'd been plucked from the real world and dropped into the centre of a deliciously sentimental novel; where the heroine, chapter by chapter, navigates through a quagmire of crazy hurdles, whisked towards her happy ending.

She'd been so focused on Mack and Katherine, and the sub-plot, she'd almost forgotten that her own fairytale was unfolding...

She was getting married.

Her grandmother's voice snapped her back to the conversation. "Sorry Nana, I missed that," Meg apologized, caught up in her own musings.

"I said, this was written in the stars."

"Oh, Nana," Meg cried, "you have no idea."

CHAPTER 33

Meg

"Wow, I can't believe how incredible everything looks! Who would have thought a place called 'The Hairy Coo' could be transformed into this romantic oasis!" Meg praised, eyes wide with wonder. The entire pub glistened with thousands of twinkling lights, while white tulle floated above them, adorning the beams. Isla even set up a wedding canopy for them to marry under, constructed with silver birch, entwined with both holly and snowberry. It was breathtaking, and perfectly suitable for a late November wedding.

"Aye, it's not too shabby," Isla agreed, setting the last of the candles on the lacy, white clothed tables. Rustic mason jars, wrapped with burlap ribbons and a sprig of holly, were delightful centrepieces.

In just a few hours, her grandmother would arrive, her flight landing in Glasgow. Kade's father had graciously offered to pick her up. She'd have just enough time to get in a good rest before the festivities began.

"It looks so magical, maybe you should consider leaving it this way permanently!" Meg grinned, offering Isla a cheeky wink.

"Ah, I'm sure my regulars would have something to say about that," Isla replied, returning Meg's smile. "They're already griping that I've closed the pub for the day."

"Well, I hope you know how much Kade and I appreciate your generosity. I can't imagine a better venue for us to marry in. We met here after all!"

"Aye, thanks to me!" Isla boasted, wrapping an arm around the bride. "Yer sure I can't convince you to join our team, Red? The queer community hands out free toasters for every pretty lady we convert."

"It's a tempting offer," Meg laughed, landing a sloppy kiss on her cheek, "but Kade's already locked it down."

"It's a sad day for gays everywhere," Isla blushed, ushering Meg to the door. "Now go on, do what you have to do. I've got everything under control. Kade will be here by 7:00 to greet early arrivals. The wedding's at 8:00 sharp. Don't be late."

"I wouldn't dream of it."

Walking through the parking lot, she was in a daze, excited, but anxious, about what lay ahead. She and Kade had spent several weeks planning everything to the letter. It was going to be a modest, intimate wedding, with family and a few good friends in attendance. Meg was looking forward to it, but not without some sadness. She'd always imagined her father walking her down the aisle, proudly offering her to the man she loved. He would have adored Kade, of that she was certain. She missed him terribly. But at least her Nana would be there, soon to be reunited with her own soul mate. She still had no idea, and Meg couldn't think of a more fitting, or romantic occasion to bring the lovers back together. It was kismet.

Kade was with his grandfather that day. She could only imagine how nervous they both were, likely sipping scotch to settle their wits. As soon as Meg confirmed that her grandmother was the mysterious Katherine, Malcolm had been rightly told. She'd never seen a man more grateful, or solicitous, than he. It warmed her heart that love could reawaken, catch fire, after so many dormant years; from the tiniest ember that never forgot what it felt like to burn with passion. He seemed a young man again, brimming with hope and yearning. The plan was to reintroduce them as soon as the ceremony was over. Only the three of them, Kade, Malcolm, and herself, were privy to the circumstances, but soon all that would change.

"I was hoping to find you here."

"Oh!"

Meg had been so absorbed, completely oblivious of her surroundings, she nearly walked straight into Lorna. She'd not seen the woman for well over a month, not since the Nathan incident. Oddly enough, while it should have infuriated her, Meg felt nothing but gratitude. Clearly Lorna had hoped for a different outcome, and Meg could only pity her. Having said that, she was the last person Meg wanted to see, especially on her wedding day.

"You know, I always imagined I would play a bigger part on Kade's wedding day," Lorna scoffed, imposing herself.

"Good Morning," Meg frowned, offering a flat greeting, firmly holding her ground. She didn't want any trouble, and she was reluctant to encourage conversation. "How did you know?" she asked quietly.

"News travels fast around here. The only thing Scot's enjoy more than drinking, is gossip. No surprise, they usually go hand in hand."

Megged shrugged impassively. "I see."

Lorna smirked, as though assessing her fortitude. "I've been trying to reach Kade, but he won't respond to my texts, or take my calls."

"And this surprises you?"

"Maybe a little."

"I may not be the one to discuss this with," Meg insisted, trying to push past her, her patience waning.

"Wait," Lorna demanded, blocking her path, "you're right."

Meg drew a deep breath, reluctantly meeting her eyes. "What is it you want from me, Lorna?"

"I just want to congratulate you...and apologize for the Nathan thing."

"Fine, I accept both, now if you'll you excuse me, I'm on a tight schedule," Meg nodded, wanting the confrontation to end.

"Have you heard from him?" she pressed, refusing to budge.

"Nathan? No, and I don't expect to. Why do you ask?"

"He was quite the mess, when I last saw him. You know, he stayed with me several days before flying back to America. I thought it the least I could do, given the condition he was in. He said that Kade lost his mind and attacked him from behind. He was lucky Nathan didn't press charges," she provoked, "Ya have me to thank for that."

"Thank you? Thank you?" Meg brayed, dangerously close to striking her. "Are you really that clueless? You can thank yourself for all the trouble you caused. None of it would have happened had you the tiniest iota of foresight! If you thought of anyone but yourself—"

"I did it for Kade—"

"You did it for yourself. You don't love Kade, you just hate to lose!"

Lorna rolled her eyes derisively, "I haven't lost anything. I don't want Kade anymore," she spat. "Nathan and I really connected. Apparently there is a man smart enough to see that I have way more to offer than you."

"Okay," Meg shrugged, refusing to be baited further. If the reveal surprised her, she refused show it.

"I'll be travelling to Virginia this Christmas. Nathan sent me an e-ticket," she offered wryly, as though the confession should upset Meg.

Meg snorted, visualizing the two of them together, vying for narcissistic privilege. *Imagine, Nathan getting a taste of his own medicine.* She almost felt sorry for him. Almost. If he wanted to dumpster dive for a woman, who was she to care?

"I should go, Lorna, I have a wedding to get ready for. Have a lovely time in Virginia. Be sure to visit the Edgar Allen Poe Museum, you'll appreciate it."

"Oh? Why would that interest me?"

"It's dark and macabre. Something tells me that's right up your alley."

Meg pushed past her, leaving Lorna dumbfounded, her mouth agape. Proud, and a little surprised she'd stood her ground, she walked away with her head held high. Maybe Scottish blood did run deep in her veins.

CHAPTER 34

Meg

Meg waited nervously in the vestibule, peaking through the small diamond window at her handsome groom, her heart beating wildly. He looked completely unstressed, smiling and joking with guest as he directed them to their seats, his parents beaming by his side. Two kilted nephews ran around the chairs, frivolously rough housing, until their mother grabbed them by the ears and plunked them in their seats.

Meg smiled to herself, warmed by the unfolding scene. Standing on the porch of her new home, four months earlier, she never imagined she'd be donning a white dress and marrying her soul mate.

"You look beautiful, granddaughter," Margie complimented, tracing her hand across Meg's cheek. "Your dress is perfect."

It was perfect. Meg had considered buying something traditional, and even found herself in an expensive Glasgow boutique, trying on gowns with puffy white sleeves, sequinned beads, pearls, and sweetheart necklines. While beautiful, she didn't feel authentic. More like a cupcake. She was never a traditional girl and her gown needed to reflect that. She ended up in a vintage shop right in Fort William, and there it was, the perfect dress.

It was a simple a-line, ivory dress, without all the "girly" embellishments. The silk halter bodice fit snugly against her, accentuating her curves, while the hem landed just above her ankles. A delicious peak at her cleavage was the pièce de résistance, something she was sure would turn Kade's head.

"Do you have something old, new, borrowed, and blue?" her grandmother asked, tucking in a loose thread on Meg's dress.

"Well, my dress is old...but new to me...so I guess that checks two boxes, and my shoes are blue." They were adorable! While she chose a modest dress, the shoes were all glam! A Jimmy Choo, sky-blue, sequinned pump, with three inch heels, four times more expensive than the dress. A ridiculous investment, to be sure, but she felt pretty.

"Maybe you'll think these are antiquated, but I'd like to loan you my pearls," she offered sentimentally, easing them out of her purse. "Your dad gave them to me for my birthday, right after you both moved in. I suppose it was his way of saying thank you. Anyway, they mean a lot to me."

"I don't think they're old fashioned at all," Meg gushed, fighting back her tears. She spun around, lifting her curled tresses. "I've always loved them. Remember letting me borrow them when I was little, playing make-believe with all your old party dresses?"

"I most certainly do," Nana smiled, clasping the choker of pearls around Meg's neck. "There, that's lovely."

"Oh, Nana," Meg sobbed, suddenly overcome, remembering all the sacrifices her grandmother made, all the boo-boo kisses, driving lessons, late night talks, and chick-flick marathons. She wasn't just her grandmother, she was like a mother, and more importantly, her friend. "I'm so grateful you're here."

"You deserve to be happy, Peanut."

"So do you, Nana," Meg nodded solemnly, the Wedding March swelling behind her. "Oh my goodness! This is it!"

Margie giggled, crooking her arm for Meg to loop. "Ready?"

"Let's go!"

Kade

Kade's eyes lit up as soon as he saw his bride-to-be. She was an absolute beauty, turning every head in the room. Her gown was better than he'd imagined, simple, classy, elegant, and Meggie wore the hell out of it. Smiling demurely as she walked up the aisle, it was obvious she'd only eyes for him. *My god, how did he get so lucky?*

As she approached, her grandmother by her side, Kade could see where Meggie's fine looks came from. Margie was a striking woman, despite marking seven decades. Aside from being more petite than her granddaughter, the pair of them were definitely cut from the same cloth.

"Be good to each other," Margie urged, handing Meg's hand to Kade. "Don't take even one moment for granted."

Kade smiled at her warmly. "Oh, I won't, I promise" he winked, inviting his woman to join him under the canopy.

"You look so handsome," Meg blushed, holding his hands tightly.

"I took a shower," he teased, shrugging, as a sea of giggles floated through the crowd. "You're breathtaking."

The officiant smiled and cleared her throat, inviting their attention.

"On behalf of Meg and Kade, I'd like to thank you all for being here this evening and for taking the time, and making the journey, not only to be a part of this celebration, but to witness a precious glimpse of their love.

Every relationship is unique, but one thing holds true: For love to exist between two people, each person must allow themselves to be vulnerable. If you ask couples, who have a strong and abiding love, what they like most about their partners, many will say that when they're with that person they don't have to pretend to be anything other than who they are. They're able to express themselves without fear of being judged or shunned. There's room inside their relationship for both of them to be unique individuals. They are free to surrender to true intimacy—to be known and loved unconditionally. Meg and Kade have both shared with me, that this is the very thing that drew them to the other.

All of us here today have our own love stories. Some are short, others long. Some are yet unwritten, while others are gently drifting from one page to the next. There are chapters in all of our stories that are sad and filled with regret — and others that are exciting and full of adventure.

Meg and Kade, we're here with you this evening because we want to support you, to celebrate you, and also to remind you that love isn't happily ever after, love is the experience of writing your story."

Kade caressed Meggie's delicate fingers, filled with more hope, more joy, than any man deserved, yet he was grateful for it.

Smiling, the officiant continued, "well folks, fate brought you together, you fell in love by chance, but you're here by choice. You're choosing each other. You've chosen to be with someone who strengthens you, who makes you wiser, encourages you to smile, and makes each day brighter. You're about to make promises, and vow to nurture each other, to advocate for your highest good, and bring joy and intimacy into each other's lives. Are you ready?"

"It's not too late to back out," Kade jested, winking at his bride.

"Not a chance," Meg giggled, nodding to the minister.

"Kade, will you share your vows with Meg?"

"I'd be happy too," he grinned, turning towards her. "I, um..."

Suddenly overcome with the significance of what he was about to promise, he hesitated. Oh, how she humbled him, this precious woman...who had no clue how extraordinary she was. There was nothing he wanted more, in that very moment, and forever more, than to be her champion. To prove to her every day how incredible she was.

Meg smiled tenderly, raising a hand to his cheek. "Are you crying?"

"Aye," he grinned, reaching for her hand. He brought her fingers to his lips, lightly kissing them. "Meggie, where do I begin...the minister talked about intimacy, but until I met you, I didn't really appreciate the significance of the word. Intimacy is like a treasure hunt, isn't it? It's mapping your lover's soul to discover vulnerable fractures, those elusive fissures she works so hard at concealing, for fear she won't be accepted...and then filling those voids with love." He took a deep breath, and collected himself, dangerously close to losing it.

"I've always prided myself on making things beautiful, what other's let fall in disrepair; of seeing the splendour and potential in things that other's dismiss. Sometimes love is like that. It almost always comes from modest beginnings, but through serendipity and effort, we shape it into something incredible. Love is a process of making something beautiful, where there was nothing at all.

Meggie, I adore you and I promise I'll always be there for you, building a home, a life together, that's safe and loving. I know that life won't always be easy, and that sometimes we'll struggle. Maybe there'll be days you won't like me very much, but I promise ya, no matter what, I'll make things right, fix what needs fixing, always giving you my best effort, along with my heart," he promised, his loyal eyes pooled with sincerity.

Nodding, the officiant smiled, pleased with his promise. "Meg?"

"Oh Kade...I never thought I'd meet a man like you. Who knew you were so poetic?" she quipped, drawing laughter from the room. "You saw something deep inside me I didn't even know existed, and patiently coaxed it to the surface. Your energy, enthusiasm, playfulness, are infectious, and you make me feel safe, cared for...adored. I don't even know how to thank you..." she sobbed, dropping her eyes to the ground. Kade lifted her chin, and wiped her cheeks, encouraging her to continue.

"You're my favourite person," she sniffed, "and I choose you to be my partner in life. I love the passion, determination, and perseverance you show in everything you do. I love the faces you make when you stretch, and how ticklish you are. I love that you never complain when I warm my feet icy feet against your bum, and how you'll scratch my back until I fall asleep. Thank you for allowing me to be my smart-ass self with you, and loving me all the more for it. You inspire me. I take you with all your faults and strengths as I offer myself to you...with all my faults and strengths. I want to spend my life with you and I promise to love and care for you as long as we both shall live...."

* * *

As guest mingled amongst themselves, Kade held back his new wife, anxious for a private moment. "Well, I guess yer stuck with me forever," he cooed, kissing her over, and over.

"I guess you are too," Meg agreed cheerfully, wrapping her arms behind him, her hands seductively lingering on his backside.

"Mmm, I'm okay with that."

"Oh yeah? What if I get really, really fat?" she goaded, pulling him tighter.

"I'll kiss every plump inch of you," he promised cheekily, "it just might take me longer."

"God, I love you," she purred breathlessly, gently nibbling his earlobe.

"If you keep that up, we may have to slip out before dinner is served..."

"Nope, we have a busy night ahead. Are you ready for the big reveal?" Meg questioned, gesturing towards Malcolm. As promised, the old man was being discreet, waiting for just the right moment. Kade could see from his body language that the poor man's patience was wearing thin.

"Aye, poor Pops is chomping at the bit. I thought he'd lose his mind today. I've never seen him so anxious."

"Let's do this," Meg giggled. Although it was the happiest day in her life, she seemed more excited to reunite the star-crossed lovers. Kade took her hand and waded through the crowd, pausing often to accept warm wishes and hearty congratulations from guests. Finally they approached Malcolm, talking quietly with Kade's father.

"Ready Pop?" Kade asked, pressing a hand between his shoulder blades.

"Yes," Malcolm exhaled, allowing Meg to clasp his shaking hand. "I've been waiting a lifetime for this."

Kade turned to address his father. "Excuse us, Dad, there's someone I want to introduce Pop to. Why don't you get yerself a pint."

Slowly they made their way towards the head table, Meg keeping pace with the old man. Margie, deep in conversation with Norma, jumped as Kade reached for her elbow, startled by his touch.

"Mrs. Miller...Nana, there's someone I'd like you to meet," he encouraged, gently spinning her around.

Margie smiled warmly at the stranger, politely waiting for an introduction, curiously examining his face. None of them spoke, breath held, waiting for a moment of recognition.

Eager, Meg stepped forward, her eyes pooled with hope, "Nana, this is Kade's grandfather...Malcolm—"

"Mack?" Margie choked, wide eyed, as though she'd seen a ghost.

CHAPTER 35

Katherine

"Hello Kat," Mack greeted fondly, cautiously taking her hand.

Margie ogled him for a moment, her mouth agape. She couldn't believe he was there, standing directly in front of her. How many times had she dreamt of that moment, seeing him again, touching him. Aside from the grey hair, and a few wrinkles, he looked the same as she remembered, strong, masculine, and handsome.

Malcolm caressed her fingers. "You look bonnie," he flattered, regarding her shyly.

"So do you," she smiled, gazing down at their hands, astonished by how familiar his touch was, as though no time had passed between them. It was the strangest sensation.

"Men aren't bonnie, Kat," he smirked, his deep, blue eyes twinkling with mischief.

"It's been a long time since anyone has called me by that name," she blushed, offering him an ironic smile, "I go by Margie now."

"You'll always be Kat to me," he said, releasing her hand, as though unsure of himself.

Confused, Margie glanced at her granddaughter. "Did you know?"

"Yes," Meg choked, close to tears. "I put it all together about a month ago."

"But how?"

"It's an amazing story, Nana, and one I'm excited to share with you," Meg promised, "but tonight let's just celebrate that we're all here, together."

Margie swallowed hard, still grappling with shock, her eyes shifting between the two men. "I can't believe this is real. Mack...is your grandfather?"

"Aye, he is," Kade assured, jovially patting his grandfather's back. "You two must have so much to catch up on. Dinner will be served soon and we've sat you side by side at the family table. Can we show you to yer seats?"

"Great idea," Meg nodded, gesturing them to follow. "Nana, your looking a little pale?" she observed kindly, "would you like some water?"

"Your damn lucky I didn't have a heart attack, girl!" Margie scolded playfully. "You shouldn't shock old people like that!"

"I'm sorry, Nana," Meg giggled, "I wanted to surprise you. Kade, will you bring Nana some water?"

"Kade, you will do no such thing," Margie insisted jauntily, "you'll bring me a scotch!"

"Make that two," Mack ordered, wrapping his arm through hers. "I think the situation calls for it."

"Tell me a situation that doesn't," Kade quipped, heading for the bar.

Mack lead her to their seats, pulling the chair out for her. Margie wouldn't take her eyes off him, for fear he might vanish in a whiff of smoke, disappearing from her life all over again.

"So why did you change yer name?" Mack asked, dropping in the chair beside her. She smiled at the accent, forgetting that she too once spoke with a thick Scottish brogue. It had been ages since she'd heard anything but flat, American intonations.

"I changed it when I started university," she admitted, allowing her thoughts to drift back. "I suppose I was being a bit rebellious, trying to assert my independence. I wasn't too happy with my parents back then."

"Aye, I suppose not."

"My mother hated it, which made it all the sweeter," she smirked. "Ann-Margaret was all the rage, everyone wanted to be like her, including me. So, since my middle name was Margaret, I shortened it to Margie. A fresh start, I guess. After awhile, it just stuck."

"I prefer to call you Kat," Mack grinned, "do ya mind?"

She pursed her lips, hesitating for a moment, secretly thrilled with the request. Hearing her old name roll off his tongue made her feel young again.

"I don't mind," she blushed, meeting his eyes. They were a long way from the past, where they'd left each other in the park, so many years before. They'd lived a lifetime in between; married, raised children, built careers, and retired, and yet, all at once, she felt seventeen; naive, hopeful, even a little anxious. After her husband died, she'd rarely dated. She had a few suitors, but none of them sparked her imagination or made her yearn for something more. In her life, only one man had ever made her feel that way.

"Mack," she breathed, as suddenly, every emotion she'd submerged, her hopes, dreams, desires, came rushing back like a tidal wave, the intensity nearly suffocating her.

"Aye," he nodded soberly, as though knowing exactly what she felt.

"I've thought about you nearly every day of my life..."

"I've so many regrets, Kat..." he confessed, slipping his hand over hers. He dropped his eyes, grasping for words, "and yet..."

"I know," she comforted, struggling with the same mixed feelings. "Life offered so many blessings in between, it almost feels disloyal to dismiss them. I loved my husband, even though our time together was short. He was good to me, and together we brought my son into the world."

"Right," Mack nodded, "My wife Fae. She was a formidable woman, kind and supportive. We had many happy years—"

"It's okay, Mack. I wanted you to be happy. I prayed for it, but that never stopped me from missing you."

"I felt the same," he offered sadly. "I waited a long time before I moved on. I wanted you so badly, I could barely breathe."

Kat stiffened, confused by his confession. The longing she'd felt, the grief of those early years, the agony of missing him, came rushing back.

"Why then?" she sighed. There was so much she wanted to ask him, so many questions that had plagued her through the years. "Why...why didn't you reach out to me? I thought you stopped loving me..."

"No," he whispered, his eyes begging her to believe him. "I never stopped."

"But...you never came back. You never even said goodbye?"

"I know. I should have. I regret not coming to see you myself. I never should have wrote you that letter. I should've realized it wasn't enough, but I was young and stupid."

Kat shook her head, trying to understand. None of his words made sense. "Letter?"

"Aye?" he nodded, "I sent you a letter. I asked Esme to give it to you before you left. I was afraid that if I went to you...our goodbye would be too painful. I—"

"You...wrote...me a letter?" she stammered.

"Yes. You don't remember?"

Kat shook her head, shocked by the admission, "I never received it."

Mack took her hand once more, his sad eyes exploring hers, "I'd wondered if that were true, but we found the letter in yer diary."

"My diary?" she gasped, recalling the desperation she'd felt that last day. *Esme*. She'd given the diary to her friend. It had felt tainted to her, and she asked her friend to get rid of it....as though it would make the parting less painful.

"Your granddaughter found it in some old boxes in the house. Esme's old house," he explained kindly, eager to catch her up. "I'm sure she wants to tell you everything, just as soon as there's time."

"I gave my diary to Esme...to destroy...but...the letter?"

"It was in the diary, hidden, I'm told. I thought maybe you'd read it and left it behind?" he asked, searching for the truth.

The whole situation was surreal, and Kat struggled for clarity. Esme kept her diary? And the letter? Why didn't she give it to her? She knew how desperate Kat felt, how hurt and angry that Mack never reached out, that he'd never even said goodbye. Maybe his letter would have changed everything.

"Kat?"

"What did it say?" she asked softly, the realization hitting her.

"I can show you, if you like. It's at Kade's house, along with yer diary."

"Yes," she gushed, taking his hand, comforted by his smile. "I'd like that very much."

Kade returned to the table, pleased to see their fingers entwined. He placed the drams on the table and smiled. "Sorry it took so long. I got distracted by my brothers. We'll be eating soon."

"That's fine, Grandson," Mack grinned. "I wonder if you and your sweet wife, would mind if we left right after dinner? We've a lot of time to make up for. Is that alright with you, Kat?" he asked, hoping she'd agree. There was nothing she wanted more then to spend time with him, and read his long lost letter.

"Wife? I like the sound of that! No objections, Pop!" Kade chuckled, tossing his grandfather a lively wink. "I'll have Angus drop you back at the house. My brother's under strict orders from his wife not to drink tonight, so he'll be sober enough to drive ya," he trilled, yanked away by a nephew, tugging on his arm.

CHAPTER 36

Katherine

My dear Kat,

Please don't think I'm a coward for writing a letter instead of talking to your face. I just don't know how to say good bye, but I also don't want you to leave without knowing how I feel. I'm not sure I'll be able to find the words, but I'll try. Meeting you was the best thing that ever happened to me. I don't know why fate brought us together, only to tear us apart, but it hurts like hell.

I thought about what you said, about how we could get jobs and stay together. About how you could go to business school, instead. Christ, I haven't been able to think of much else. The selfish part of me wants to say 'to hell with it', and take a chance, but I can't do it. You're the smartest person I've ever met and you need to go to school. You need to become a doctor. It's what you've been yearning for your whole life. I don't want to be the reason you give up your dreams. If only your dad didn't have to transfer. If only we were older. I do love you Kat, but I have nothing to offer you. Not here. Not right now.

I know this hurts you. God, I could see it in your eyes the last time we spoke. It crushed me to witness it. I felt like I was letting you down, but I know that letting you go is what's right. You're parents want to help you with school, and I think it's important to let them. But I have an idea. Perhaps I can save for the passage to America, over the next few months. You can get settled in school and get established, and when you're ready, you can send for me. If we could made things work out here, why not in North Carolina? We could pick up where we left off.

I don't expect to hear from you until you get to America. I know you'll be busy, but please reach out to me as soon as you can. Maybe it's too little too late. I hope not. I know I was a jerk, and if you never want to speak to me again, I'll understand. I won't like it, but I'll not pressure you.

I'll end now, but I will leave you with this. You're my soul mate, Katherine Margaret. I know this as sure as anything. I want to marry you.

Forever Yours,

Mack

Kat set the letter down, dabbing her eyes with a tissue. *She never knew.* There were so many feelings fighting for consideration, she could barely sort through them. "Mack, I don't know what to say?" she choked, wishing the words would come.

They were sitting in Kade's living room, Mack on the sofa beside her. It was late, and she was suffering from jet lag, but nothing could make her leave his side, not before unraveling the mystery. Why didn't Esme give her the letter? And if she'd read Mack's words, would she have acted on them? The answer was a resounding yes. She would have sent for him. She loved him desperately. Oh, how she'd suffered, lost and confused for months and months on end.

"It was all true, Kat. Every word."

"So I thought you stopped loving me, and you thought, after reading your letter, I didn't want you anymore..." she grieved, her body numb.

"Aye, that's what happened."

"Why do you suppose Esme held the letter from me?" she asked, desperate to recall their last meeting. It was a long time ago and so many of her memories had faded.

"I'm not certain. Perhaps she was envious?" he offered gingerly, as though more was on his mind.

"Envy?"

He shrugged indifferently and continued. "I'd not thought of this in years, it seemed so incidental—"

"What is it?"

"After you'd left, Esme reached out to me," he swallowed, pausing to gather his thoughts. "She seemed lost without her best mate, and I admit, I'd considered finding solace with her...but I was only looking for a friend. She was the only person I knew who loved you as much as I..."

"I understand," Kat soothed, reaching for his hand. She hated him struggling so.

"We'd met a few times, at the old diner. It didn't take her long to reveal her true intentions. She came on strong. I was pissed that she was being so disloyal to ya, Kat. She was no friend to ya."

Kat dropped her eyes, trying to process his words. It made her sad, thinking about the deception. First, holding back the letter, and then making a pass at Mack. It was no surprise that Esme never returned any of her letters. Perhaps she'd been riddled with shame? Or maybe she just didn't care. Either way, Esme single-handedly kept them apart. The betrayal was heartbreaking.

"It's so disheartening," she admitted, burdened with sadness. "All those years we spent apart, all because of a young girl's jealousy?"

"Aye, It's true," he sighed. "Even though I'd moved on…married my wife, and raised my wee ones, I still woke up every morning and met the mirror with longing for ya, Kat." She met his gaze, her heart swelling with love.

"You did?"

He nodded. They sat in silence for a moment, their breath shallow, wanting more, but both too nervous to ask. Finally, Mack cleared his throat, breaking the spell.

"I have something for you," he grinned, reaching into his jacket. He pulled out her locket, freshly polished. It gleamed in the firelight, as he held it in front of her.

"Is that…my locket?" she asked, reaching out her hand. She easily opened it, like she'd done many times before, caressing the photos inside. "How? Where did you find it?"

"Your Meggie had it. That's how I recognized it. It was hanging around her neck."

"But, I thought I'd lost it?"

"She found it in an old dressing table, the one she brought from home," he explained, taking it from her. "May I?"

"Yes," she whimpered, leaning towards him.

"There," he smiled, allowing it to fall against her chest, "back where it belongs."

"I was devastated when I couldn't find it. It was the only photo I had of you," she confessed, reaching for his hand. "I never thought I would see it again."

"If it hadn't resurfaced, I might never have found you," he said softly, easing closer. Kat raised a hand to his cheek and leaned in for a kiss, gently pressing her mouth against his. Tingles flirted down her spine, their chemistry unchanged since their first kiss.

It had been many years since arousal had knocked on her door, but it wasn't unwelcome.

"Kat!" Mack chuckled, easing out of her kiss. "I don't remember you being so bold!"

"I'm not a young girl anymore," she smirked, placing a suggestive hand on his thigh. "It's 2018, Mack, women are allowed to make the first move. Besides, we're not getting any younger, we don't have time to waste!"

"Aye," he laughed, caressing her shoulders. "What do ya suggest?"

"Well if it's not too forward, Mr. MacDonald, may I boldly suggest you take me to bed."

CHAPTER 37

Meg

"Well, here we are Mrs. Campbell," Kade rejoiced, carrying Meg over the threshold. She giggled as he set her gently on her feet, astounded by what she saw. Their bedroom had been highjacked and completely transformed into a romantic oasis. Dreamy, white holiday lights had been carefully woven around a brand new, four poster bed, dressed in a luxurious duvet donning peacock colours of purple, teal and gold. A fire, blazing in the hearth, invited an ideal setting for a passionate night. Their wedding night.

"Wow, this is gorgeous!" Meg gushed, approaching the bed. "Who did all this?"

"It's my wedding gift to you, Meggie. Did you not see your sister-in-laws slip out earlier? I arranged for the new frame to be delivered and assembled while we were celebrating, and then they popped by to make up the room," Kade replied proudly, thrilled with her response. "I hope you like it. I handpicked everything myself."

"It's perfect," she assured, touched by the sentiment. "You can add decorator to your resume. I can't believe you this for us. What a wonderful surprise to come home to."

"You deserve it, wife," he purred slipping in behind her. He brushed aside her silky hair, landing a kiss on her neck, a desperate moan escaping his lips. "God, I've been waiting all night to get you alone."

"Say that again..." she whispered, shivering from his touch.

"What's that?" he asked softly, caressing her shoulders with a feather stroke.

"Wife," she smiled dreamily.

"Ah, wife, wife, *wife,*" he purred, offering her sweet kisses after every word; across her shoulders, around her neck, softly trailing his way up her chin. "Wife, wife, *wife,*" he echoed, finishing with a delicious, lingering kiss on her mouth.

"Kade," she mewled, enjoying his seduction. Lacing his fingers in her hair, he pulled her chin back, trailing his tongue down her neck and cleavage, earning a deep, sexy sigh from her.

"I need to get this dress off you, Meggie," he growled, blindly tracing his fingers down her back. "That's a lot of buttons," he smirked, devilishly eyeing her.

"Oh...no..." she giggled, remembering how he dealt with the last dress that got in his way. "Kade..." she warned skittishly, "you can't..."

"I can..." he teased, distracting her with another kiss. "You don't plan to marry again, do ya?"

"Never," she promised, playfully squirming out of harms way, "but it's so pretty..."

"Aye, but I like what's underneath so much better," he insisted, pressing her helplessly against the bed post. Slowly, he ran his hand up her thigh, pressing his palm against her mound before slipping inside her panties. Sharply, she pulled in her breath, stunned by the contrast of cold fingers on hot flesh.

"That's the response I'm looking for," he groaned, penetrating her with two long fingers. He wrapped his free hand around her hip, inviting it to the party, and leisurely rubbed her clit to tease out an orgasm. Her legs shook beneath her as his hands worked in unison, determined to bring her pleasure. She held tightly to the post, his erection pressing into her ass. Knuckles growing white, she steadied herself as a climax bloomed from her centre. Moaning her approval, she tipped her head back, savouring the wave of spasms, and her first orgasm as a married woman.

"I'll never tire of hearing you cum," Kade panted hotly, biting into her neck. "Now about these buttons?"

"What buttons?" she shrugged, no longer giving a damn about the dress. Within seconds he jerked against the fabric, relieving the satiny buttons of their duty. They flew in every direction, as the silky dress fell to the floor. She stepped out of it, mindful not to catch her heels in the fabric.

"That's better," he stared eagerly, his erection tented under his kilt. "It's a shame this was hidden all day."

"Yes, I'm sure your family would have approved of me marrying you in my underwear," she quipped, walking towards him. Aggressively she pulled him towards her, crushing him with her kiss. "I want to taste you," she purred, dropping to her knees. She raised his kilt and gripped his ass, surprised to see he wore nothing beneath, and eased him into her mouth. His sweet, briny taste coated her tongue, and she invited him deeper into her throat, with nothing on her mind but offering pleasure to her husband.

"Meggie..."

She loved him with her mouth, drawing him deep and then pulling up on the shaft, his approving moans encouraging her. He rocked his hips, mindful of choking her, his strong fingers knitting through her hair.

"God, that mouth," he growled, gazing down at her longingly. "Oh Meggie, when you look at me like that...I feel like I've died and met an angel." He eased himself away, and raised her to her feet. "But, I'll not consummate our marriage in your mouth," he chuckled, "no matter how tempting it is. Lie down on the bed, my love."

She did as she was told, slipping back the duvet and spreading herself over the crisp, cotton sheets. Moaning, Kade eased her panties over her ass, kneeling on the floor in front of her her. He kissed her thick thighs before roughly spreading her legs, tasting her with his tongue. She raised her hips, wordlessly begging him for more. Happy to oblige, he danced his tongue around her folds, pulling her labia into his mouth, darting his tongue into her hole.

"You taste sweet, so warm and wet," he groaned, blowing his cool breath over her heated sex. She squirmed beneath him, anxious to be fucked. He was in no such hurry, taking his sweet time. He stroked her again and again, his eager tongue flicking against her clit, penetrating her with his fingers. Her womb was on fire, a yearning from deep within. Close to the edge, her hands pulling at the sheets, she writhed beneath his mouth.

"Cum for me, wife," he begged, increasing the pressure, his fingers milking her g-spot. She bared down, her jaw clenching from the insane pleasure, as another climax shuddered through her. Kade raised to his feet, dropping his kilt to the floor. In one, practiced motion, he flipped her on her belly, sliding her to the edge of the bed. Knowing what he wanted, she perched on all fours, presenting her swollen pussy for him.

"Oh Christ, woman," he hungered, eagerly pressing inside her.

"Yes, oh god, yes," Meg panted, aroused further by his need. He rocked against her, his hips pounding against the fullness of her ass, again and again, his strong hands gripping her shoulders tightly, desperately seeking release.

It was sexy as hell, how he could take her so aggressively, and still make her feel safe. She loved how unrestrained he was, certain she would meet his passion. He'd always treated her that way, celebrating her strength, intelligence, and sexuality. There was something profoundly seductive about that. A shrinking violet no more, he bed her well, his strokes unforgiving and powerful, intending a violent climax. He shifted his grip to her ass, pressing hard against her, releasing a deep, primal moan, his cock convulsing against the swollen walls of her sex. Releasing a scream of her own, she pushed back against him, her body insisting on another orgasm.

Kade

After lovingly tucking Meggie in, Kade climbed in beside her, wrapping his naked body around her. The embers in the hearth cast a soft glow throughout the room, offering them a warm, romantic ambiance to fall asleep to. It was very late, and they were completely exhausted after the days festivities. He was about to fall asleep, when Meggie turned over, resting her head against his shoulder. She touched his cheek, and he could just make out her smile in the dim firelight. He sleepily smiled back, his heart filled with peace. There was nothing else she could offer him that would make him happier than he was in that moment. She trailed her hand down to his chest, curling his chest hair with tentative fingers.

"Kade," she hesitated, sighing apprehensively.

"Aye? Meggie what is it?"

"You know how I said I wanted to rent out the front bedrooms. A B&B?" She offered sleepily.

"Yeah."

"We might need to rethink that..."

Amused, he eyed her curiously, wondering if she was delirious, already halfway to dreamworld. Why on earth was she thinking about renovations?

"Oh?"

"For the nursery," she replied, her voice barely a whisper. He chuckled, now certain she was dreaming.

"Shhh, Meggie," he soothed, tenderly adjusting her covers. "We've plenty of time for that."

"Probably less than you think," she giggled softly, snuggling closer. Kade stiffened, wondering if his own fatigue had him hearing things.

"W...what?"

She raised her chin and smiled, "I'm having a baby."

"You're pregnant!" he gushed, leaning over her. "When, how?"

She shook her head, stifling her laughter. "Well, I think you know the how part. The when was a few months ago, in the kitchen. If you recall you just had to have me, right there on the formica table."

"Oh...aye," he smirked. "I do recall that day. Why didn't you tell me?"

"Honestly?" she asked, her smile fading. "I didn't know until recently. Besides, I wanted to wait until after the wedding. Consider this *your* wedding gift, my love."

"We're going to be parents," he beamed, still recovering from the shock. "A wee, little lad."

"Or lassie—"

"You know, Campbell men haven't sired a lassie in three generations, my love. I promise ya, it'll be a boy!"

"Either way, I'll be happy," she whispered, drifting off to sleep.

He pulled her in for a cuddle, his strong hand protectively covering her womb. "Me, too, Meggie. Me too."

CHAPTER 38

Epilogue

Mack

"Well Dad, I have to say, you look ten years younger," Norma observed, straitening his bowtie.

"I feel ten years younger, daughter!" Mack boasted, brushing her hands away. "Now stop yer fussing. This is as good as it's gonna get."

"You look great, Pop," Kade smiled, handing him his suit jacket. "Now let's get you married."

"Aye," Mack smiled, accepting a kiss from his daughter. He was as happy as he'd ever been. If someone had told him six month earlier that he'd be getting married again, he would have told them they were off their heid! He'd already had one good marriage, and thought that was well enough. Never in his wildest dreams did he imagine his beautiful Kat would find her way home again.

He'd asked Kat to marry him only a week after Kade's wedding. To others it might have seemed rushed, even a little impulsive, but not to him. He didn't want to spend even one more minute without her. They'd lost enough time.

They'd stayed at Kade's house that week, exchanging stories about their lives, laughing, crying, enjoying good food, and of course, making love. He was pleased he still remembered how everything worked, and that his tired, old body was able to keep up, even without the little blue pills. It helped that Kat was one of the sexiest women he'd ever laid his eyes on. In spirit, she was still the lovely lass he'd fallen in love with; but made better over time. Seasoned with wisdom and life experience, she had a grace about her that transcended physical beauty. She shone from the inside out, a kind woman, completely comfortable in her own flesh; spiritual, confident, and intelligent.

He proposed to her the night before she was due to fly home. They were cuddling on the sofa, enjoying mulled wine and listening to a 60's play list; The Beatles, Elvis, Herman's Hermits, Petula Clark. All the classics. Kat was restless, struggling with mixed emotions. On one hand, she'd had the best week of her life, she told him, and the thought of leaving was weighing heavily on her. On the other, she had a life back home, good friends, a bowling league, her volunteer work. Mack appreciated the dilemma. It wasn't the first time in her life she'd have to leave everything behind. The last thing he wanted was to pressure her. They'd even talked about Mack flying home with her, but it would take weeks to get a passport. He'd never been out of Scotland in his life.

In a quiet moment, Mack had pulled a beautifully wrapped gift out of his sweater, and offered it to her. He told her that, years earlier, when he'd given her the little locket, he'd promised that one day he'd give her something grander. He could tell she was surprised, but accepted it with humility. Inside was a solid gold bangle, encrusted with diamonds. He and Kade picked it out together a few days before, when Meg and her grandmother were enjoying a day trip to Inverness, a boat cruise on Loch Ness.

He'd asked her to look inside, to read the inscription. It read simply: *Soul Mate.* Then he popped the question. He said that when she'd left, all those years ago, she'd been given no choice, her power stifled, and he would never do that to her again. The decision was hers, and hers alone. He told her it didn't matter where they lived as long as it was together. He would follow her to the ends of the earth if he had to; he just wanted to live out the rest of his life in her arms, as her husband, and she his wife. Without hesitation, she said yes.

It had taken them a few months to sort things through. Kat returned home and tied up loose ends. She put her house on the market, and within a few weeks it sold, for way more than she'd hoped. They spoke nearly every night over *FaceTime.* They'd even gotten a wee bit naughty. Who would've thought the old folks still had it in them! As soon as Mack's passport came in, he flew to America to help her sort though her things and pack up what she wanted to ship to Scotland. They worked hard those few weeks, but they were a good team, and as exhausted as they were, they were motivated by love. It offered them a renewed sense of energy, a vitality they hadn't felt in years.

So here they were, now early spring, getting married only fifty-eight years after falling in love, his bride seventy-five years young. When one of his sons asked what his rush was to get married, Mack told him Kat was pregnant. That shut him up good and fast, the wee scunner.

"Ready Pop?" Kade shook his hand, pulling him in for a warm embrace. "I'm told that Meggie has arrived with yer bride. We need to get ya to the front of the chapel."

"Okay, grandson. I'm ready." Mack stood tall, straightening his suit jacket. "Let's not keep her waiting."

Katherine

"Welcome to the family, Katherine!" Norma swept in and gave her new step-mother a kiss on the cheek, rubbing away the red impression her lipstick left behind.

"Thank you, Norma. I appreciate that," Kat replied, through misty eyes. Years ago, when she'd imagined her wedding to Mack, she never pictured his grown children there. She was grateful they'd accepted her, supporting their father's happiness. It couldn't be easy for them, she thought. They were likely missing their mother that day. She sent a silent prayer to Fae, that she'd raised such fine children, and had given Mack such a wonderful family.

The last five months had been a whirlwind. It had not been an easy road to their wedding day, made even more challenging by their age. She certainly didn't have the energy she used to, but Mack was a big help. Between the two of them they'd accomplished a lot. She'd sold the house, along with most of her possessions, with the exception of her personal items, and together, she and Mack moved to Fort William.

Meg and Kade were living at the Sealladh, and Kade's house was offered to them. They wanted to be closer to Meggie and the baby, and to help out in the Bookery, so it was the perfect choice. Kat was happy with the decision. As much as she respected the love that Mack shared with his deceased wife, she didn't want to move into the home they'd shared, and raised a family in. Mack agreed to the fresh start whole-heartedly, and offered his own Glencoe house to his newly wed granddaughter to rent.

"The service was perfect, Nana," Meg gushed, slipping in beside her. "You both looked so happy."

"I am Meg, and yes it was a perfect service. We wanted it short, sweet, and romantic. I did a Catholic wedding once already. God should be happy."

"Nana!" Meg laughed, surprised by her tenacity.

"I'm serious," Kat chuckled. "Besides, Mack's not Catholic, and let's be honest, neither am I anymore."

It had been 40 years since she'd stepped inside a church. Not since her mother's funeral. Mary had died the same year as Kat's husband, 1978. It was a dreadful year. Her mother had taken ill, and moved in with her the last year of her life. She'd been divorced from Kat's father for eight years. It turned out, Douglas had been having an affair for a very long time, since before his transfer to North Carolina. The woman he'd fallen in love with was also a professor at Edinburgh, who'd transferred to Duke six months prior to him. It didn't take long for Kat to piece it together; the urgency for the move. Douglas hadn't been thinking of his daughter's education at all—he'd been following his cock.

Her father carried on the affair for many years, until the spring of 1970. His lover, tired of being his mistress, had given him an ultimatum. He filed for divorce and married her within the year. Kat was bitter for a long time. She'd been forced to leave behind the love her life so her father could get his rocks off. It was all so sordid, and thoughtless. She'd refused to address him for many years after that, and had not even spoken to him at Mary's funeral. He died in '85, the year her son graduated from high school. They'd reconciled shortly before his death. His 'new' wife had just left him for another man. He was heart broken. Kat, unwilling to carry the burden of anger any longer, invited him back into her life. While they didn't enjoy a close relationship, it was peaceful. Douglas might have died with a heavy heart, but her conscience was clear. She'd forgiven him.

"How are you feeling, Meg? Not too tired?" Kat asked, placing a gentle hand on her granddaughter's belly. A timely kick made them both smile.

"Baby is very active today. Must be all the excitement!"

"I'm sure it is. You've been on your feet a long time. You need to sit," Kat lovingly scolded.

"I will Nana, as soon as we get to the pub. Did everything get taken care of, with the envelope I gave you?"

"Yes, Peanut. I can't wait for the surprise!"

"Me too!" Meg blushed, massaging her belly, the way expectant mother's do.

"Well, ladies," Mack interrupted, Kade by his side. "It appears everyone is leaving the chapel. Shall we make our way to the reception?"

"Yes," Kat agreed, embracing her new husband. "I'm looking forward to our first dance as man and wife."

"Aye, and I'm looking forward to afterwards, the consummation part," Mack winked, pulling her in for a kiss. "D'ya think our guests would mind if we left early?"

"I'm sure they'll understand," Kade chimed in, his face boasting the pride he felt.

"Are you ready then, Mrs. MacDonald?" Mack smirked, offering his hand. "Shall we go to the party?"

"Yes, husband. Lead the way," she accepted, giddy as a school girl.

Kade

"Can I get you another lemonade?" Kade offered, rubbing his wife's feet in his lap. It was the least he could do for her. She never complained, in spite of how busy she'd been; running the shop, and helping to settle their grandparents in. She was a trooper.

"Ahh, that feels nice," she whimpered, eyes closed. Aroused by her moans, he quickly stiffened beneath her. She had that effect on him, even at nearly seven months pregnant. He couldn't get enough of her.

"Aye, you like that do ya," he flirted. She opened one eye and smirked, shaking her head at him. "What?" he asked harmlessly, though there was nothing harmless about him. His thoughts were far from innocent.

"You're such a horn-dog."

"That's true. Would ya have it any other way?"

"Not a chance," she laughed, gently pressing her foot against his crotch.

"Keep that up and I'll be massaging more than your toes."

"Later, if I don't fall asleep on you again," she grimaced, likely recalling the last two times he'd tried to seduce her at bedtime. The poor woman could barely stay awake past nine anymore, so they'd been forced to adapt to early morning love-making. Made no difference to him, but Meggie wasn't a morning person, especially since he'd knocked her up. Nausea wasn't a turn on, apparently.

"No matter, I'll just raise yer nighty and do my business," he teased, earning a well-deserved smack. He raised his hands in surrender. "I'm kidding!" Meg leaned in for a kiss. Wrapping a hand through her hair, he pulled her towards him, enjoying the softness of her lips. God, he loved her.

"Hello everyone," his brother Angus voiced into the mic, wincing from the feedback. He'd been chosen master of ceremonies that evening, not because he was the wittiest, but because he was granddad's favourite; at least in the top ten.

"I hope everyone is having a grand time. Thank you, Isla, for the amazing meal. You've out done yourself again—," he complimented, to thunderous applause. Isla, arm around her new girlfriend, raised her hand, waving off the thanks. She was glowing, but it wasn't from the praise. She was in love, and Kade was thrilled for her.

"The bride, and her groom, will now cut the cake...and I've been told to ask everyone to gather around. There's a wee surprise for ya all."

"What kind of surprise could be inside a cake?" Kade asked, eyeing Meggie for enlightenment. Maybe some sort of American tradition? She shrugged, gesturing him to follow, not bothering to slip her shoes back on to her swollen feet.

The wedding cake was simple but lovely; ivory, elegant, two tiered, with a gorgeous ribbon of fondant crowning it. Meg offered her grandmother a smile, as Kade sidled up beside her. Everyone had gathered.

"So, traditionally the wedding cake is a symbol that the bride and groom will forever provide for each other, but this time it's a little different," Angus continued addressing the guests. "Earlier this week, the bride's granddaughter, our one and only Meg, had a routine ultrasound. We understand she asked the technician to place the gender of the baby inside a sealed envelope?"

Kade glanced down at his wife, his smile raising. *What had she done?*

"Neither Kade, nor Meggie, knows the sex of their wee one, but this very special wedding cake will now reveal to all of us whether it's a boy, or a little girl!"

"Really?" Kade asked, pulling his wife closer. "Did you plan this?"

Meg nodded. "Nana and I did. She gave the envelope to the baker. It will either be pink or blue inside."

"That's amazing, but I assure you it'll be blue," Kade said, convinced he, along with his father and brothers, only carried boy sperm.

“So, Nana, and Pops—will you do the honour?” Angus asked, handing them the knife. Pop looked almost as excited as Kade felt.

“One, two, three—It’s blue!” Cheers rang out while everyone congratulated Kade and Meg with the news. He leaned over and kissed his wife. A boy was exciting news, but a girl would have sent Norma over the moon. He saw his mother standing across from him, and shrugged. Wiping her tears, Norma smiled, offering him an enthusiastic thumbs up.

Angus, waiting for a dip in the excitement, chimed in once more. “Now, go ahead and cut the bottom tier, folks, and share a piece of your wedding cake,” he encouraged, "then we’ll have a toast!”

Pop took his bride’s hand, and together sliced into the second tier. Lifting a small piece in front of them, the crowd gasped. It was the colour of bubblegum.

“What the hell?” Kade searched his wife’s eyes, desperate for a swift explanation. She clapped her hands, as tears rolled down her cheeks. “Meggie?”

“Twins,” she gushed, falling into his embrace. “I’ve known about these little nuggets for months, but I wanted to surprise you.”

“Months? And you knew the genders, too?”

“No, I wanted that to be a surprise for us both!” she cried, “Kade, we’re having a boy, and a girl!”

“Jesus, woman, you’re full of surprises.” He planted another one on her, this time with more passion.

“So now what colour do we paint the nursery?”

“You mean what colour do I paint the nursery?” he teased.

"You should know by now, that by we, I mean you."

"Aye, I should know better," Kade chuckled, caressing her swollen belly. "I don't mind. I'd do anything for you and the wee ones."

"I'd like to propose a toast!" Thom interrupted, raising his glass. "Here's to Pop and his beautiful bride, Kat. Congratulations! We're all so pleased you found each other again, and that you'll live out your lives in love!"

"Here, here!"

"Wait, I'm not done," he continued joyfully. "Norma and I couldn't be more excited to welcome these beautiful new grand-babies in June. Twins are an incredible blessing! Cheers to all!"

Shouts of "cheers" rang out as wedding guests clinked their glasses and offered congratulations all around. Kade eased his way through the crowd to greet his mother. She pulled him close, landing a sloppy kiss on his cheek.

"You'll have yer million dollar family all at once," Norma praised.

A glorious smile lit up his handsome face. "I may need a million dollars! I've got some mighty swimmers!" he boasted proudly. "I'm happy, Mum."

"It's as it's meant to be. You'll be a wonderful father, my boy."

Meg

Rocking in the chair Kade had lovingly restored, Meg held her precious daughter against her breast, softly humming a lullaby. The sweet noises Gracie made reminded Meg of a hungry kitten.

The twins were a week old. They had a bit of a scare during

labour. Her contractions started two weeks early, and her son, the unlucky twin on the bottom, was showing signs of distress. Her doctor thought it best to perform an emergency c-section. Thankfully her babies, born three minutes apart, were as healthy as could be, so any discomfort she felt was inconsequential.

"You're a hungry girl," Meg cooed, drunk from Gracie's scent. "You need to save some for your brother."

"How's our girl?" Kade whispered, approaching cautiously, his boy in his arms. The little cherub was fussy, but not yet crying.

"She's going to need a change," Meg shrugged, wincing as she raised Gracie to her shoulder, encouraging out a burp.

"I can take care of that. She doesn't scare me—," he teased warmly, delicately brushing Meg's bangs aside. She was in desperate need of a haircut.

"Give her time. Teenage girls are a handful."

"Aye, but she'll have me wrapped around her baby finger."

"—just like her mother?"

"Exactly like her mother," he smiled.

They swapped their offspring, Meg pressing her son to the second breast. He latched on instantly, happy to be in his mother's arms. She smiled down at him, still baffled by how much love she already had for her children. Although she'd only known them a week, she couldn't recall what life had been like before them. She was hopelessly in love, bewitched by two perfect souls, Gracie, and sweet little Robby, named for her father.

"Look at Robby, happy as a clam. He sure loves the breast."

Meg raised her eyes and smiled. "He's like his father."

"In that case, he'll be a smart little man, too."

"And modest."

"Of course," Kade nodded proudly. I'm going to put Gracie to bed. Come and find me when your done?"

"Yes," Meg nodded, barely registering his words, too wrapped up in the bliss.

Once she'd laid Robby next to his sleeping sister, she found Kade in the kitchen. He'd prepared her a snack. She eagerly picked up the sandwich, taking a huge bite. She was famished! If it wasn't for Kade keeping her nourished, she was sure she'd die of starvation. Feeding two babies was draining.

He lingered thoughtfully for a long moment, holding her hand lightly. "You look beautiful."

"Oh this? I call it *exhausted chic*. I haven't showered since yesterday."

"You still look beautiful, even with barf in yer hair," he chuckled. "Finish your food, I'll help ya bathe later."

"Okay," she sighed, dangerously close to tears. She loved how he loved her.

"You know, in all the excitement, I forgot to give you yer gift."

Surprised, she cocked her head, trying to read him. "What do you mean?"

Raising from his seat he fell in behind her, kissing her crown before dropping something cool around her neck. It fell against her chest with a light thud, a beautiful gold locket, shaped like a heart.

"Kade, it's perfect," she sobbed, no longer able to hold back her tears. "Thank you."

Kade knelt in front of her. "No, thank you. How do ya thank a woman for blessing you with a family? Meggie, do you know what today is?"

Confused, she held the locket against her heart. "No."

"It's been a year since we first met."

She shook her head in disbelief, suddenly flooded with wonderful memories. *Had it only been a year?* How things had changed since the day she'd stood on the front porch of her decrepit, little cottage—now their beautiful family home. Kade rested his head in her lap, allowing her to stroke his hair. Her heart was full. She knew, beyond any doubt, that she'd been guided by fate to bring her Nana home; then rewarded with a love of her own.

The End

Visit jennifervettor.com to connect to her social media.
Join her email list for information on new releases,
recommendations, contests, and hot topics!

43810874R00165

Made in the USA
Middletown, DE
30 April 2019